"Less well known than *The Handmaid's* [...] [its] vision, . . . Suzette Haden Elgin's *Na[...]* tribulation in a world where . . . wome[n...] Elgin's heroines do, however, have one set of weapon[s...] own." —**Sandra M. Gilbert and Susan Gubar,** *New York Times Book Review*

"I urge [*Native Tongue*] upon you. . . . Elgin has carried current [views] on women to their 'logical' conclusion. . . . She takes up everything from religion to sex. Above all, she understands that until women find the words and syntax for what they need to say, they will never say it, nor will the world hear it. . . . There isn't a phony or romantic moment here, and the story is absolutely compelling." —**Carolyn Heilbrun,** *Women's Review of Books*

"*Native Tongue* brings to life not only the possibility of a women's language, but also the rationale for one. . . . [It is] a language that can bring to life concepts men have never needed, have never dreamed of—and thus change the world." —*Village Voice Literary Supplement*

"This angry feminist text is also an exemplary experiment in speculative fiction, deftly and implacably pursuing both a scientific hypothesis and an ideological hypothesis through all their social, moral, and emotional implications." —**Ursula K. Le Guin, author of** *The Left Hand of Darkness*

"Published in 1984, *Native Tongue* got it right. Despite many gains, the status of women today remains precarious as ever. Female friendships are as vital and sustaining as water and air. And in the power and precision of language, one can begin to change the world." —**Maggie Shen King, author of** *An Excess Male*

"Elgin's novel will inspire those who believe that women's words can change the world. Read it!" —**Marleen S. Barr, editor of** *Future Females, the Next Generation: New Voices and Velocities in Feminist Science Fiction Criticism*

THE NATIVE TONGUE TRILOGY
BY SUZETTE HADEN ELGIN

NATIVE TONGUE

THE JUDAS ROSE

EARTHSONG

NATIVE TONGUE III

EARTHSONG

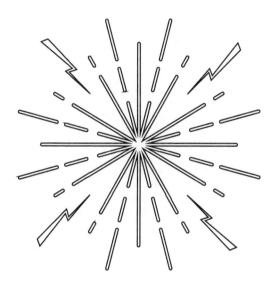

SUZETTE HADEN ELGIN
FOREWORD BY KAREN LORD
AFTERWORD BY SUSAN M. SQUIER AND JULIE VEDDER

FEMINIST
PRESS
AT THE CITY UNIVERSITY
OF NEW YORK
NEW YORK CITY

Published in 2019 by the Feminist Press
at the City University of New York
The Graduate Center
365 Fifth Avenue, Suite 5406
New York, NY 10016

feministpress.org

Second edition
First Feminist Press edition 2002

First printing July 2019

Cover design by Suki Boynton
Text design by Drew Stevens
Corn wreath logo by Suzette Haden Elgin

Library of Congress Cataloging-in-Publication Data
Names: Elgin, Suzette Haden, author.
Title: Earthsong / Suzette Haden Elgin.
Description: Second edition. | New York, NY : the Feminist Press, 2019. |
   Series: The native tongue trilogy ; 3
Identifiers: LCCN 2019021245 (print) | LCCN 2019021816 (ebook) | ISBN
   9781936932672 (E-book) | ISBN 9781936932665 (pbk.)
Subjects: LCSH: Women linguists—Fiction.
Classification: LCC PS3555.L42 (ebook) | LCC PS3555.L42 E37 2019 (print) |
   DDC 813/.54—dc23
LC record available at https://lccn.loc.gov/2019021245

FOREWORD: EVOLUTIONARY SONG

When Suzette Haden Elgin created the language Láadan for her trilogy of novels *Native Tongue* (1984), *The Judas Rose* (1987), and *Earthsong* (1994), she had an agenda in mind. The complexity, depth, and thoroughness of her linguistic invention were intrinsic to the books, but went far beyond the requirements of plot because Láadan was intended for use in the real world. Elgin's declared aim was to test four hypotheses:

> (1) that the weak form of the linguistic relativity hypothesis is true [that is, that human languages structure human perceptions in significant ways]; (2) that Goedel's Theorem applies to language, so that there are changes you could not introduce into a language without destroying it and languages you could not introduce into a culture without destroying it; (3) that change in language brings about social change, rather than the contrary; and (4) that if women were offered a women's language one of two things would happen—they would welcome and nurture it, or it would at minimum motivate them to replace it with a better women's language of their own construction.[1]

Elgin notes that her experiment is based on a theory that "women are distressed because existing human languages are inadequate to express their perceptions." A women's language, crafted purposefully to fill that lack, should alleviate that distress. A language that could effect that level of change in individuals, and in a society, should spread, or inspire imitators and improvements at the very least.

To Elgin's credit, Láadan has survived and is still considered noteworthy by writers today. In a 2012 article for *The New*

Yorker, Joshua Foer gives an example of Láadan as a woman's language:

> Many conlanging projects begin with a simple premise that violates the inherited conventions of linguistics in some new way. . . . Láadan, a feminist language developed in the early nineteen-eighties, includes words like *radíidin*, defined as a "non-holiday, a time allegedly a holiday but actually so much a burden because of work and preparations that it is a dreaded occasion; especially when there are too many guests and none of them help."[2]

And, in a 2019 article for Literary Hub, Rebecca Romney comments triumphantly on that same term, *radíidin*, in the subtitle of her essay: "There's even a word for emotional labor!"[3] *Emotional labor* is our modern, two-word English phrase for the unsung and unseen effort involved in maintaining the image of the consummate hostess and homemaker, an effort that is dismissed by patriarchal society as part of "women's work" if it is considered at all.

Unfortunately, noteworthy is not the same as widespread. Elgin admitted that the ability to test the first three hypotheses depended on the success of the fourth hypothesis. Only if enough speakers took up the language would there be sufficient, non-anecdotal data on its effects on society. However, she imposed a limit of ten years—from the 1984 publication date of *Native Tongue* to the 1994 publication of *Earthsong*—and by 1999 she was referring to the experiment as a failure.

But were ten years and one trilogy really enough? Both Elgin and Foer warn that constructed languages, once released into the real world, go beyond the control of their creators in unexpected and sometimes unwanted ways. Klingon (from Star Trek) and Elvish (from The Lord of the Rings trilogy) have had more success, but that success was won over several decades with greater exposure via books, television, movies, and enthusiastically precise cosplay. Furthermore, though we may not have *radíidin* in our present-day vocabulary, we *do* have *emotional labor*—so perhaps, given time, patriarchal English could be sufficiently modified to present the feminist worldview without taking up an entirely new lexicon.

Elgin would have drafted *Earthsong* well before the 1994 deadline for her experiment, but it reads as if she was already anticipating failure, moving on, and perhaps hinting at another hypothesis for the final novel of her trilogy. On Elgin's future Earth, Láadan has done its work, but more work remains to be done. The importance of communication and language recedes into the background, and a new problem is highlighted, but this one has no time limit on the solution. The novel, in both story and structure, is an exploration of the power of small adjustments over a long period of time. Gradual change over generations is the key—slow and meandering, but as inevitable as waters run to the sea. It is an epic without heroes, or rather, with so many collective heroines that the transforming force becomes radically multiplied and virtually unstoppable. There is no ten-year plan with this revolution via evolution.

In *Earthsong*, Elgin shifts her focus from language to our culture of violence. Science fiction is filled with stories about intelligent alien life that is either unwilling or afraid to make contact with Earth until its denizens evolve into truly civilized beings. Our species' habit of war has been portrayed as a plague to be quarantined, or an unfortunate phase that this unruly, adolescent humanity must pass through unassisted on a journey of self-determination and self-control.

Earthsong's central premise is that by ending hunger we will also end violence. Evidence already exists that what we ingest can affect how we behave. Early exposure to lead—inhaled or consumed—can permanently damage the developing nervous system and can cause behavioral problems. However, Elgin offers no explanation for the link. She merely presents the task, framing it as a communication during a "vision quest" from deceased great-grandmother to living great-granddaughter, and sets the characters on a journey to find the answer.

Readers don't *need* an explanation. They can suspend disbelief and easily accept that the command of an ancestor, shaped not only by a lifetime of experience but also by a new and near-omniscient perspective on human history, will seem illogical to the living. Adults do not tell a child exactly what to do, but tell them whatever is necessary to get them to do it regardless. Ancestors speak the truth in words their offspring can understand, and leave them to learn in time all the nuances and depths contained in that truth.

Beyond the story, hunger also makes sense as a symbol or metaphor. We humans have many more hungers than mere food, and the world is wounded by our appetites. If we could solve the problem of our runaway consumption, it might not lead immediately to peace, but it could certainly help us to avoid our own destruction. If we are children, we are babies who have to be weaned and trained not to soil our own nest. The metaphor expands in the choices Elgin's characters make. The initial tests to replace food with alternative nutrition are solitary, isolated, and passive. The process that is eventually implemented is social, cooperative, and active, thereby sating several other human hungers, such as the desires for companionship, achievement, and creativity.

The solution in *Earthsong* is not only to end hunger but also to rid humanity of the fear of hunger. That fear allows others to have power over us, to construct and manipulate systems that deliver life necessities. Examples of invented scarcity in the real world include food deserts in impoverished neighborhoods, high food-import bills in small island states, and severed supply lines in besieged and blockaded territories. Removing that fear instantly shifts the balance of power, destabilizing economies and established systems of control, and it is fascinating to see how this plays out in Elgin's novel. A children's song at the end of the story reveals how insidious that fear of hunger can be, and how we might train ourselves out of it. The lyrics tell children (and adults) being weaned from "mouthfood" to hold a pebble in their mouths to calm hunger pangs. This is not true hunger, but a combination of psychological yearning and physiological reaction that will disappear when the adjustment, or evolution, is complete.

But our fears, like our hungers, are many and varied. The real world and the causes of our urge toward violence are far, far more complicated, and the changes required of us, individually and collectively, can feel too massive to even attempt a start. Elgin reminds us, both then and now, of how a feminist r/evolution can be achieved with small steps and by indirect means. *Earthsong* contains a new paradigm of change, where violence is not employed to destroy violence, nor power to eliminate power. This approach, rarely celebrated in the genre of science fiction, provides a necessary counter to the patriarchal myth that elevates singular heroes, utter conquest, and the swift construction of an unassailable Utopia upon a shining hill.

The end of hunger. Equality for all. World peace. Phrases that sound like a beauty pageant wish list, with goals that can only be reached in a vision or a dream . . . or in the best of imaginative science fiction. Speak words crafted to help us better understand ourselves and each other. Keep the communal joys of eating, but switch to a mode of consumption that makes instead of takes. Wait for no hero; do what you can with the ordinary, the many. Or in other words, beyond symbol and metaphor, gradually make this world into a place where everyone has a voice, a community, and a purpose.

In hard times, readers hunger for hopeful fiction, and *Earthsong* provides all that and more.

Karen Lord
April 2019

Notes

1. Suzette Haden Elgin, "Láadan, the Constructed Language in *Native Tongue*," Science Fiction Writers of America, 1999, http://www.sfwa.org/members/elgin/Laadan.html.
2. Joshua Foer, "Utopian for Beginners: An Amateur Linguist Loses Control of the Language He Invented," *The New Yorker*, December 24 & 31, 2012, https://www.newyorker.com/magazine/2012/12/24/utopian-for-beginners.
3. Rebecca Romney, "This Science Fiction Novelist Created a Feminist Language from Scratch," Literary Hub, January 15, 2019, https://lithub.com/this-science-fiction-novelist-created-a-feminist-language-from-scratch/.

EARTHSONG

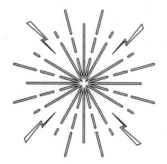

FOREWORD

My name is Nazareth Joanna Chornyak; I was a woman of the linguist Lines. I died of a broken heart in the summer of 2289, at Chornyak Barren House, on that day when all the Aliens suddenly returned to their homeworlds; I was one hundred and twenty-one years old at the time. One minute the Aliens were there—in the conference halls, in the government facilities, in the Interfaces of the thirteen linguist Households—as they had been for two hundred years and more. The next minute, hoverlings were just above the lawns and parks and buildings and the Aliens were hurrying out to them, carrying with them only their portable atmospheres, leaving everything else behind, boarding the hoverlings and disappearing toward the motherships. Without one word of explanation to the linguists or to anyone else, they were simply gone. And so was I.

It was bad timing on my part. If I had known the Aliens were going to leave, I would have died the day before, or the day after. I would never deliberately have done anything so gaudy as seeming to be a part of their exodus. Many people assumed that the shock of seeing the two Aliens-in-Residence abandoning the Chornyak Interface killed me; they were wrong. I was out in the gardens, gathering an armful of roses; I didn't even see the AIRYs leaving. It was nothing more than an unfortunate coincidence, you perceive.

When I died, I was expecting a number of different things. Or perhaps not exactly *expecting* them . . . "expecting" isn't the right word. I mean that I knew there were a number of possibilities, and that I was expecting some member of the set proposed by my own culture.

There's the one where you die and it's like a guillotine of darkness . . . the whistle through the air, the instant of agony, and then nothing at all. Clearly, if that's accurate we'll never know it. There's the one where you're met by choirs of angels, the feathery kind with harps, and led off to a heaven of white and pink and gold where the blessed spend eternity praising God. There's the one where you wake up again as a cockroach or a cow or, if you've been good enough, as some new and different human being. There's the one where you're caught up into a sort of mist and you waft about as one infinitesimal part of an infinite but disembodied Oversoul. There's the one where, if you're a man, beautiful maidens feed you fruit and honey and goodies while others like them sing and dance for you . . . what that one is like if you're a woman, I have no idea. Certainly no adult woman wants young boys to feed and entertain her. There's the one that is the guillotine of darkness in reverse—a sort of guillotine of light. There's the horrible one that has hell in it, with devils tormenting you in a lake of fire . . . and the equally horrible one where the blessed lean over heaven's parapets and watch the goings-on in the lake of fire with smug *satisfaction*. I was expecting one of those, or some variation on one of those.

I was *not* expecting what I actually got. The idea that you find yourself first at a sort of waystation where you're offered a triple choice—go on, go back, or stay and help—was new to me. *You can go on*, something said, *to What Is Ahead . . . but you can't know what that is. Only that it's a great improvement on where you've been. You can go* back *to where you've been, and do it all over again; you can make better choices than the ones you made the previous time, and perhaps be more satisfied with the results. Or you can make the third choice: stay right here, and help, when you are* called *upon for help.*

The dead are not allowed to intrude upon the living, I was told, and I was glad to hear it. But from this place (not exactly a place, but that will have to do) they can respond when they are properly petitioned. As I was properly petitioned by my stubborn great-granddaughter Delina, with a little help from those who became her friends in spite of her awkwardness.

4

I didn't leap at that third alternative, though in the end it was the choice I made. As I've already told you, I died of a broken heart.

I had spent more than a century patiently trying to help, and being thoroughly disgusted at the results. I tried so hard, I dedicated myself to the task of setting an example of what *could* be done, of what would *work* and would repay the investment of energies. I never forced people over fences; I took the fences down and said to them, "Now there is a way for you to go forward." And I failed. Again and again and again. It was like being Chief Nanny For Life in a gigantic nursery school. It broke my heart, and I never did come to understand it; in many ways, the older I got, the more it baffled me. The way people suffered . . . the stupid hurtful things they did, to themselves as much as to others . . . it was always a mystery to me. And I really, truly, had thought that when I died—no matter which version of the "Afterlife" turned out to be accurate—I would be able to think: "Well, I've done all I can; now it's up to somebody else." Even if the somebody else turned out to be me as a cockroach, or whatever. I had never thought of it being me as *me*, me as Nazareth Joanna Chornyak, if you understand what I mean.

(Probably you don't understand. There's no reason at all why you should understand.)

Being dead does make it harder to *tell* this story. I can't just send it off to a publisher or call up somebody from the newspapes and share it with them; I have to rely on those among the living who are willing to do those things *for* me. The mediums; the channels; all the varieties of trancers. But they are astonishingly numerous, and that's not the real problem. I can tune in a trancer and start dictation as easily as I tuned in the channels on my comset when I was alive. The real problem is the language. Not the words *I* say . . . and that's wrong, I don't use "words" anymore, but it's the only way the trancer knows to put it . . . the problem is the words and the body language that are generated at the other end of the language transaction. They're almost never the *right* words and body language.

I spent my entire life as an interpreter and translator of

languages, both the languages of Earth and those of other worlds, and the problem is one I know well. That makes it no less frustrating. When the trancer's language has no words or bodyparl for what I want to say—to give what I want to say a surface shape, in sound or in writing—then the message gets garbled, and there's nothing I can do about it. It happens all the time. As if it weren't bad enough that I was a failure all my life long, now I am forced to face the fact that I continue to be a failure in death. It's almost enough, sometimes, to make me wistful for the guillotine-of-darkness alternative. Almost, but not quite. Knowing for *sure* that you have all of eternity to do better in makes you more comfortable with failure.

Suppose I only want to tell you where I am and what it's like here . . . suppose I just want to describe my surroundings to you. I have tried many times, with many trancers. The versions they have produced (doing their very best, I know) have been as varied and as different as all those proposed versions of the Afterlife. And none has come even remotely close to being what *I* perceive! That is the nature of this kind of communication. The trancer who is telling you this now will write that I am in a sort of *office*, high above the Earth and all her colonies and all the sister planets and galaxies, sitting at a sort of desk and looking out a sort of window through which I can . . . somehow . . . observe all the countless billions of creatures as they go about their affairs below. That's a very silly and inaccurate metaphor indeed, but it's the best she can do.

Translation, you know, is not a matter of substituting words in one language for words in another language. Translation is a matter of saying in one language, for a particular situation, what a native speaker of the other language would say in the *same* situation. The more unlikely that situation is in one of the languages, the harder it is to find a corresponding utterance in the other. And my poor trancers have almost no data in the banks of information in their brains that match what I try to give them; they *have* to fall back on metaphors.

As human beings always have. Unable to perceive anything remotely corresponding to the actual Holy One of the universe, they have used the metaphors of The Stern Father, The Tender Mother, The Oriental Potentate, The Conquering Warrior, The Many-Armed Dancer, The Plumed Serpent, The Whirling Lightning . . . it's a long list. None of these is even approximately accurate, but all of them at least make it possible to *talk* about what is and isn't holy. And that's a start. In the same way, this trancer's metaphor of the Heavenly Office Overlooking All the Worlds will serve us well enough for the moment.

But I know that this story is going to be disorganized. That it will come to you through many different voices all trying to give utterance to the single instrument that is *my* "voice," speaking in their own various native tongues and with their own varying degrees of skill. I know there's no way I can make the story come to you in tidy chronological order, as do the books of the ancient novelists; it will have to come in chunks and pieces tumbling out of time, beyond the reach of my planning or my control. I know from experience that pieces will leak through which seem to be unrelated to the tale I'm telling; I know that pieces I *intended* to give you will get lost and then turn up, mystifying those who hear or read them, in the unrelated tellings of others. All of this is to be expected, and it can't be helped. I hope you will be patient with me, and that you will make allowances for the difficulties I face in this curious situation. I hope you will be patient with the trancers as well; they do their best, and they are not trained linguists. (Not that it would necessarily improve matters if they were. A linguist trancer would probably make even worse messes, imposing an order that I never intended, cut brutally to fit the current theories about reality and—heaven help us all—the latest and most fashionable theoretical models in linguistics.)

I want to answer a number of important questions for you. I want to explain to you why the Aliens abandoned humankind, and what that meant for us, and how it turned out in the end. I want to tell you how the worlds—that had been almost Edens for a while—far too quickly returned to the crime and misery that had always been humankind's lot. I want to tell you about the coming of the Icehouse Effect, which put a cruel end to the lives of so many millions before it was over. You may not particularly want to know what happened to Láadan, the language constructed by the women of the Lines to express the perceptions of women, but the story is also important. You may not be curious about these things—but unless you know about them, you are blind and deaf and numb in the world.

And then there is the story of the founding of the Church of Our Lady of the StarTangle, and the flying chapels it sent out into the far reaches of space, and the story of the Music Grammar Teachers. I want to tell you about all of that. I want to tell you about PICOTA, the Pan-Indian Council of the Americas, and how they helped the rest of us in a time when help was desperately needed, without worrying about whether help was deserved. So many stories; so much information!

I promise you; I give you my word. If you will give me your perceptions for a while, for so long as it takes you to read this book . . . if you will bear with me as I try to speak to you from beyond space and beyond time . . . if you will use your magnificent human brain to fill in the empty spaces left by this method of taletelling that is the only one available to me now . . . it will be worth it.

I promise you; you will not be sorry.

I promise you; it will *help*.

PART ONE
WHAT THE FIRST TRANCER SAID

CHAPTER 1

Delina had been prepared for resistance; it was no surprise to her. She knew very well that if she hadn't been from Chornyak Household the sorters at the door would never have let her pass. They would have listened silently while she told them what she wanted, and then she would have been handed over to the patient crew that was trained to soothe Anglos and send them mildly bewildered and placid on their way. But she *was* a Chornyak, and for centuries Chornyak Household had been more powerful than the governments of many an entire world; that had gotten her past the first hurdle and braced for the next. And she was prepared to return resistance *for* resistance. She had the fearsome stubbornness that went with being a linguist, and with being a woman of the Lines, and with being someone who had always been, and was always going to be, unpopular. Delina lived in resistance as fish live in water. She would have been at a loss without resistance to brace herself against.

She had already faced and overcome obstacles as complex as anything she was likely to face here at the PICOTA domes. First she had needed the backing of the other Chornyak women, and that had been terribly hard to get. They had scoffed and mocked and teased and threatened and reasoned, and tried every sort of persuasion available to them, before they gave in. Delina didn't blame them for that. In their place she would have done the same.

Then she had lost precious time convincing the Chornyak men who were legally responsible for her behavior that the surest way to punish her was to sit back and let her suffer the humiliation of her inevitable failure. That had worked—but only, she knew, because of the turmoil the worlds were in, with all but the most basic commerce and science thrown into chaos by the abrupt departure of the Alien partners. Without that enormous distraction she could never have persuaded the men to let her do this; they would undoubtedly have had her sedated and confined to Chornyak Barren House until she gave in and gave up. She had succeeded because the men were frantic. In the context of their vast despair, her fool's errand had been on the scale of a fly buzzing around a window, not worth the time and energy it would have taken to stop her. A fly that couldn't just be swatted absentmindedly into oblivion, because she was a *family* fly.

And finally there had been the matter of getting past her own terror of being *perceived* as foolish, made stronger because she was weak from grieving for Nazareth. That had perhaps been worst of all, with the tapes playing over and over in her head. Fretting and prophesying at her. *They'll think you're ridiculous. They'll laugh at you to your face and make jokes about you behind your back. You look stupid, and you're going to look stupider before it's over. What if you fail? What if you* have *taken up a fool's quest? For the rest of your life, they'll remind you of it! And you'll* deserve *their ridicule . . .*

It was hard to ignore all that; it was hard to be militantly confident, with all that going on. Resisting your *self* is being trapped in a feedback loop that is at once somewhere and nowhere . . . like shoving honey. It had been almost too much for her, stubbornly struggling against her own stubbornness.

She stood quietly before the old man the sorters took her to, therefore, pleased to have come so far so quickly. Pleased to be already standing in this room that was filled with the soft light from the rainy day outside, streaming in through the skylights in the dome's ceiling. The walls were the color of sunbaked earth; the rug under her feet was the color of sand, patterned in turquoise and dark brown and a deep rich red, woven on the PICOTA looms in ancient patterns that she found pleasing. She had seen the room before on the comset, many times; she had never before been inside it. When the children in her Homeroom had come here on the traditional field trip, Delina hadn't been allowed to join them.

She had been needed for a contract negotiation over a dull grayish rock that the Aliens (for some reason she no longer remembered) had wanted to buy in large quantities.

She had expected to have to fight her way past half a dozen seasoned gatekeeps before she was granted an audience with the chief of the PICOTA. The Pan-Indian Council of Tribes of the Americas was not a sewing circle; she hadn't thought it would be easy to get through to the man who ran it. But here she was, and she had let enough politeness time go by; it was time she spoke up and explained herself.

"You can tell me to go, Mr. Bluecrane," she said, standing at a cautious distance from the round table where he sat, knowing he would have been told of her errand—and her determination—before they brought her to him. She spoke courteously and carefully, a small and stocky and not particularly pretty woman surrounded by much larger males, her chin up, her eyes level but not seeking Will *Bluecrane's* eyes. Only the trembling of her hands betrayed her fear. She said, "You can tell me to go; but I won't leave. You can have me taken away; but I will come back. I want to be sure you understand that."

"Delina Chornyak," said Bluecrane, trying to sound less cross than he felt—because she looked so small and so worn out, and because he understood what the departure of the Aliens had meant for the linguists—"this is a waste of your time. And mine."

Delina sighed, and looked down at her hands. Traitor hands! Shaking; making her look weak; letting her down. She clasped them behind her back, where they would do her less harm. "Even so," she answered him, steadily. "Even so. I will stay, whatever happens."

"I don't believe you."

The words fell one by one, cutting the air, each one a separate sharp knife of sound. Will Bluecrane was a master of resistance himself, and he had several decades of experience that Delina lacked.

When she made no response except to raise her eyes again and look calmly straight ahead, Bluecrane began rubbing his hands together. Slowly; rhythmically; hand by hand; it was the sound of someone walking through tall grass. Delina knew what that meant. He was following the rules, but he wasn't comfortable about it, and he was thinking hard. It was better than she'd hoped . . . perhaps he was as soft of heart as her sources had told her he was. *Please*, she thought. *Let it happen that way; let it be like that.*

"Explain it to me, Delina Chornyak," he said to her, folding his arms over his chest and leaning back in his chair. "I'd like to hear it from you directly . . . in case you have been misunderstood."

She told him what she had told the sorters, straight through without hesitation; she'd rehearsed the lines so long, waiting for this moment, that she knew them as she knew her name. And he said nothing at all, even when she got to the end of her speech.

He gestured with his chin then to the younger men waiting nearby, and they stepped up, one to each side of Delina, ready to escort her back down the central hallway to the exit corridor and straight out into the dreary day outside. She stood taller, holding her lower lip tight in her teeth, and Bluecrane made an exasperated noise, and glared at her.

"I wouldn't advise you to come back again," he said sternly. "I would advise you to go home and take up some project that has a better chance of succeeding than this foolishness. Here you are, part of a family whose entire existence was to deal with the languages of Aliens—and now the Aliens are gone, and for all we know they will never be back. Here you are, part of a solar system that for all we know is going to be blasted into dust by those same Aliens this afternoon, or tomorrow morning. And you're *here*, pestering me? There's more than enough trouble on this world at this moment, Delina Chornyak, without you adding to it! Go home!" He sighed, and he leaned forward and folded his hands on the table. "Go home, and stop piling trouble on top of trouble."

"I am here *because* of all that trouble," she said, struggling with the words because they sounded so arrogant, saying them all the same because being perceived as arrogant was part of what she had to do and couldn't be avoided. "I'm here to *get help*. Please— let me try."

There was another tiny movement of the old man's chin, and the sorter on Delina's left touched her shoulder softly with his fingertips. She raised her eyes and looked directly at Bluecrane then, holding the gaze long enough to make her point but not so long that it was insolent, saying, "You're *wrong*, Chief Bluecrane; you are making a mistake." And then she turned quickly so that the sorters wouldn't be obliged to touch her more, and she followed them out of the room.

When they came back and told him what had happened—that the moment Delina reached the edge of their land she had taken a quilt from the pack strapped to her shoulders, wrapped herself in it, and sat down on the ground in the pouring rain, a careful few inches past the PICOTA property line—Bluecrane laughed and told them not to concern themselves about it.

"She'll get very *wet*," they said.

"A woman of the Lines? Nonsense."

"There's nothing between her and the rain but a *quilt*."

"You watch," said Bluecrane. He chuckled, much amused at the ignorance of these two entrusted with the guarding of his personal time and space. And as he had predicted, although the rain went on all that day and all through the night, when the sun came up again the quilt was still dry. And Delina was still there.

"What is she doing?" the old man asked every now and then as the day went by. The answer was always the same.

"Nothing. She's doing nothing at all."

"Is she eating?"

"No . . . but she's taking water."

"Is she all right?"

The sorter shrugged, and made a noise deep in his throat.

"Well?"

"There's something wrong with her back; you noticed that. Her spine is twisted."

"So?"

"So it's possible that it hurts her. Sitting there like that, hour after hour."

"Has she complained? Has she cried?"

"No."

Bluecrane sighed. Damn the woman, and all the Chornyaks,

and for that matter, all the linguists. Only linguists would have allowed Delina's back to go untended. Only linguists would have had enough power to get *away* with it; it had to be a violation of a dozen laws protecting children. He had far too much to do to have this nuisance added to his list. But when the sun falling through the skylights began to slant toward midafternoon he said, "Call the law. Tell them we don't want them to do anything. Tell them she has her family's permission, improbable as that seems; the Chornyak men must all have gone out of their minds. Tell the law not to come—we don't need them."

On the third day he himself went out to talk to her, hunkering down beside her and looking carefully off into the middle distance so she wouldn't be embarrassed.

"Daughter," he said to her this time, because she had begun to earn his respect, "how long is this going to go on?"

"As long as it takes," she said. And then, "As long as it takes, Grandfather."

His breath was long and slow in the silence. All around them the grasshoppers were making leaps, their landings much louder than could be justified by their size and weight. He had always thought that they sounded like popcorn popping. A big rust-colored one sailed onto his right thigh, and he let it sit there; it wasn't bothering anything, and grasshoppers don't eat bluejeans.

"You are an Anglo," he said.

"I know that," she said. "And you are an Indian. There's nothing either one of us can do about it."

"Our ceremonies are useless to Anglos."

"I don't think so, Grandfather. Anglos are human beings. They are just like you, and just like all your relatives."

He frowned, distracted for a minute, wondering why the rain didn't bother the grasshoppers, sure that when he was a boy grasshoppers had sheltered from the rain like any other creature with good sense, wondering when the grasshoppers had changed and why he hadn't noticed. And then he said, "But their *souls* are very different from ours."

"I don't think so, Grandfather," she said again. And she added, "My greatgrandmother Nazareth Chornyak didn't think so, either. And she'd better be right, or we are all in terrible trouble."

Will Bluecrane's mouth tightened, deepening the net of wrinkles all around it. Bringing her greatgrandmother into this was pulling rank. She was getting above herself, doing that. And he got up and went back into the domes and left her there.

The next day the sorters had something new to tell him. "She's stopped drinking water," they said. "And last night she did not lie down."

"Not at all?"

"Not at all. She sat there all night, just as she has been sitting all through the days. She made the necessary trips into the trees . . . except for that, she didn't move."

"She is being a lot of *trouble*." the old man said crossly, and they nodded their full agreement. "But let me tell you . . . she won't keep this up for very long. Not without water."

"Maybe the law should come take her away. For her own good."

"Not yet," said Will Bluecrane firmly. "She is a very determined woman; unless she learns this lesson, she will just come back and try again."

"I don't like this," said the older of the two sorters. He was Will's own grandson, George William Bluecrane, and he had a tendency to presume on that relationship when he was worried. "This is not a way a woman should behave. I am absolutely sure it's going to lead to trouble, sooner or later."

"I don't like it either," Will told him. "But George—liking or not liking it has nothing to do with anything."

"What will the Chornyaks say, if one of their women dies outside our door, while we do nothing?"

Joe Brown, the other sorter, laughed softly. "What will the Pan-Indian Council say," he asked, "if the Chornyaks don't come and take their demented woman away from our door—where she is a great nuisance—and look after her properly?"

Will Bluecrane rubbed his hands together slowly in the silence that followed this exchange, until his grandson broke it by asking him straight out: "Why *haven't* the Chornyaks come? Why are they letting one of their women do this foolish thing?"

"Because," Will told him gently, "they are in great trouble, and they don't have the time or the heart to deal with her."

Their faces told him that he hadn't explained anything and that it would be best if he did, and he said, "*Look* . . . the linguist males have always known themselves to be critical to damn near everything that went on in the entire universe . . . the economic universe . . . and now nobody needs them any longer. They're useless now. Superfluous."

"They know as much as they ever did," Joe Brown pointed out.

"That's so. Sure. But without Aliens, who needs speakers of Alien languages? It must be like losing both your legs at once, with no warning—very disorienting. The men are paying Delina Chornyak's behavior no attention because panic, not reason, rules them right now. Give her another day; give *them* another day. We will see what happens."

"Maybe they're *hoping* she'll die here. It would be one less problem for them to deal with. You know how the linguists are."

"Joe Brown," Will snapped, "don't *you* add to my burdens! Have the decency to keep your bigoted ideas to yourself."

The next morning it was raining again, a cold steady rain that felt more like November than August, and he went out again to talk to stubborn Delina. He saw that her lips were dry and cracked and that she had begun to shiver inside her quilt. She had made no trips into the trees the night before, he knew.

He didn't hunker down beside her this time, and he was no longer concerned about sparing her embarrassment. He stood just far enough back so that she could look at him without craning her neck, and he glared at her fiercely through the rain. "Delina Chornyak," he said to her sternly, "you are being a damn *nuisance*."

She grinned up at him. "Yes," she said, "that's true. But be fair, Grandfather! I did warn you."

"I am not your grandfather."

"The well-bred Indian does not make fun of the ignorant Anglo woman who means well," she said, her lips twitching at the corners in a way he had always approved of in women.

"You will die out here, if you go on without drinking water."

"I don't think so, Grandfather."

"And now you are talking nonsense!" he snapped. "You are delirious with thirst, you foolish woman! As you said yourself, Anglos are human beings. Pay attention to me now: if you don't take water, Delina Chornyak, you will die."

"You won't let that happen," she said gently.

"I *will*."

"I don't think so, Grandfather."

"You *look* foolish, too," he told her, with as much scorn as he could manage. "There's water running down your face and dripping off your nose. You should see yourself; you'd be embarrassed! Pull your quilt up over your head and keep yourself dry!"

She dropped her eyes, but she made no move to shelter herself; the rain poured over her head and streamed down her back from the ends of her long brown hair. She looked half-drowned, and she was so pale through her sunburn that she had the color of faded yellow leaves; it was not a color that suited her. It seemed to him that her left shoulder, the one that was lower than the other, was pulled more sharply toward the ground than it had been when she stood before him in his office; it seemed to him that the quilt had hid her crookedness up to now, and that it was an ominous sign that it did so no longer. He didn't like the way she looked. It worried him, and he resented the way that the picture she made, sitting there in the rain, was being burned into his memory.

He went away again, and went about the business of being chief of the PICOTA. It was a lot of work, it always had been, and it required all his attention, but his mind kept wandering. And when night came and Delina still had neither gone away nor taken food or water, half of what he should have done that day was not yet done and the other half had been done badly.

The woman who came to see him just after dark was neither young nor beautiful. Nor was she respectful. "Will Bluecrane," she said to him, arms akimbo and both hands braced on her ample hips, "this has gone on long enough! That child is going to die on our doorstep, and how are you going to live with yourself *then*?"

"She's thirty if she's a day," he said, "maybe forty. Did you notice her neck?"

"Do not try to distract me," she told him grimly. "I'm *serious*."

"She may be pretending, Anne," said Will. "There may be a device in her quilt that puts water directly into her veins, for instance. There may be—"

"You've talked to her! Does she look to you like someone who's had water lately?"

"Ah, but Anne, remember . . . she's a linguist. From birth they're trained in bodyparl, trained to use it the way you'd use scissors or a computer. They can look any way they *like*, and no layperson can spot them when they choose to be deceptive."

His wife snorted. "Myths!" she said. "Claptrap! Government propaganda! Who do you think you're talking to?"

"And Anne," he went on, ignoring that, "she *has* to be in touch with Chornyak Household. Because not one of her people has come near her in all this time or so much as called to ask how she's doing. Do you really believe they'd do that if she wasn't reporting in regularly? As Joe Brown says, love, they may hope she dies out there—but believe me, they wouldn't risk being perceived as neglecting her. Not the linguists."

"But, Will—"

"Furthermore, it's true that the Aliens have gone away, but they might come back; and if they do, the Chornyak men will need Delina again. She's valuable property, and they always hedge their bets."

"Will Bluecrane, *you* with the wooden head, will you rein in your mouth, please, before it runs off with you? I can hear people now . . . 'Poor old Chief Bluecrane . . . he used to be somebody you could look to for guidance. He used to be a man with a good *mind.* And now just look at what he's become, in his second, or maybe his third, childhood.'"

His eyebrows went up; she wasn't kidding. "What is it?" he asked. "I'm right, Anne; you know I am."

"That's all beside the point. Maybe she could be fed somehow

. . . be given water somehow . . . without our knowing. I'll grant you that. Maybe she *can* shape her face to the lines of thirst and misery, as you say. I don't think that's happening, but I'll grant that it's possible; I've heard the stories. And the linguist women spend . . . spent . . . half their lives shut up in interpreter pods . . . for all I know, it's no hardship for her to sit out there day after day. But there's something else."

"Oh, lord," said Will mournfully, covering his face with his hands, "let there be nothing else!"

"How much do you know about the women of the Lines?" she demanded. In what he had always referred to as her "I am Anne Jordacha Walks Tall Bluecrane—*hark!*" voice.

"Not much. And I have no wish to know more, considering the example that sits outside."

"Then let me tell you this: they are never idle. *Never.*" She put the palms of her hands flat on the table and leaned toward him. "By the time a linguist female is twelve years old, if her hands are not needed for some other activity, they are busy at needlework! Always! No woman of the Lines sits more than three minutes without taking out a needle or a hook or some other tool of the crafts they practice. And Delina Meloren Chornyak has sat out there four days with her hands folded in her lap. *Folded!*"

Will was stunned. She was right. This was the piece of information that mattered, and it had gone right past him. Like an untrained boy, he had neglected the first and most basic principle of knowing-what-is-going-on: ANY MISMATCH IS A WARNING SIGN. He'd known, but he hadn't thought of it; to his shame, he knew that he never would have thought of it. The woman could have turned ninety, sitting wrapped in her quilt by his door, and he would never have realized that she should not have been sitting there *idle*. He put his chin in his hands and talked to the table top, talked to his wife's spread fingers and the blue veins on her hands. "I am not fit to be chief of the PICOTA any longer," he muttered.

"True," said Anne decisively.

"I'm old. My mind wanders."

"That, too."

"I will go out and talk to her again," he said. And then he

jumped, startled, as Anne smacked the table with the flat of her left hand.

"Addlepate!"

"But—"

She did it again, and ignored his scowl. "Will, for heaven's sakes, let me go bring her in here where you can be comfortable while you talk to her!"

"*Oh*, no!" He shook his head firmly. "She expects me to go out there and hunker down and do monosyllables and wise grunts and noble platitudes at her, and she's earned that. I'm not about to disappoint her."

His wife cocked her head and stepped back, her hands once more on her hips, and stood there looking at him as if he were a very rare and exceedingly nasty bug; she blew through her lips in total exasperation.

"I don't care," he told her. "This is an Anglo woman, and she is busting her tail trying to be *her* idea of a Native American doing a sacred fast, and I'm not going to make her feel like a fool by acting normal. I will go out there and meet her expectations as best I can."

"And then?"

"And *then* I will bring her in here. Where we can *both* be comfortable."

"But only for a couple of hours," she said.

"Why do you say *that*?"

"Will, that poor child came here asking for our help with a vision quest. She's already done most of one on her own. If you wine her and dine her and tuck her into a nice soft bed for the night she'll have to start all over. That's not only ridiculous, it's *cruel*. Bring her in, mumble significant mumbles, give her a little plain water, find out what is to be done next, and then get on with it." She sat down on the edge of the table and looked at him hard, but her voice was tender, and as she talked he began nodding his head, because she was right. "My love," she said, "this is a very brave young woman, but she can't go on forever. Nobody does *two* fasts, back-to-back . . . and I'm afraid she would try, if she thought it was expected. Think, please, dear man, and take care."

When he dropped down on his heels beside Delina this time, he knew by the ache in his heart that he *was* getting old. He was supposed to be tough; he wasn't supposed to go all over liver and lilies like this. She would have been disappointed in him if she'd known.

"Granddaughter," he said, keeping his voice stern, "you have convinced me."

"It *took* long enough," she answered, her voice both hoarse and cross.

"Yes, I agree; it did. But you must realize . . . for centuries we've had Anglos dropping in wanting to . . . oh, dance with a kachina, maybe. Wanting to spend the Christmas holiday in a sweat lodge—an *outdoor* sweat lodge, mind you, not the kind *we* use. Wanting to hang by a hook from a tent pole. You know the kind of thing. And they always foul it up. And then they have to be rushed to the experts. And we have to do extra ceremonies—at great expense of time and money and energy, which we cannot afford—to purify all the things they've made messes of. It would be one thing if it did them any good, Delina Chornyak . . . it never does. It's important for us to discourage them."

"I understand," she said. "But I'm sure this isn't going to start a new fashion, Mr. Bluecrane. You're not going to have Anglos dropping in by the dozens wanting to sit outside the door for a week, fasting. There's no call for it. And I am *not* going to foul it up—I promise you."

"There was a story about you on the comset," he said.

"The world has turned upside down, and they call *me* news?" She was shocked; the possibility had never occurred to her. "What are they saying?"

"It's pretty much a muddle, but I *think* the gist is that you believe some PICOTA insult caused the Aliens to leave, and you're doing a protest demonstration."

She laughed, and he found that comforting. If she could still laugh, she wasn't too badly off.

"One of your relatives will have planted that tale?" he said.

"Probably. I should have expected it, I guess; it's a lot less embarrassing than the truth would be."

"Will you come inside now, child?" he asked her. "And sit for a little while in comfort, while I send for the people who know how to do the ceremony you want? Can you stand up?"

"Perceive!" she said, and she stood, with the quilt still draped around her. The quilt—blocks of black and white sea waves in the dolphin curve that evokes love's most ancient and basic chord in humankind, on a ground of dark blue—was as bright as if no single drop of rain or ray of sun had ever touched it. "Perceive—I'm standing up!"

It was true. She wasn't steady, and she wasn't graceful, and her head was as bedraggled as the quilt was fresh and fair, but she was on her feet. And he had not had to help her.

"Come along," he said gruffly, turning his back so she wouldn't see the tears in his silly damn eyes, and he led her inside to get on with it, fast, before she grew any weaker.

He sincerely hoped that she was going to live through it. He sincerely hoped she was going to survive the sweat lodge, which she would *undoubtedly* insist on doing outdoors, in the rain. He sincerely hoped he wasn't going to have her death on his conscience, and on his wife's tongue, for all the rest of his life.

CHAPTER 2

"Delina," said Nazareth, "this is really excessively dramatic."

That hurt. The sound Delina made was a tiny gasp of pain, as if she'd been suddenly slapped. *Not even "Hello, Delina Meloren." Just "This is really excessively dramatic."*

The dead woman stood near a line of big cedars, in a thicket of sumac blazing scarlet and lemon-yellow and burnished gold around her, close enough for Delina to see and hear but well beyond any possibility of touch. *"Do not approach her,"* the medsammys had said, *"and if she approaches you, do not back away. Find your place, and stand your ground."* The spot Delina had chosen was well out into the middle of the field where, if she tipped back her head, she could see the tall buildings of the city rising up in all directions beyond the trees and hills that bordered the PICOTA lands; she hoped it *was* her place.

Delina was far past both hunger and thirst now. As clean both inside and out as a synthodiamond, riding on a high keen wind only she could feel or hear, she scoffed at her greatgrandmother and declared that she was no more melodramatic than *Nazareth* was.

"I beg your pardon?"

Can you really shock the dead? Can you startle them into begging your pardon? Delina smothered the laugh that threatened to break loose, and explained.

"Dropping dead in a rose garden," she said, "at the very moment the AIRYs are leaving us forevermore—the very moment they *cease* to be Aliens-in-Residence and become Aliens-in-Absentia?

Seeing them off by expiring among the flowers at the mere sight of their backs? You call that dignified, Greatgrandmother? I call it *tacky*. And I call it outrageous, too! And irresponsible. *Especially*. I call it irresponsible. How *dare* you do that to us!"

"Delina, dear love," Nazareth answered calmly, drawing her shawl more tightly around her shoulders, as if she felt the chill, "is that any way to talk to a dead person?"

Delina's eyes narrowed and her lips thinned, and she almost backed up a step before she remembered: *Stand your ground.* Nazareth wasn't asking a serious question, she was teasing an outrageous child; but she was going to get a serious answer all the same. She paused a minute to think, to shape the words that she would say, and then she answered with great care.

"I don't *know*, Greatgrandmother," she said, "I truly don't. How *do* people talk to a dead person? I've never talked to one before. Books about manners don't mention it. You're the only person I ever knew who claimed it was possible, and you gave me no instructions. I've had to just do the best I could, all on my own, and for you to stand there being flippant at me isn't helpful. Or called for, in my opinion."

Nazareth raised her eyebrows. "When?" she asked. "When did I ever tell you that it was possible to carry on a conversation with the dead?"

"You didn't say it in so many words, Greatgrandmother."

"I thought not."

"But you gave me the *impression* that you believed it could be done. Lots of times. *And*, you said it was narrow-minded to assume that it couldn't be done just because it hadn't been."

Nazareth's lips twitched, and she stood tapping them with her two forefingers, studying Delina for a moment, before she spoke again. "It appears to me that you are genuinely angry with me," she said slowly, "and that's astonishing. I had every right to die, like any other human being. But you're angry."

"I'm *furious* with you!" Delina declared, raising her chin and looking the old woman right in the eye, so far as it was possible to do that at this distance; she was sure her *intention* was clear. "And I am here to tell you that you're not going to get away with it!"

"That's why we're here."

"Exactly."

"You couldn't have just . . . oh, done a séance, for instance? Or brought in a Ouija board, or a crystal ball, or some goat entrails? You had to go bother all the Indian Nations?"

Ah! There it was—the explanation for her greatgrandmother's uncooperative behavior. The reason there'd been no greeting, no friendly preamble, let alone any sign that she was happy to see Delina again, as Delina rejoiced to see her. Delina was supposed to have managed this alone, without "bothering" anybody. Without washing the Chornyak linen in public. Without making a spectacle of herself, or of the Households.

Delina firmed her lips to a thin line, and opened her mouth for a cool and dignified reply, but there wasn't strength enough left in her to bring it off. Shuddering all over, she wrapped her arms tightly round herself and rocked from side to side, whimpering, her face screwed into a tight knot of misery.

"Delina Meloren," Nazareth said quickly, "my question must have been badly put!" She stepped out of the sumac thicket, narrowing the distance between them a little, saying, "You realize that once I was past ninety I no longer concerned myself a great deal with people's 'feelings' . . . perhaps I've lost the knack. I didn't intend to cause you pain, but that's no excuse. Delina, can you tell me what hurts you so?"

"Greatgrandmother," Delina managed finally, through teeth clenched against the shaking, "I'm not stupid; I'm not ignorant. I tried everything. I did try. *Everything!* Respectfully. With an open mind. No matter how the others looked at me, or how they talked. And none of it worked. Maybe because I did it wrong; I don't know. But it failed. All of it. The Ouija board *sassed* me . . . have you ever heard of such a thing as that?" She swallowed hard, and went on, "*And* I had to put up with the entire family . . . everybody but Willow, bless her . . . treating me as if I'd gone mad, instead of helping me. Telling me I was out of my mind with grief . . . lecturing me solemnly about how much you would have disapproved of my behavior . . . telling me I was letting you *down!* Dosing me with potions that would gag a maggot, choke a snake—"

27

"But *child*," Nazareth broke in, "what on earth did you tell them you were doing?"

"I told them I was trying to get in touch with *you,* Greatgrandmother, because we needed your advice! What else would I have told them?"

Nazareth blinked. Frowning, lips parted, shaking her head slowly, she started to speak. "You should never have said that you—" And then she stopped, and started over in a different tone of voice. A crisp one; all business. "Please go on," she said. "The Chornyak males did not shut you up and *declare* you mad, as I would have expected them to do. The women of Chornyak Household have all grown so puny and so peaked that they are no match for you. The people of the PICOTA did not send you packing. You stand here before me apparently at liberty to do whatever you damn well *please.* That being the unlikely lay of this land, child—go on!"

"I could scarcely have said that now I had no work to do I'd decided to take up parlor games," Delina said flatly. "There *was* no plausible explanation, except the plain and honest truth. I told them—and it was accurate—that no proof exists either for or against the possibility of communicating with the dead. I told them I needed to talk to you. And I told them I didn't intend to give up until I was convinced it was impossible. Nobody encouraged me; on the other hand, nobody *stopped* me. I framed it as a scientific hypothesis, you perceive." She took a long deep breath and let it go, shuddering. Remembering. "Meanwhile, while you have been lollygagging around heaven, or wherever you are, the whole *world* has gone mad, and for all I know, all its colonies as well! *Shame* on you, Natha!"

Nazareth considered that for a while in a silence of a sort that Delina had seen many hundreds of times before and had often seen followed by spectacular fireworks. She faced her greatgrandmother with her head flung back, as defiant as she could manage to be under the circumstances. Remembering what the Indian medsammys had told her about the necessity for utter faith, utter confidence, utter trust. *"We have no reason,"* they'd told her, *"to believe that those who live in the spirit world look at things the way* we *do. Why* should *they? But we know one thing: hypocrisy and false manners are no use with them at all."* She stood quiet and alert, waiting, listening to the wind telling her she was doing *fine,* until Nazareth spoke again.

"And so, Delina Meloren, for sweet sanity's sake you decided on a vision quest in the ancient Indian fashion? This follows?"

Delina could have explained that it was the dreams that had made her decide to do it. Dreaming night after night of blue corn and red corn, black corn and purple corn, fields of short stubby corn growing implausibly in hills of plain dry sand, and never the tall lush green and yellow Anglo corn of Kansas planted in dark rich ground in long logical rows, her mind had *finally* gotten through to her. Had gotten past all her . . . terrible irresistible pun . . . all her reservations. But she was not going to explain. Her greatgrandmother was dead; she had the advantage. Presumably she knew all the answers before she asked the questions.

Delina stood there as silent as granite, glaring at Nazareth. Noticing that the Indian medsammy was right . . . Nazareth looked nothing like an apparition. She looked perfectly ordinary, and a bit tired. She trailed no clouds of glory. She wore a nondescript and ordinary-looking gray dress—not the garment she'd been cremated in, Delina was certain of that—and an equally ordinary shawl was around her shoulders. You couldn't even see through her.

"Greatgrandmother," Delina said, aware that she was wringing her hands and not able to stop, wishing desperately that at least one of the other women of her household stood beside her, "I am *so* angry with you!"

"Yes, dearlove. I notice that you are."

There was a gust of wind, and leaves tore away from the sumac and whirled up into the cedar trees like a necklace of brilliant fetish birds; the cedar moaned as the wind went surfing through its broad green arms. It was getting colder, and darker.

"All my life," Delina said bitterly, "I heard just one line . . . 'Nazareth will not leave us till we can spare her.' And then, on the very day when we need you more than any other day, on the very day when the whole world turns upside down, you *die* on us!"

"Well, Delina, I am sorry," Nazareth told her, "and I am sorry you've had so hard a time. Still . . . *I* never said that line, you know. Not once. Other people said it. And the way I died . . . that wasn't deliberate."

Delina's laugh rang out harsh and sudden, startling the grasshoppers into leaping, all at the same time, all around her.

"I don't believe you for one *minute*, Greatgrandmother!" she cried. "Don't try that with me! You were out there in the roses. You looked up and saw the AIRYs waltzing across the lawn and whoopsing away with no explanation. And you said to yourself. 'Well, I certainly don't want to have to deal with *this* mess!' *And* you dropped dead on the spot with a sheaf of roses tastefully draped over your thighs! That is what *really* happened!"

There was another long silence, punctuated only by the chill wind in the cedars and the occasional thunk of a landing or a taking off.

"Delina."

"Yes, Greatgrandmother Nazareth."

"The dead do not argue. Tell me why you've . . . what is this you've done? Summoned me, I suppose. Tell me why you've summoned me."

"Don't you already know? Isn't that part of it?"

"Part of what, child?"

"Part of being dead?"

"If it were, would I tell you?"

Delina thought about that, and shook her head. "I guess not," she said. And then, from out of a lifetime of love: "Natha? Are you all right?"

"Yes, Delina, sweet child; I'm entirely all right. Now . . . tell me, please, with no more carryings-on."

"All right," Delina answered. "I'll ignore the facts of all this. I'll behave as if I were at . . . oh, at the State Department. I have three questions for you."

"Ask them."

"One: I want to know *why* all the Aliens left. Two: I want to know if they are coming back—or if they are going to do something else to us, something dreadful. And three—more than anything else—I want to know what to *do*. At least where to begin. How to *start*." She moaned, then, and put both her hands over her face, and stumbled three steps backward, trying not to fall down, thinking: *Oh, damn, now I've done it! And that was four questions, not three!* If it hadn't been so long since she'd taken any liquid into her body she would have been weeping, but there was nothing left to serve her for tears. "Don't you *dare* disappear on me again!" she said desperately. "I am doing the very best I *can!*"

It didn't happen; when she looked toward the cedars again, Nazareth was still there. She looked as if her patience were wearing thin, but she was still there.

"Oh, Natha," Delina said mournfully when she had caught her breath, gripping the earth beneath her with her bare feet, curling her toes into the dirt to keep her where she was, "we are so bewildered! The men are *no* help; they have all the authority to do things, but they just mill around bleating and blustering, and when we make suggestions they wave their arms at us like we were cattle they were trying to shoo into a field . . . I think they're in shock, Natha. As many weeks as have gone by since it happened, I think they're still in shock."

"That's possible," Nazareth answered, nodding. "It's a hard and shocking time for humankind, Delina; there's been no preparation for this. No warning. Plenty of ancient stories about the *arrivals* of alien beings, but none where they settle in for generations and then leave without a word. Shock is appropriate. Not useful for getting on with it, I realize—but appropriate. Understandable."

Delina let her hands fall to her sides, and she settled herself to speak with more composure. She wondered if she dared go closer to Nazareth; she longed to. But she was afraid; better to stay where she was. "You know, Natha," she said, "better than I do, that the men always believed the time would come when the Aliens would tell them all the secrets. Would explain all the science, all the technology, they'd kept from us. When they would stop treating us like cute little children playing grownup. I think *all* the men, not just the men of the Lines, were convinced of that. And now here we are, knowing no more than we ever knew, and they're gone!"

"What are they doing . . . the men, I mean?"

"They go off in corners in little bunches, and talk to each other ... they get drunk, and talk to each other. They have meetings, and talk to each other. They're *stuck*, somehow! And supposing we women could do any better, there are no mechanisms in place to let us try. It's the same way in every one of the houses of the Lines ... chaos ... and I suspect it's even worse everywhere else. Somebody has to do something, Natha, we have to find a way to go *on*. We linguists are the only ones who know *every*body in power ... I think it has to be us, I really do. Please, Greatgrandmother, can't you—isn't there some way you can come back again?"

Nazareth clucked her tongue. "Don't be absurd," she said crossly, ducking to avoid another flight of sumac leaves. "Of course not!"

"Suppose we made you a shrine, Greatgrandmother. I am *quite* serious. Suppose we made you a shrine, and we really did come each day and tend the shrine and make our respectful greetings to you?"

Everything fell silent around them while Nazareth thought that over; it was, after all, a fair question. But in the end she shook her head, and Delina nodded.

"All right, I'll accept that," she said. "It makes sense. But then please answer my questions. Why, after interacting with Earth and its colonies for more than two hundred years, did every single Alien leave us? At the same exact minute, and, for all we know, forever? Throwing all the worlds into turmoil? Why? What does it mean? They knew, Natha—they knew what the consequences would be, for us, and they had no more evil among them than humans have. Why did they do it? What is going to happen? And what are we to *do*?"

And Nazareth told her; it didn't take long.

There was thunder off in the distance; once, twice, and then in a long rumbling roll that went on and on. The leaves went dull as the sunlight was cut off by the clouds. And the rain began falling again as Delina listened, nodding now and then, holding her lower lip tightly in her teeth, trying to make sure every word was etched in her memory. She was not so naive as to count on doing this twice in a single lifetime; she knew Nazareth. Suppose the summoned dead ordinarily popped in and out like robobuses; nevertheless, Delina could well imagine her greatgrandmother refusing ever to participate in this most ultimately bicultural process again. And the medsammys had told her she must leave her wrist computer hanging in the bundle in the sycamore, along with all the rest of the mechanical trappings she'd had with her. She just had to *remember*. She focused her windswept mind to that, and hung on for dear life.

Will Bluecrane would never have asked another Indian for a report on a vision quest. Never. Even the thought of doing such a thing was improper. But with Anglos you *did* have to ask, because otherwise you couldn't be sure what sort of messes they'd gotten themselves into, or what needed to be done to set matters right. Reluctantly, therefore, because Delina had shown herself worthy of a different sort of treatment . . . but still, he couldn't risk letting her suffer harm . . . he asked her.

"My greatgrandmother came," she said.

"And that was what you were hoping for, I believe."

"Yes, Grandfather."

He waited, and she looked at him gravely for a minute before the grin he found so delightful happened. She was no prettier than she'd been when she first showed up to torment him, but right now she had the uncanny translucent elegance that goes with a sacred procedure done properly and all the trimmings laid on. She had not only survived, he told himself with satisfaction, she had *improved*. And that was how it was *supposed* to work.

"Chief Bluecrane," she said, "your medsammys supervised me sixty-seven ways from breakfast and back again. I promise you . . . there's nothing you need to clean up, nothing that has to be repaired. It's all taken care of. You don't have to ask me any more questions."

"You're *sure* of that?"

"Certain sure. Of course I'm sure, or I'd ask for help. I came here asking, remember? I didn't decide I'd just make it all up as I went along. You can check with your people, Mr. Bluecrane;

they'll tell you that I'm all right and nothing has to be done. No repairs required; no loose ends. They were very careful, and I was very careful. And Greatgrandmother was very careful, you may be sure. And I found out what I needed to know."

The old man sighed, long and slow, and crossed his open palms on his broad chest, beaming at her with very genuine pleasure.

"I'm glad," he said. "I'm very glad. And I am proud of you, Delina Chornyak."

Delina looked at the floor; like any linguist woman, and like any woman disapproved of long term, she had had too little experience of praise to know what to do with it.

"What will you do now?" he asked her.

"Go home." She looked up at him, frowning. "I'll let you know how it turns out."

His eyebrows went up. "Explain, please," he said.

"It's important for the men at Chornyak Household to believe that I've had an awful time and been properly punished for my impudence. I have to go home in disgrace, you perceive . . . humiliated . . . barely able to face them . . . cured at last of my absurd ideas and ashamed I ever had them. That's what I promised I would say, whatever happened, and it's what the women who've been covering for me are entitled to. I have to convince the men that I've learned my lesson and am deeply sorry for my behavior."

"That's called *lying*," said Will.

"Yes. It certainly is. And I don't do it well. But most of it will be done for me. Some of my aunts and greataunts, chattering about my deep regret where the men can hear them, will do it."

"I'd have thought the men would know . . . they say you cannot lie to a linguist."

"That's so," said Delina. "Unless"—and she looked at the floor again—"you are also a linguist."

Will nodded; perhaps it was true.

"You will tell the women the truth, though?"

"Oh, yes!" she said. "Not the little girls, because that's not fair—you can't give them responsibility like that, not against the inquisitive efforts of skilled adult males. But I'll tell the women."

Will wondered what the women of his own house did behind *his* back, hoping the gulf was not quite so wide as the one at Chornyak Household. Presumably the fact that the males and females of the linguist Lines lived in separate buildings made gulfs easier to carve out and maintain.

"Do you think the women will believe you, Delina?" he asked.

She shook her head, her eyes not seeing him. "Probably not. I'll have to find a way to convince them; it won't be easy."

"Good luck to you," he began, thinking he'd throw in a few more wise sayings just to round things off for her, and then he stopped, realizing that she wasn't hearing him, either; she was thinking of something else.

"I have a message from Nazareth Chornyak Adiness for *you*," she said, surprising him. "Brace yourself, Grandfather."

"I'm braced, Delina. Braced and curious. Tell me."

"Greatgrandmother said—and told me to tell you she had said—that the women of the Lines must begin taking husbands from among the PICOTA, if your men can be persuaded. Even if they will not come live in the Households and our women must go to them instead, it must be done. That alliance must begin, as quickly as possible, she says . . . because there is more trouble coming, and it will be needed."

Will Bluecrane nodded slowly, rubbing his chin with the back of his hand; it made sense. He could see it. It was going to be a matter for much argument, because the prejudice against linguists was far from gone . . . on the other hand, it was the marriage of the highest of technologies. And no doubt there *was* more trouble coming; in his experience, there always was. "Stars and bionic garters!" he said. "Shall we begin with me?"

"You have a wife already, Chief Bluecrane."

"My misfortune, Delina."

"And hers," she said, chuckling.

"Go home, child," he said, thinking what a shame it was that she wasn't pretty. Life would have been so much easier for her if she'd been pretty. He wondered how her husband treated her, and how he had been persuaded—even in the bizarre context of Main

Houses and Womanhouses and Barren Houses that passed for "home" with linguists—to let her hare off to the PICOTA domes on her errand with the dead.

"Go home," he said again, gruffly, "and eat, and drink, and rest. And then we'll talk about this business of future alliances. And Delina . . ."

"Yes?" She swayed where she stood, and he reached out and steadied her, carefully.

"Will you be all right?" he asked. "Shall I send someone along to see you safely home?"

"Nobody will mind if I'm a little wobbly," she said, "and I don't require any fussing over. I'll be fine."

"I am told that you were obedient, and respectful, and brave," he said, pleased to see her cheeks turn dull red. "That's satisfying to me; if you had died, or been a smartass, I would never have lived it down."

"Thank you; I'll remember that while I'm being humble at home."

"Just one more thing."

"Yes?"

"I am *also* told by our . . . what is it you call them? Medsammys?"

"Medsammys, yes. From 'medical' . . . and 'samurai.' Elite class with the power of life and death."

"Appropriate for ours, Delina?"

She thought a minute, and then shook her head. "No; not appropriate at all. I'm sorry! It's habit; a discourteous habit of reference that I promise to give up. What was it that your healers told you?"

"That you could have accomplished exactly the same thing with a ten-day fast in your *own* tradition. Maybe some sacred music with it, for buffering."

"Really?" It was the first time Will had seen her falter.

"They say so. They say that for such as you—a discourteous habit of reference I promise to give up in my turn—it's the long fasting, not the rest of the gewgaws."

"I didn't know that," said Delina slowly. "If I'd known, I would not have troubled you."

But I dreamed of Indian corn, she thought. *And Greatgrand-mother Nazareth did not say we must begin marrying theologians and musicians. She chided me for "bothering" the Indian tribes, but she said we must marry men of the PICOTA. Perhaps,* she thought, careful not to let it show on her face, *perhaps you are wrong.*

"That's all right," he said. "But remember it, please. For next time."

CHAPTER 3

FROM THE ARCHIVES OF: Chornyak Barren House
ENTRY OF: Delina Meloren Chornyak

You can't just get up in the morning and say to yourself, "Well, time to start saving the solar system!" Never mind the logic or illogic of it, never mind "modesty"; they're not relevant. Even if you knew beyond all *question* that you had the power to do it, you couldn't tackle the task that way and still function. You wouldn't be able to tolerate even five minutes of leisure, you perceive . . . you'd be saying to yourself, *How can you sit there and* read *(or take a bath, or talk to a friend, or anything else not indisputably critical to survival) when you* could *be saving the* worlds? It would be like knowing that you were on the right track to finding a cure for a cruel disease, only worse. You'd work night and day. You'd work while you ate. And still, *still*, you would feel intolerable guilt.

That won't do. The work will never get done, that way. You have to step outside what you're doing and look at it *from* outside, even while you are most deeply occupied with it. You have to learn to perceive it as a scientific project, as a theoretical investigation, as research for the sake of research. You have to rope it off in your mind as if it had nothing to do with anything, with maybe—*maybe*—a slim potential for practical application, far down a long and unforeseeable road.

I approached the problem Nazareth set for me, therefore, as I would have approached any problem in linguistic analysis. As if I had been searching for the answer to . . . oh, let's say, the problem of English predicate order before nouns. Why do we say "little brick house" but not "brick little house?" Why "tall blond man" but not "blond tall man?" I set to work to find out how to save humankind from catastrophe in exactly the same way I would have searched for those word order rules:

Record the data.
Look for pattern(s).
Extrapolate.
Solve for the missing item(s).

Plus the extra step every woman of the Lines learns early: *Find the one critical end of the tangled string. The one you pull to make the entire knotted mess fall in orderly disorder at your feet.*

I'm well trained; I knew better than to hurry. Nazareth had never let up on reminding us that you have to plan *far* ahead: not in terms of years or tens of years, but in terms of *centuries.* Strange as it seems, when the human lifespan is rarely more than one hundred and fifty years, it has to be like that. We know from bitter experience that planning based on shorter chunks of time leads only to dead ends and a step back for each step forward, with success becoming a matter of blind chance. I knew all of that. On the other hand, I knew I had no time to waste.

We linguists were going to be all right for a long time. The excellent fees we'd always earned and our skill in investing them, together with our frugal lifestyle, meant that there was money enough to maintain all thirteen Households of the Lines for generations. I could see that we might have to cut back on our charities; I could see that we were probably going to be hated again, more than ever; but we wouldn't have to go without anything we ourselves needed. And our underground and earth-sheltered buildings would continue to protect us against riot and disaster.

But the ferociously busy trade between Earth and her colonies and the Alien worlds hadn't employed only linguists. From the top government officials who hired us, all the way to the people on hourly wages who built the interpreting booths where we spent most of our time, that trade had represented a good three-fourths of the solar system's economy. You couldn't rip it out of the fabric of daily life and expect the remaining rags and tatters to sustain all the billions who had depended on it. Most of the people who'd been thrown out of work when the Aliens abandoned us would have had meager savings, if any. The social welfare systems would take care of them after an equally meager fashion when their funds were gone . . . for a while. For a little while.

The Aliens hadn't taken away any of the gleaming gadgets they had given us to make our lives easier, but we knew the gadgets would break down (everything does, eventually) and they would wear out, and we didn't know either how to repair them or how to make new ones. The borrowed Alien science had been left behind, too, but we had always used it by pushing buttons that read PUSH and pulling levers that read PULL. Not by knowing what we were doing! I was at the breakfast table the Sunday morning when Jorn Benjamin Chornyak told the sorry tale of our attempts to find *out* what we had been doing—when our scientists broke open the units that the buttons and levers were mounted on.

"There was nothing inside!" Jorn said, leaning over the table, his voice thick and harsh. I had often heard Jorn distressed or angry; you can't be Head of all the Lines and live placidly. But I had never heard him sound like he sounded that morning. Total silence fell in the diningroom then, you can be sure. Even at the tables near the outside walls, where you sit if your goal is to eat fast and escape, people put down their knives and sporks and they listened.

"There wasn't anything there," he went on, in that curious voice that said, *I can't take much more of this, I've already borne more of it than I can bear.* "Nothing at all. And you know what that has to mean. Either the Aliens did everything themselves, and the buttons and levers and studs on the units are like those on children's toys—*connected* to nothing at all, put there so that we human beings could play 'just pretend'—or the connections are in a form we know nothing about and don't even know how to start looking for."

People said the kind of things you say in such situations:

curses; lamentations. From beside him, Jorn's youngest son asked, "What's going to happen with all that stuff?"

"Well," Jorn answered, giving his scrambled eggs one vicious stab after another, "what do you *suppose* is going to happen? When the gadgets stop working, they'll be useless, of course!" And he added, "They've sent crash teams into the planet archives . . . we'll have to find out how we *used* to do things. We had ways of getting by, before they gave us all the pretty toys; we have to find out what they were, and learn how to make use of them again."

"And the colonies?" somebody asked from a far corner, hesitantly. "Will we be able to stay in contact with them?"

Jorn shrugged. "I don't know," he said. "Nobody does. Maybe the metacomsets will go on working for the next hundred years while we figure out how they're made and how to maintain them. We were *told*, when they were installed, that they were a permanent modification to our information networks; maybe it's true. And maybe it was a lie, like telling little kids 'sure, there's a Santa Claus'; maybe they'll all quit tomorrow morning and we'll be cut off except for the kind of primitive communication across space we had in the twentieth century. I do not have the least idea. Nor, so far as I know, does anybody else."

I was frightened; we were *all* frightened. All day and all night we heard the flyers coming and going, seemingly without ever a break; all day and all night, every computer channel was up and running and sending FULL messages when you tried to access it. People were moving back and forth; information was moving back and forth; international organizations and interplanetary ones were busy. A great deal was going on. But we know it would be childish to assume that those who were running all the frantic hum of activity knew what they were doing. At least I had that small advantage—I did know what I was doing. I had my information from a source that was beyond challenge.

"The Aliens left us," Nazareth had said to me, standing there by the cedars looking just as alive as I did, "for just one reason:

because their governments have put the Earth and all its colonies under quarantine for their intransigent *violence*."

I tried to interrupt, but she made the PanSig BE-STILL-TILL-I-AM-THROUGH gesture, using both arms to make it as emphatic as possible, almost losing her shawl in the process, and she never paused until she *was* through. Earth and Mars and Venus, Gehenna and Strawberry Fields and Luna, Jupiter and Xa and Horsewhispering—every single planet and every last asteroid!—we had all been classified by the consortium of Alien governments as *plague* worlds. They perceived us as pocked and raddled and warped, filthied by a disease that made us do one another deliberate harm, often taking pleasure in the doing. None of us were going *out*; none of them were coming in. Quarantined! Like the lepers of the most ancient histories. And quarantined we would stay, she told me solemnly, until we cured ourselves.

"How?" I got in that one word. "*How?*" *Where is the end of the string?*

And my greatgrandmother said: "Find a way to put an end to hunger, Delina Meloren."

Just like that! No details; no instructions. Just: Find a way to put an end to hunger.

They asked me later whether she was unable to tell me more or just unwilling, and I said angrily, "How in Gehenna's name would I know *that*? I'm a linguist, not an anthropologist of the culture of the Dead!"

Because they were also linguists, even in that time of terrible worry they were intrigued by the lexical possibilities, and they stopped to play with the pieces a little . . . "Thananthropologist?" "Thanthropologist?" But I didn't join in that discussion. I had an opinion, and I intended to express it. "It is my personal opinion that she was *unwilling* to say anything more," I told them. "You know how she is. Was. Is? 'Nobody understands or values that which just falls into their laps,' she was forever saying. Right? And consider this: if there is a rule—a law of the Afterlife—against such telling, how could she get away with explaining to me why the Aliens have abandoned us? If she was allowed to tell me about the quarantine, why not the rest of it? I think she could have told me what to do, step by step, down to the last detail! I really do. I think she just *wouldn't.*"

"Delina," they objected, "you can't know that! Surely, if she could have helped us—"

"Perhaps," I said flatly, cutting off the romances. "When I am dead, I will know." And I set the question aside; it had no relevance.

I couldn't see the crucial connection between ending hunger and ending violence, myself. It wouldn't have been my guess. There were so many far more obvious string-ends. Changing the school curriculum, for example. Creating a soap-op to play daily on the comsets, with nonviolence as its theme. Vaporizing Gehenna and all its sadistic and masochistic citizens; hunting down everyone Gehenna-like on other worlds and treating them the same way. Things like those would have come to my mind, and perhaps I would have been desperate enough to accept even that last one. But ending hunger? I didn't understand.

I didn't let it bother me. We've all seen a seemingly trivial verb ending or postposition turn out to be the one bit of information that brings a grammar of rigor and elegance out of hopeless confusion. I was willing to take the connection on faith; it came from a reputable source. And so I put the libraries onto my wrist computer—it was slow, but at least it didn't keep telling me it was FULL—and I set to work.

My libraries had abundant data on both hunger and experiments in stamping it out. The pattern displayed in that data was so prominent that I didn't have to look for it; it leapt out at me on its own during the second routine sort, preflagged.

First: There would be a "new food." Fish flour. Pulverized gwabaroot. Liquefied algae. Whatever. *Second:* The new food would be provided at little or no cost to a hungry population. *Third:* The people would reject it despite their hunger, because in the context of their culture it was repulsive to them, or in some other way totally unacceptable; they would go hungry rather than eat it. A few exceptional individuals might make a sensible decision and survive, but most would choose to starve. *Four:* Everybody back to the drawing board!

Over and over again, those same four futile steps.

You might think—certainly *I* did—that people who are in the extremes of hunger will eat anything. They *won't*. I learned that people have gone hungry trying to survive on soups made of grass and bark and weeds, all the while surrounded by a wealth of nourishing food readily available to them in the form of millions of fat grubs and worms. Other populations (including some for whom the grubs and worms were an everyday part of the diet) have died surrounded by animals that would have fed them well—because they were *sacred* animals and killing them was forbidden. I found account after account of prisoners condemning themselves to die of severe illness or frank starvation because the food their captors provided to them was contaminated by filth or vermin. None of this is logical, but it is all a matter of record.

Cannibalism has always been a logical option; no more land wasted for burials, less waste of other resources for cremation. And human flesh (though it tends to have high concentrations of toxic chemicals that must be neutralized before consumption) is a superb food. But people *would not eat it*. Even in populations that considered the corpse nothing more than a corpse, and the spirit that had made it a person entirely gone, not one in ten thousand would use corpses as a food source even in extremis. Even in cultures where sacred rituals occasionally required the tasting of human blood or flesh (these were rare, but I did find a few), no sane person would touch either one for the single purpose of survival.

The databanks had reviews of science fiction novels about societies whose governments recycled corpses for food, keeping that a secret from their populations, only to collapse into chaos when the secret was discovered. But there were no records, even in formerly confidential files, of any *actual* society trying such a thing. (I found that strange, over so many hungry millennia; if it has been tried, however, the information is now lost or is not

44

accessible to us.) Nor had any society which, like ours, could grow human beings in test tubes, ever grown them in an altered form . . . without brains, say, except for the primitive areas that keep the organism functioning . . . as a way of bypassing the constraint on cannibalism and providing a reliable supply of wholesome food.

I discovered that I am also subject to these limits, and that I am not one of those exceptional persons who would consider the matter logically and survive. I could eat grubs, but there are insects I could *not* eat. I could not eat human flesh. I could not eat a tubie, not even knowing, as I do know, that although in every other way they appear just like us they are without souls. I don't believe I would feel any differently about eating a tubie that had been grown as a kind of advanced vegetable.

I floundered about in all this data, you perceive; I think it would be reasonable to say that I *wallowed* in it. Getting nowhere! I was like someone who goes to look up one word in the dictionary, and hours later is still at the comset following just one more interesting pathway through the word-wilderness. I wasted endless hours. But we must remember: if it had been even a few months earlier I couldn't have done it at all. I would have been on duty most of the hours I was awake, in the interpreting booths. I would have been up at five a.m. and off in the Chornyak flyers, and I would not have gotten back till after dark, often not till after midnight. I would have been wholly engaged in the interminable business of interplanetary commerce and diplomacy; we women of the Lines had never had any time for projects of our own before the Aliens went away. And although I was accustomed to compiling and searching large historical databases associated with languages, I had never before tried to research the history of *people*. Bumbling about as I did, baffled by the absence of coherent structure (and unable to spot it where it existed, I'm quite sure!), it's fortunate that I had abundant time; I needed it.

It embarrasses me that even though I had seen the pattern clearly—and had seen that it always failed—still, I fell immediately into the same old weary trap, asking all the same old wrong questions. Monkey see, monkey always and forever do. Like all the others, I looked for a "new food," a universal food that every culture would turn to willingly, that would be available everywhere at little cost. I pored over botanies of the colonies, grabbing at every bush or sprig or fungus that I thought might show promise. I spent hours struggling through books for which I didn't have even roughly adequate preparation, about the *synthesis* of foods. There was a three-day stretch when I did nothing at all but search for information about a plant called jelloweed, alleged to grow in almost total darkness and drought, in any soil, in any weather. Only to find out in the end that it offered about eighteen calories to the unsavory pound.

I got lost in the data-collection stage and forgot about problem-solving, you perceive. Only when I had bank after bank of this useless information stored and classified and analyzed, only when there was literally nothing new to add, did I accept the fact that I had to start over. Only then did I force myself to ask the right questions. And only then did I remember the principle I should have *started* with: Chomphosy's Law. Which says: "Don't learn ways to get more of what you want; learn not to *want* it." The question wasn't "How can people get more food to eat?" The question was "How can people eat less food and still thrive?"

It shames me that it took me so long to frame that very obvious question. But once I'd asked it I knew what to look for in the libraries: *a population of humans who ate much less then the ordinary population, who did so voluntarily and happily, and who thrived nonetheless*. Once I had that for search target, things moved more swiftly, because there had always been such populations. Puttering along beside the rest of us, their behavior not really noticed because we were used to politely ignoring it. From the beginning of recorded history, the population of religious—the *monks* and *nuns*, the professionals of religion—had fit my search specifications down to the last detail.

Even so, I almost missed it; I almost went down one more garden path. The proposition fairly glowed at me, it was so clear and so obvious: *when you have a sufficiently powerful religious faith, you need very little food*. Think of the holy women of medieval Europe who are said to have taken almost no food throughout their adult lives—nuns, every last one of them. Catherine of Siena, for example, who as a teenager took only bread and water and raw vegetables, and as a grown woman nothing but communion wafers, plain water, and a few leaves of bitter herbs. Catherine remained healthy, vigorous, happy, and hearty. How could I *not* have thought that religion was the key? (You can perhaps imagine how appalled I was at the idea that Nazareth expected me to find a way to bring about a religious vocation in the motley populations of the known universe!)

I was almost ready to go back to the PICOTA domes and try to summon my greatgrandmother one more time—or to try (with little confidence, but greater courtesy) the ten-day Anglo fast Will Bluecrane had sworn would achieve the same result. I wanted to tell Nazareth Joanna Chornyak, who had been Nazareth Chornyak Adiness and perhaps had been pushed into understandable imbalance by that foul marriage, that she was not only dead but *mad*. I was almost ready to give up, frankly, when the computer's search for items involving both diet and religion tossed me a little paragraph from the 1980s about the Benedictine Abbey of Bec-Hellouin, where a Doctor Tomatis cured a desperately ill population of previously hearty monks by *restoring their former practice of spending eight hours in every twenty-four in Gregorian chant.* A new abbot with "modern" ideas had called those eight hours wasted time and ordered the practice dropped. When it was begun again—though the brothers continued with a diet any number of investigating doctors had called "insufficient to support life," and a schedule so heavy on work and light on sleep that those same doctors had declared it impossible—the good monks of Bec-Hellouin returned to the blooming health they had previously enjoyed.

I read the paragraph and smiled over it; it had a certain charm, but not much detail. I stored it only because I am thorough and because it met my search criteria. I went on to other material that seemed more promising. It was that close; I nearly missed it! And then that night my sleeping brain put it all together for me, and I sat bolt upright in my bed with the *answer* to my question ringing in my ears!

Catherine of Siena and her sisters, many of whose diets were not just scanty but repulsive. The monks of Tibet and Laos, all the Buddhist monks of the world, getting by blissfully on rice and the occasional green onion. The yogis of India, living into their nineties and well beyond on a cup of rice a day, and perfectly contented when that wasn't available. All these holy ones shared a powerful religious vocation, true . . . but they had something *else* in common. For every such population, I was almost certain (and when I checked, I found that I was right), there was frequent exposure to *chant*.

I knew—I hoped I knew—what it had to mean. The monks of Bec-Hellouin, too weak to lift their heads one week and out chopping wood the next, with no change whatsoever in their diet to account for the difference, had gotten their nourishment not from the scanty food they ate but from the eight hours of Gregorian *chant*, just as Dr. Tomatis had claimed. And that was the key. Of *course*!

I got up in the pitch darkness and went up on the roof, because I was too agitated to stay in my room like a sensible person; and I worked frantically, wrapped in my technoquilt against the winter air, until the lights began to go on all around me near dawn.

It was all there. It had always *been* there. Photosynthesis, taking nourishment from waves of light as plants did, appeared to be impossible for human beings; there is no evidence that populations spending many hours in light need any less food than others. But the parallel—nourishment from waves of *sound*!—was a different matter. I couldn't believe that I'd been so stupid, that I hadn't seen it sooner. It had been right there under my nose the entire time, while I fiddled about with jelloweed and the synthesis of yams.

And that, you perceive, is how, after many false and foolish starts, I finally hit upon the idea of *audio*synthesis.

To the women yet to be born,
Delina Meloren Chornyak

48

CHAPTER 4

When Delina finished talking, not one of the women spoke; silence hung over the parlor, where they sat in their customary needlework circle, like low fog. She had expected it, given what she'd had to say; she sat waiting, as silent as they were. Until Brandwynne Chornyak looked at her long and hard, made an exasperated noise, and turned instead to Willow.

"Willow," she asked, "what do *you* think of all this? You must admit, surely, that it sounds like the most utter nonsense. We understand that you feel obligated to support your sister, be she ever so ridiculous. But—"

Willow cut the older woman off right there; she had listened that long out of respect for Brandwynne's years and experience, but enough was enough.

"I don't agree," she said firmly, "and I'm not saying that just to 'support my sister,' as you put it. I don't think that what Delina is saying is ridiculous. Her *source* is an odd one, for sure; for her to claim she can talk to dead greatgrandmothers bothers me, too. But what *difference* does it make?"

"That seems obvious enough!"

"Brandwynne, it seems obvious to you because you're using an old chunk of furniture sitting there in your mind gathering dust, with a sign on it that says: NO SANE PERSON BELIEVES THIS. Please try dusting if *off* for a change! Consider the information, on its own, *as* information. I don't care if Delina found the idea for audiosynthesis under a rock. I don't care if it was written in seed pearls on the back of a rattlesnake. The point is, it *works*; and it is probably the most important scientific discovery since fire. I'm not going to sit here and let you trivialize it."

Brandwynne laid her work down in her lap, careful not to drop stitches, and looked at Willow as she had looked at Delina. Piercingly. As if she were an ancient manuscript, almost obliterated by time and accident, to be painfully deciphered. Outside, a fierce wind rattled the windows and sleet swirled in white clouds; there was unscheduled severe weather again. They were going to have to get used to that.

"Willow, do you mean that seriously?" Brandwynne asked slowly, her brows drawn together in a frown that surely hurt her forehead. "It's not just loyalty to Delina? It's not just a need to *do* something . . . anything! . . . to put an end to this eternal waiting around for the men to get things moving again? I could understand that, Willow, I really could. We all feel like we're hanging somewhere in midair, on hold."

"I say it all and I *mean* it all, as seriously as my heart and mind can manage," Willow told her. "Suppose Delina actually summoned Greatgrandmother Nazareth from wherever she was at the time, got her to answer her questions, did the research, tested the results, and reported to us. More power to her. Suppose on the other hand that the chat with Greatgrandmother was a hallucination brought on by what Delina had been through at the PICOTA domes—and she brought back the answers, did the research, tested the results, and reported to us. More power to her anyway! It's the *information* that matters."

Glenellen Adiness spoke then, drawing her stole closer against the icy draft from the window at her back. "Come now, Willow," she objected, "you can't possibly mean to tell us it's not important to know whether we can communicate with the dead or not! I can think of any number of individuals I'm ready to summon this very afternoon, if that's actually possible!"

Delina was miserable. Her head ached, and her back hurt her. All the nerves that were improperly wired were sending her false signals, set off by strain that had lasted too long; she needed to lie down. She hated being on *display* like this; it had been going on for what felt like hours. And next would come the interminable grilling . . . she hated that, too. She understood why it was necessary. Like Brandwynne, she recognized the urge they all felt to run off in random directions shrieking, "Do something! Just *do* something!" They had to be very careful; they had to be very sure. But it was hard, all the same.

It seemed to her that Nazareth could have the decency to . . . oh, rap on the window, perhaps. Ideally, Natha would have popped in and presented her personal endorsement, sparing them all this misery and shaking a few preconceptions loose as she went; Delina would have been so very grateful if she'd done that. Failing that, she could at *least* have made some small gesture to shore things up, instead of abandoning her poor messenger to merciless interrogation. *Probably she refuses to go out in the storm,* Delina thought crossly. *Probably she's scared she'll get her protoplasm frozen off!* But miserable or not, abandoned or not, it wasn't fair to let Willow do all the work.

"Glenellen," she said, hoping it was going to make at least a little sense, "you're right. Of course you're right; of course that's information beyond price. But I would like to set that question aside, for right now. I can tell you in complete honesty that so far as my own perceptions are concerned, Nazareth was *there*, and she spoke to me, exactly as you are speaking. But Willow's right. That isn't what matters right *now*. Just as it doesn't really matter whether ending hunger will bring the Aliens back or not."

"Delina, you—"

"I'd like to think it would," she said, ignoring the attempt to interrupt, determined to get to the end of her argument, sure that if she stopped she'd lose track, "because life alone in a universe of Terrans is not the life I *know*, and it frightens me. But it's not what matters now. Someday we can return to the question of whether we can talk with the dead or not. Someday we will find out whether this one measure will put our lives back as they were. But I am absolutely certain that those things will wait. Right now, what matters is that I went into that room for thirty days—"

"*Lying* to us!" Jenny put in sharply, stabbing her embroidery with her needle as if it were something she intended to kill, and wincing when the sharp point found instead the fingertip she'd had poised underneath a small spray of blackberries. "Claiming that you were making a 'religious retreat'! And dragging *Willow* into your lies, Delina!"

It was true; she had done that. It had made her half sick, because they did *not* lie to one another. That was one of the pillars shoring up their lives. But she had not had any choice. Because if Willow hadn't been the one bringing Delina's meals on trays and taking them away again untouched, someone would have interrupted the experiment before the first week was over. *I lied. I did lie, and it makes my heart sore. But what else could I have done? Great-grandmother, would you* please *knock on the window? Just once?*

"I went into that room for thirty days," Delina continued, slogging on. "I took no supplies except thirty days worth of plain water and thirty days worth of plain chant . . . Gregorian chant. I ate *nothing*, nothing at all, for thirty days; I listened to that music instead. And I not only did not lose weight, dearloves, I gained a pound and a half! That proves that audiosynthesis is possible for human beings; it proves that we can do it. *That* is what matters. Because the economy of this world has fallen to pieces around us, and people *are going to be hungry*! You know that as well as I do!"

And she stopped, completely out of breath and out of courage.

Sarajane was past eighty, and not happy with the turn taken lately by Earth's affairs. The stress and worry, the not knowing what was going to happen next, had been wearing her out; *she* had lost a good deal of weight. "Delina Meloren," she said slowly, "it is precisely because what you are telling us *is* so important that we have to be certain. That we have to devil's-advocate at you."

"I know that," Delina said. "I understand, and I agree. I just wish I could somehow say it better. More clearly."

"Things are going to be grim, Delina," said Brandwynne, "just as you say. We all know that. Famine is coming now for many of the worlds, sure as summer, especially for those that have been specializing in a single crop to maximize their profits. And that means that we *must* not waste the little time we have, dancing down some foolish garden path you saw in a . . . heaven help us all . . . in a *vision*."

"From the point of view of science," Delina insisted, "it really and truly does not make *any* difference how I got the idea. I will accept the possibility that it came straight from my own mind, if that's your preference. I find it unlikely, myself. Why would I, all of a sudden, become someone capable of great scientific discoveries? Or *re*discoveries, to put it more accurately? But I don't *care*, you perceive; decide that question as you like, I won't argue. From the point of view of science, then: if waves of light can be converted to energy to support life—as is done by plants every day, without disconcerting anybody—there's no reason why waves of sound can't function in precisely the same way. To the mind, a perception is a perception is a perception, after all—whichever sensory system is involved, it's all converted to on/off signals."

"But why . . ." Sarajane leaned forward, frowning, and the ball of blue yarn in her lap fell and rolled away across the floor, ending up under Brandwynne's rocker. "Why has something so obvious not been discovered long long ago?"

"It *has*!" Delina said. "It *was*! I told you . . . I *meant* to tell you!"

"You did tell them, darlin'," said Willow, at her side. "*I* heard you, if nobody else did."

"Holybook after holybook, Sarajane, there's a section that tells all about it. Not usually in a way that's easy to understand, holybooks being as they are, but it's *in* there. And from the beginning of history the holy *persons* have said to us, in so many words: live like we do and you won't need much to eat."

"Gregorian chant!" Brandwynne said, raising a knitting needle high. "Yogis . . . buried for weeks at a time, and so on . . . *they* don't listen to Gregorian chant."

"Want me to take that one on, Delina?" Willow offered.

"No. Thank you, but no." Delina shook her head and tackled it herself. "Brandwynne," she said, "there are two important points. First: because Gregorian chant comes out of my own culture I assumed it would be the form of chant my brain could use most readily. That was an obvious strategy. Second: the yogis are doing something different. They're shutting their metabolisms down to coma level or below so that they won't *need* much of anything to sustain life. I wasn't interested in that; I'm still not interested. And I'm sure it's irrelevant to this discussion."

Brandwynne nodded, conceding the point. "You're right, Delina," she said. "You're quite right. My apologies."

The lights flickered, went out, and came back on again as the solar generators took over. Sarajane clucked her tongue, and she spoke for all of them when she said, "How nice not to have to be out in that!" The government had always tried to schedule the storms, storms that Earth needed, at times that would not inconvenience most of its population. But they'd rarely been able to extend that courtesy to the linguists, whose presence in the interpreting booths had often been required around the clock. Every woman in the room had memories of terrifying trips in the flyers and vans through storms no one else would have dreamed of venturing out in; it *was* nice not to have that to deal with, even temporarily.

"Delina?" It was Brandwynne again. "What do you want to do now? What do you want *us* to do now? Assuming we accept the idea that you're correct about this process . . . this audiosynthesis . . . and I think that we all agree we *must* do that, unless we can prove you wrong . . . what should happen next? How do you suggest that we proceed?"

"More testing," Delina told them, not meeting their eyes, frowning down at the blanket corner she was turning with her crochet hook. "More testing, right away. We need the answers to a long list of questions."

"For example?"

"For example," said Delina, "*I* can do audiosynthesis, but can everybody? For example, is it something only adults can do? Or only adult *women* can do? Neither is likely, but we have to find out. For another example, does the sound source have to be chant?"

"I thought you were *sure* it did!" Glenellen protested.

"No, I'm not sure at all." Delina shook her head. "The only actual experiment, the only account I could find that came from documented historical materials in the libraries instead of from some sort of oral tradition, was the incident with the monks of Bec-Hellouin. *They* used chant. To keep the variables as few as possible, so did I. To say the sounds *must* be chant on that basis alone is leaping to conclusions. Maybe it's true, maybe not; we need to *know*. Consider: in the late twentieth century this country had what the medsammys called an 'epidemic of overweight' in the population. In spite of extraordinary interest in careful eating and fanatic exercise regimes. Remember? And consider: it was in the late twentieth century that a constant supply of music was available even for very poor people."

"Because for the first time," Willow said, "the machines for that purpose were available for almost no money . . . so that *everybody* could afford them."

"That may be only coincidence," Delina noted. "Maybe the two things are unrelated. But we have to check, because that music was, ninety-nine percent of it, *not* chant."

Glenellen's voice was filled with frank awe. "Do *you* mean," she demanded, "that all those people who spent half their lives dieting were canceling the diets' effects by listening to music? Is that what you're suggesting?"

"That was the time of Muzak!" Brandwynne pointed out. "Why didn't everyone working where that dreadful canned stuff played incessantly gain weight, too?"

"I think you have to participate," said Delina carefully.

"Participate? What does that mean, Delina? Please, Delina, look up—you could crochet blindfolded, you *don't* need to watch your hook, and you know it! What does it mean, you have to participate?"

"You can't just *hear* the sound. You have to listen; *really* listen. Or make the sound yourself the way the choirs in monasteries do. It can't just go on around you; you have to pay attention to it."

And then she added hastily, "I *think*! You understand . . . this is why I say, more testing. We need to know: what *kind* of sound must it be? How often? For how long? What is the formula for converting units of sound into calories . . . is it the same for everybody, for example? Is it a straight measure—so many minutes of the right music equals so many calories—or does it vary according to circumstances?"

"What else?"

"I don't want to make another speech. Please . . . no."

"What *else*, Delina?"

"For example, what if the diet is *mixed*: part music, part mouthfood? Will that work? Can it be done? And what about such things, such critically important things, as vitamins and minerals? Can you get them from sound or must they come from another source? We know it's all right for thirty days, because Willow and I checked my blood levels at the beginning and at the end, but does that hold up long term? We don't know these things—we have to find out."

She dropped her needlework and put both hands to her face. "You perceive!" she said, looking around the circle from one woman to another, feeling that if she could not convince them she would die of frustration, furious with Nazareth for doing nothing to make it easier, "I need *help* from you! I don't know the things we have to *know*, and I can't find out by myself! Please—I really do believe we must get started on this. Please, dearloves." She let her hands fall and looked at them, baffled. *What else could she say? What else was there to say?* "Please," she said again, pleading with them, and so tired, "it's not *trivial*."

"Well, of *course* it's not trivial!" said Willow crossly. "They know that, Delina! The fussing isn't because they think it's trivial."

Delina bit her lip, not caring that she'd already bitten it raw, and took a deep breath. *I have a good mind*, she thought. *I am articulate; I think before I speak, and I speak the truth. Why am I so bad at making myself understood?* It was an old question, and one she had no answer for; she suspected that if she'd had to rely on English rather than Láadan she would have been a woman with one of those labels attached. *Borderline personality disorder. Hysteria.* She put it out of her mind. She had to finish this. She had to do it properly and completely; she had to get it *over* with. She had begun seeing double, and she could feel the muscle spasms building in her face and neck; if this went on much longer the others would see them, too. She wasn't willing to let that happen.

"Some of the questions," she told them, "we won't be able to answer. Not yet. We can't find out whether audiosynthesis is something only adult women can do, because we have no way to test it with a man or a child. But we can *assume* the most economical result because it makes no sense not to; we can assume that every human being past needing breast milk has the ability, and proceed on that assumption until there's evidence to the contrary. It will be a long time before we can know the *specifics* for certain . . . like how much music equals how many calories, that kind of thing. But we can do the basic testing right now. We can *begin*, and establish a foundation to go on from. We can each take one of the variables, you perceive, and test systematically for that single item."

The women murmured their agreement all round the circle of chairs. The procedure was the same one they used in the investigation of languages; they understood what she was proposing and knew how to proceed.

"And there's one more question," Delina added, stammering, the words tumbling over one another in her haste to get it all said and escape from the room. "That is . . . there will be *lots* more . . . but there is this crucial one: After we do the testing, after we have the information, who do we tell?"

Who do we *tell*?

Willow reached for Delina's hand and held it tightly; she had seen the tightening muscles, and seen her sister go white. But she spoke to the others. "I haven't bothered her about it," she said. "I saw no reason to."

"Haven't bothered me about it? About what?" Delina was bewildered, and she stared at Willow in dismay. "What are you talking about?"

"Delina, sweet child," said Sarajane gently (and from her vantage point no doubt a woman in her thirties could still be called a child), "that's a question you needn't ask. You didn't really think, surely—"

Willow interrupted her; it was a measure of her distress that she could be that rude. "I'm sorry, Sarajane," she said first; but she interrupted all the same. "She really *did*. She really did think that we could do the pilot testing, combine our results, write it up on a chiplet, and send it off to . . . oh, say, the United States Department of Agriculture."

"Wait!" Delina objected. "Wait a minute!" She was outraged. Why *did they insist on talking about her as if she weren't there at all? They were forever doing that.* "I hadn't decided it just like that, Willow," she said. "I wasn't *sure.* I suspect that we'd best tell one of the senior men, and have *him* take the information to the government, to save time. If we do it ourselves, they'll only call in the men to explain it anyway. The question is, which *one* of the men? Which one is the most likely to—"

She stopped, sensing something in the quiet room where the only sound was the hissing of sleet on glass and tiles, and she saw that they were all looking at her with an expression she knew too well. That expression that said: *You poor silly baby with your poor silly baby brain; fortunately for you, we grownups love you.* She had been facing that expression as long as she could remember.

It had been there when she'd had to explain what she was doing with Ouija boards and Tarot decks and runestones; it had been there when she'd pleaded for them to cover for her while she went to the PICOTA for help. It had *always* been there, whenever she spoke her mind, so that sometimes she thought she should just keep silent . . . except that if she did, how could she be sure things would get done? It gave her a sick feeling, thinking how it would have been, a number of times, if she *hadn't* spoken up and faced that look.

When she was a child, her father and her uncles had given her the solemn charge of making certain that Willow understood the basic concepts of linguistics. For a while she'd been fooled, because at first they'd taken the trouble to deceive her; but then they'd stopped bothering and she'd realized from their bodyparl that the task was a fake. Twice each month she'd been called on to report on Willow's progress; twice each month, she'd done it dutifully. And that *poorsillybaby* look had always been on their faces as they let her go through the routine. And now here it was again.

"What is it?" she asked fiercely, sorrowfully, wishing she could get things *right* once in a while, wishing she could go talk to Nazareth about it, wishing she felt like someone who belonged in this world. "What am I doing wrong?"

They looked at Willow, and Willow looked stonily back, furious with them. She saw no reason for that expression. Many times what Delina said was what everyone was thinking, it was just that only Delina had the courage to admit it. And many times, even when what Delina said struck all of them as absurd, she turned out to be right. Why didn't they *learn*? It was worse than the standard ridicule from the men, which could be ignored. Because it came from other women, it hurt Delina badly; knowing they loved her only made it hurt worse. Willow had no intention of helping them. She watched while they tried to figure out who should say it, and she welcomed their discomfort; every one of them was dear to her, but she saw no excuse for the way they treated Delina.

She had said that once to one of the oldest women at Chornyak Barren House, a woman gone now nearly ten years, and the answer had come straight back in the frail thin voice: "Willow Joanna, they treat your sister *exactly* as they have always treated Nazareth." And she had realized, amazed, that it was true, and that if it continued to be true, and if she lived to a sufficiently old age, the day would come when Delina would finally be treated with a kind of terrified respect. Exactly as they had treated Nazareth.

Except that unlike Nazareth, Delina was barren, and that meant she had not had to face a marriage to a man she neither loved nor respected, chosen for her by some other man, with all the problems that were guaranteed to follow. Nazareth had not been that lucky. And Willow was glad of it, because if Nazareth hadn't had children, Willow and Delina would not have existed.

Brandwynne did the honors, eventually. "Delina," she said, "let's go on supposing that you're right, and that we can determine the answers to many of your questions. Well enough to serve, as you say, as a foundation to build further investigations on. Dear-love, when we have that information, we will have to hide it. You must understand; we can't *tell* anyone."

Delina was shocked; she did not mince words. "What *wicked-ness*!" she said. "What *evil*!"

"Come now, Delina!"

"To know that adult human beings can thrive without any nourishment but music, and not to tell? That's not even *decent*! Explain yourself!"

"Delina Meloren . . ." Brandwynne was faltering now, and she looked at Willow pleadingly; but Willow ignored her, and she had to go on, like it or not.

"Delina, if you are right—and if we tell—the men will find a way to *stop* it."

Willow was delighted. It sounded even stupider said aloud than it had sounded inside her head. Never mind that it was entirely true. Like every truth that can be handily labeled "a conspiracy theory," it sounded stupid all the same. So stupid that Delina stared at Brandwynne absolutely speechless.

"Delina," said Willow, willing to help now that Brandwynne had had a chance to feel what it was like to be embarrassed by a truth, "they *would*, you know. The men . . . the government . . . the scientists. My dear, they would find a way to regulate it. To keep it for just a privileged few. To make it cost money. To *tax* it. It's obscene, and they would have a hundred elaborate rationalizations about how what they were doing wasn't *really* what it appeared to be at all, but they *would stop* it."

"No."

"Oh, yes."

"It's *information*, nothing more," Delina objected. "It's not like a . . . a strike, or a revolt. There's no *way* they could stop it."

Willow let go her sister's hand then with a last affectionate pat, and picked up her needlework. "Delina," she said, keeping her eyes on her knitting, "think."

"I *am* thinking. I have *been* thinking! I have thought till my brain aches in my head! And you cannot tell me that anyone is going to stand over people with guns and force them to eat food!"

"Well, you haven't thought some of the things you *should* have been thinking," Willow told her. "Nobody is suggesting that people would be forced to eat at the point of a gun; when did our men ever have to resort to anything as crude as that to accomplish their goals?"

Delina said nothing, and Willow went on. "Think, for example, what happened with medical care. It wasn't because people couldn't learn to do it themselves that men made it a crime to practice medicine 'without a license,' and set the cost of the license so high that most people couldn't even dream about getting one. And made it impossible to order medicines without a medsammy's permission. And sent women to prison for tending other women in childbed. And set up a system with the greed so tightly locked into it that it was like fouled pond water in August . . . hopelessly polluted."

Tears were pouring down Delina's face now. Partly because she was humiliated to have been naive *again*, to have failed again to see what was so obvious. Partly because she was humiliated to belong to a species capable of such meanness. Partly because she was just so worn out, and because she hurt.

I cannot bear it, she thought. *I cannot, cannot bear it.* But of course she knew that she could, and that she would. She knew her mind and her spirit; they would fail her, as they had failed her all her life. Other people, facing trouble, could count on succumbing gracefully to nervous collapses and convenient amnesia; not Delina. Her mind and spirit would *not* break and release her into some peaceful insane serenity. She would go right on knowing, right on remembering, and right on being responsible for her share of the load.

"All right!" she wailed, beating with one fist on her thigh. "All right, Willow, and all the rest of you, you can stop smirking at me now! Of course that's how it is; you're right. I am stupid not to have perceived it from the very beginning! I'll grant you all of that and whatever else you want to add! But *tell* me, then: whatever in all the world are we going to *do*?"

She stared at them in the silence, waiting; the wind had fallen back to gather itself for a fiercer rush, and the silence was a new sound.

"Suppose we handle it as we handled Láadan," said Brandwynne, finally, tentatively. "Suppose Delina is right."

("May the Holy One let her be right!" someone said.)

"Suppose we teach audiosynthesis to the women and girls of the Lines, just as we taught them Láadan. And then we'll find a mechanism for spreading it far and wide. Until it has gone *so* far and *so* wide that by the time the men find out about it, it will be too late to undo what we've done."

There were frowns on all their faces, and Delina said what they all were thinking. "But Brandwynne, the Láadan project failed. Why would we try that again, when it has already failed us once?"

They had been so sure that women outside the Lines would welcome Láadan, would welcome a language constructed specifically to express the perceptions of women, once they knew it existed and had ways to learn it. They had been so certain that it would be the same blessing for other women that it had been for the linguist women. And they had been so wrong in those certainties.

"It wasn't a failure for us!" said Glenellen indignantly. "It has been a triumph, and a blessing!"

"Yes," said Delina, "and so might it be a triumph and a blessing if every woman of the Lines could do without her food ration and give it to others who need it—but it would be the same sort of failure Láadan was. Remember how ridiculous we felt? There we were, the foolish women of the Lines, with our language for *all* women, that we'd slaved over in every spare minute for a hundred years and more, offering it to women everywhere—at great danger to ourselves, I remind you . . . and they didn't give a *fig* for it!"

"They took it up for a while," Sarajane chided her.

"Uh uh," Willow scoffed. "For a year or two. While it was the very latest thing. And then, with very few exceptions, they forgot all about it."

"I don't understand why that happened," said Delina softly. "I never have. Do any of us understand it?" But nobody answered her.

"Perhaps it was not a failure," Brandwynne said, if it will provide us with the model we need *this* time! Perceive—the two projects are very different. Láadan is a *language*. Constructed to express the perceptions of women and save them vast amounts of linguistic work they must otherwise do, yes, and valuable in our eyes. But it is clearly something most women are willing to do without. The problems they have with existing languages apparently don't bother them as much as the prospect of having to learn a new language does. Humiliating for *us*, and a humbling experience, but there it is. But nourishment for their bodies, dearloves, and for the bodies of their children? It's not the same thing! Hunger is a powerful motivator!"

"Maybe," said Delina slowly; beside her, Willow was smiling, and nodding yes. "At least it would save us from having to start all over—we know the Láadan model as well as we know our heartbeats. We could use the channels we've already established."

"Well, then," said Brandwynne briskly, "that's settled. And now we have work to do, work that won't wait. How shall we divide it up?"

CHAPTER 5

"What distresses me," Sarajane told Delina fretfully, "is that I go right on *feeling* hungry!"

She sat cross-legged on the high narrow bed in the small sickroom, with her chin in her hands and her knobby spine bent in a comma; she wore nothing but the bedsheet she'd wrapped round her body underneath her arms. She looked like a plucked chicken with braids. But she didn't look the least bit *sick*. Suppose some of her numerous progeny decided to visit? Delina wasn't sure that even the blisters marring the delicate lacework of wrinkles on the old woman's face—blisters put there deliberately, with the help of a handful of poison ivy—would convince her sons and grandsons and greatgrandsons that she needed to be kept in bed. "Dear Sarajane," she asked, "couldn't you try to look just a little sicker?"

"Don't change the subject, child!"

"But—"

Sarajane waved one impatient hand. "Put it out of your *mind*, Delina Meloren!" she said emphatically. "If any of my relatives, or anybody else's relatives, stick their noses in here, they'll find me gasping for breath and delirious, you have my word on it! But I don't want to talk about that now. *Trust* me; I've been misleading men for more than eighty years!"

"Oh, law . . . I'm sorry, Sarajane," Delina said, feeling foolish. She *was* sorry. Talk of teaching your grandmother to suck eggs.

"I should hope so!"

"Yes, ma'am. And I am at your service."

"I want to know how it's all going, that's all," Sarajane declared.

"Nobody's given me any kind of report for days. I want to know how we're all getting along!"

"We're sailing through it," Delina said. "Except for Brandwynne."

"Brandwynne?" Sarajane's eyebrows went up. "But Brandwynne's strong as oxen! What happened to her?"

"You know Brandwynne."

"I do indeed; I've changed many of her diapers in my day. And what precisely has she done this time?"

"How about if I just quote her?"

"Good enough . . . what did she say?"

"She said, and I quote: 'Seventy-two hours have gone by and I've gained three ounces; I'm convinced. And now I have work to do.' And out she came."

"You talked to her about variables?"

"I did," said Delina.

"And?"

"And she told me that given the number of design flaws in our experiment, one more would make no difference—and she talked about extrapolation. And, as I said, out she came. Prepared to claim, if anybody questioned her about it, that she'd been misdiagnosed."

"Drat the woman!"

"Yes. But the others are holding on and doing just fine, and Brandwynne's making herself useful."

"Doing what?"

Delina laughed softly. "Petitioning the men to let us attend their meetings," she said.

"She doesn't think they're already befuddled enough?"

"She started out with the idea that it would keep them from getting suspicious about what we're up to here at Womanhouse . . . which is an irrelevant worry, I think, given the way they're occupied, but Brandwynne is an i-dotter and t-crosser about that sort of thing . . . and then she decided that we *ought* to attend the meetings, and she buckled down to petition seriously. And she may be right."

"Hmmmph."

"Well, it's possible. Things are happening so fast out in the worlds . . . everything's sort of melting down, you know? Maybe we *should* go. As for the others, still hanging in there—they're like you. They go on feeling hungry."

"It bothers me," Sarajane said crossly, and she grabbed a pillow to clutch against her flat chest.

"I'm sorry you're uncomfortable," Delina said. "I wish I knew a way to do something about it."

"No, no . . ." Sarajane made the hand-waving get-away-from-me gesture again. "That's not what I mean, child. What I mean is: it's going to make it hard for us to *teach* this process, if the hungry feeling just goes on and on."

"I warned you about it," Delina reminded her.

"So you did, but that doesn't make it any easier. Did knowing about it make it any easier for *you*?"

"No," said Delina, and she sighed softly. "It didn't help."

"I know, *intellectually*, that I can't be hungry. I'm weighed every morning, and I've been gaining weight. Obviously I'm getting more than enough nourishment. But it's like you told us it would be . . . my mouth is lonesome." She chuckled, and hugged the pillow tighter. "Only you, Delina," she said, "would have put it that way! But it's accurate. My mouth *is* lonesome. My mouth, and my tongue, and my teeth. I lust after biting and chewing and swallowing, you perceive. I dream about the way good chocolate feels, melting on my tongue, and the taste of freshmade spicebread . . . and butter melting on hot bread! Oh, how I crave the taste of butter melting on hot bread! I'm downright *depraved*, Delina! I admit it."

Delina smiled, thinking how ill the word fit her, and told her that such evil would no doubt be remarked on far and wide.

"But think, child!" said Sarajane. "I'm *old*! I'm supposed to be pretty well impervious to lust! It must be a good deal worse for the young and truly passionate, don't you suppose? Delina, if everyone who tries audiosynthesis is going to have this problem, we'll have a lot of resistance to deal with."

Delina sat down beside her on the bed, wishing she dared rub the knobby back and sure she'd do it wrong if she tried. She would ask Willow to come do it instead. "Sarajane," she said, "I don't know if that mouth-hunger is ever going to go away for people who've always eaten traditional food. It's habit, you perceive. It's a lifetime of enjoying the way food feels in your mouth and throat, and the smell of food, and the way food looks, and the pleasure of eating with others. But I don't think it *has* to be that hard. Tiny kids don't have that lifetime of conditioning to overcome; infants suck their thumbs to soothe the mouth, but they don't know anything about any food but milk."

"And people involved in famines? They'll be all ages, you know; they won't just be infants and tadlings."

"Yes. But they'll be people who have no food, or almost none. They won't have to make a deliberate effort not to help themselves to food, Sarajane, the way we've had to—because there won't *be* any. They won't have to struggle against temptation. And where, before, they *suffered* from hunger, they won't suffer anymore."

"You hope."

"I hope, yes," Delina agreed. "And so far, so good, Sarajane! Willow is doing just as well on Mozart and Calendia as I did on Gregorian chant. Jenny is enjoying herself and staying bonniful on Ozark ballads and baroque bluegrass. Glenellen is having to work hard to pay sufficient *attention* to the popdrivel she's testing, and she's lost a few ounces as a result, but the evidence seems clear enough: *any* music will do, if it's music the listener is willing and able to attend to."

"Even wicked music? Even the latest sadistic popballads from Gehenna?"

Delina shivered. "I don't know . . . I suppose so. I'd like to believe that such stuff would be like spoiled food and make the people listening to it sick, but I'd wager that's just sentimental pap. We couldn't be that lucky, could we? I don't plan to test for it, however. I'm just happy that any and all music seems to serve."

She grinned at Sarajane. "Beauty," she said, "is apparently in the ear of the beholder. Behearer?"

"Beholder, Delina. Beauty held with the eye; beauty held with the ear; beauty held with the hand. It's all beheld. And it's wonderful that it works out this way—that it's not just some very *narrow* range of music that will do!"

"Yes, it is," Delina said. "It's what you would expect—the most economical solution, you perceive—but it could have gone the other way, and it would have made things so much harder." And she added, "It would take training . . . lots of it . . . to get by as many religious do, on a drone note or two. None of us needs to try that. But the *principle* would be exactly the same as for any other musical sound."

Sarajane sat up straight, wiggling her shoulders to ease them, and beamed at Delina, who was grateful that there were no observation windows for this sickroom; she had rarely seen anyone look so superbly healthy as Sarajane did now. All the signs of strain she'd been showing were gone. "To think that I have lived to see this day!" the old woman said gleefully. "To think that a Chornyak woman should have done *this*!"

Delina immediately looked hard at the floor, and Sarajane could not keep from laughing.

"You did do this, you know, Delina Meloren!" she said. "You can try to slough it off on Nazareth, but it was *you* who got this project off the ground, not your greatgrandmother. We've not seen hide nor hair nor ghostly trace of *her*!"

"You don't believe I talked to her, do you, Sarajane?"

"Not for one minute! I don't pretend to know what happens to the dead, my dear, but I don't believe they're available to the living. But—" She stopped, and reached over to pat Delina's hand. "But, I agree with Willow. It makes no difference. If it makes you happy to think you and Nazareth had a chat, don't let me lessen that happiness. The information is all that matters, and *it* appears to be valid, praise be!"

Delina said nothing; you do not argue with old people. And she blamed Nazareth, who had let her down abominably. Not one thump on a window. Not one noise in the night. As Sarajane said, not one ghostly trace.

"Delina?"

"Yes, Sarajane?"

"Will you get me a different chiplet, please? I am so tired of the one that's been playing all these days, I cannot tell you *how* tired!"

Delina hesitated, and Sarajane's face changed; she narrowed her eyes and stuck out her chin. She had the chin the St. Syrus Line was famous for—sharp and sturdy under a generous mouth and a nose that came to a point.

"If Brandwynne can say that seventy-two hours convinces her, and she quits," she announced emphatically, "*I* can say that seventy-two hours of one music chiplet convinces *me*. Even though I won't quit."

"Sarajane," Delina began, "I would have liked to know—"

"You would have liked to know whether the same music, over and over for thirty days, would serve. Of course you would! But you said yourself: any music serves *if* the listener is willing and able to attend to it. Delina, I am *not* willing, or able, to listen to that same stuff any longer!"

Delina drew a breath, intending to plead, but Sarajane put her hand firmly over the younger woman's mouth.

"Hush!" she said. "We have told you over and over again—you cannot expect other people . . . *normal* people . . . to behave as you do. I'm quite sure that in my place you would actually have listened to those same three hours of music for thirty days, just to settle the question. I freely admit that you would have. I *won't*. And I want to point out to you, Delina Meloren Stubborn-As-Any-Mule Chornyak, that we have at least fifty years, and more likely two hundred and fifty, in which to settle all these fine points. Now get me a different chiplet—the same *kind* of music will be fine, but a different set of pieces—without any more fuss. Please. I'm miserable enough, me and my lusting mouth, without having to be bored on *top* of it!"

It was frustrating to have to admit it, but Delina knew Sarajane was right. If they could have just handed the audiosynthesis information over to the government to be taught solar-system-wide on the comsets, it would have been one thing. A *swift* thing, perhaps. To do it secretly, on the other hand, was going to take a lot of years; they did indeed have plenty of time to work out the details. She said it aloud then: "It will take a lot of time, doing it this way."

"Yes, it will."

"During which many people are going to die of hunger."

"Yes. That's true. And you are not to torment yourself about it."

"Suppose the next thing we do is send the information to all the women of the Lines, using the recipe codes," Delina said slowly, half to herself. "They'll know how to go on with it immediately, and they'll understand why it's urgent. We can get every linguist woman trained in audiosynthesis inside a year. And we can find a way to get the food that we free up that way distributed secretly, to people who need it, and the money we save invested for the project. I'm sure we can."

She stood up abruptly, managing to trip over the leg of Sarajane's bed in the process. Her voice was stern as she grabbed at the wall to get her balance. "I don't accept that," she said flatly.

"Don't accept what? That you're not to torment yourself?"

"No—what I don't accept is the idea that we have to sit by and watch people starve when we know how to *prevent* it."

"Delina!" Sarajane's voice was sharp now, and her face was troubled; she knew what a nuisance it could be to have Delina dead set against something. "I tell you now, and I want you to listen to me: secrecy is the *only possible way* this can be done!"

"I know that," Delina said. She stood against the wall, leaning her head back against it. "I should have realized it all along; I don't know where my mind was. I suppose I just wasn't willing to face it . . . I wanted this to be a fairy tale. But perceive, Sarajane . . . the person who's being nourished by the sound doesn't have to know that it's happening . . . she just has to be made to *listen*, and the nourishing takes place. It can be a secret, and stay a secret, and we can nevertheless keep people fed."

"How? Tell me how we can do that!"

"Give me a little time, dearlove. There's an idea nibbling at me; I can't quite perceive it clearly yet, but it's there. Let me work on it."

"Muzak didn't do it," Sarajane said, cautioning her. "Remember that, Delina! People didn't gain weight because music was just played at them endlessly, if that's what you're thinking of."

Delina smiled at her, and offered no argument; she could feel her mind trying to get through to her once again. Whatever it was, in a little while she'd have it. "I'll go get you a different music chiplet, now, Sarajane," she said.

"Thank the saints," said the old woman. "I'm grateful; it will be a tremendous relief. But there's just one more thing."

"Anything," Delina told her. "Anything that's possible— you've got it."

"Like an answer to a hard question?"

"For sure. If I know it. Try me."

Sarajane cleared her throat and hesitated, hugging the pillow hard, and Delina saw the worry on her face. She had been nearly carefree, but that was gone now.

"What is it, Sarajane?" she asked, thinking how very much she loved her. "What's bothering you?"

"There's something I want to know," said Sarajane slowly. She let the pillow go and put both hands to her face. "Delina, I want to know—what will people be like, after this? People who've only known their mother's milk, and then audiosynthesis? People who've never known mouthfood . . . what will they be *like*?"

And then as the silence went on and on, she said, puzzled, "Delina? Delina—did you hear me?"

It was as if all the breath had been knocked out of her body, or all the blood drained away; Delina was suddenly so weak that she literally could not stand. She let herself slide down the wall, slowly, cautiously, a boneless thing making do with gristle and the *memory* of bones, and sat on the floor, bracing herself with both hands, while Sarajane stared at her in amazement.

"Delina Meloren, for the sake of all the suffering saints, what is the matter?" she cried. "Are you sick, child?"

Delina answered her in a voice that was almost a moan: "Oh, Sarajane, she's done it again!"

"*Who? Done what?*" Sarajane smacked the bed with her hand and sat bolt upright, losing her sheet in the process. "You will explain yourself this minute, Delina Chornyak!"

"I'm sorry."

"And you *should* be sorry!" Sarajane grabbed the sheet and

wound it round her more tightly, tucking in the last corner and edge so that it would stay put. "I *will* be sick, if you go on like that!"

Delina drew a long deep breath and swallowed hard. "I should have known," she said wonderingly. "It shouldn't have been possible. But, Sarajane, my greatgrandmother has suckered me *again*!" She saw the exasperation on the other woman's face, saw her start to speak, and raised a hand to stop her. "No," she said. "Please. Wait, please—I *am* going to make this clear. Just give me a minute to catch my breath."

"One minute," said Sarajane grimly. "*One*. Not a second more!"

"Consider, Sarajane, what Nazareth always told us. That to make a plan succeed you must hide it, inside a plan that is itself hidden inside a plan, and the more layers, the better. That the way to bring about change is not to lift people over the fence but to take the fence down and let them notice that there's no longer anything stopping them from going forward. That—"

"Delina," Sarajane said, her voice now genuinely angry, "you cannot *imagine* how little interest I have in a catalog of Nazareth Chornyak's pithy sayings!"

Delina paused, and raised her eyebrows. "Are you saying that I must stop going on and on and on about it, and get to the point?"

"You know I am saying nothing of the kind," Sarajane answered her, gently. "Of course not. I am speaking the simple truth, child. Nazareth's . . . admonishments . . . cannot be the reason you turned white and very nearly passed out on me a minute ago. Forgive me for sounding harsh; it's because I'm concerned. And," she added, "because I'm too addled to know I'm not hungry."

Delina got up, moving as if it hurt her, trembling. She went and sat down beside Sarajane on the bed and said, "Would you hold me just for a minute? Would you? Please?"

Sarajane gathered her close without a word, and sat stroking her hair and murmuring soft comforting nonsense, until Delina sighed and said, "Thank you. I think I'm put back together now."

"Are you sure?"

"I'm sure. You can let me go; I'm prepared to talk sense."

"Good! I'm prepared to listen." Sarajane sat up straight, settled her pillows behind her at the head of the bed, folded her hands, and gave Delina her full attention.

"I was just so angry, you perceive," Delina began. "Every single time, all my life long, I've thought: *After this time, Nazareth will never be able to trick me again.* You know? She never lied; it's not that. But the truth she tells isn't the *real* truth! There's always another truth behind it, or tangled in it, one that's more important. I always think, *Next time, I'll spot that truth first.*"

"Delina, dear child . . . Nazareth is *dead*," said Sarajane softly. "You've got the wrong tense."

"For sure. And all the more humiliating, therefore. Bad enough that I never got the hang of it while she was alive . . . this is worse!"

Sarajane made one of the sounds that means, "I am listening," and nodded encouragingly, trying for patience.

"When Nazareth told me—or, if you prefer, when I had the hallucination that she was telling me—that the key to ending violence was to end *hunger*, I didn't understand. I told you all, when I was talking about it at the meeting—it seemed to me that there were many other things we could have done that would have been more obvious and speedy remedies. I understood how *wonderful* it would be if people no longer had to face hunger. I understood that it would perhaps mean more leisure, perhaps less greed. But human beings have fought bloody wars over many things of far less importance than food! I didn't see how ending hunger was the answer to my *question*. I just took it on faith, Sarajane; I didn't argue, and I didn't demand an explanation. Greatgrandmother has . . . *had* . . . that skill—of convincing people that she spoke the truth."

"Yes. She did. And very useful it was, too, over the years."

"Sarajane, it wasn't until you asked that question—*What will people be like, after this?*—that I suddenly saw it. And I was so angry to have been fooled *again*. It was like something had hit in the pit of my stomach, with no warning! It . . . it just knocked me over!"

"I saw that. But I don't follow you yet, child."

"I don't know how to say it. I don't have the right words."

73

"Try, please, Delina. I've been an interpreter for eight decades and more . . . I will follow you."

"Well . . ." Delina reached over and took Sarajane's hands. "The problem, the terrible problem that human beings have always faced, is that it seemed as if violence were somehow part of the *definition* of being human. Getting rid of it . . . it's like getting rid of *lungs*, somehow."

"Go on."

"So . . . remember how, after we women began speaking Láadan, and after our little girls began growing up speaking it, how we changed? It wasn't that we were *the same women with a different language added on*, Sarajane: we were *different*. So different that the men could no longer bear to have us with them for more than half an hour at a time . . . so different that they built the Womanhouses for us, to keep us separate. Remember?"

Sarajane smiled at her. "There are concepts that cannot be expressed in a language because it would self-destruct; there are languages that cannot be used in a culture . . . because it would self-destruct."

"*Now* who's reciting the pithy sayings of my greatgrandmother?"

Sarajane laughed. "I am. It's so handy, you perceive . . . you have to wonder, did she stay up all night polishing them? But go on, please; I shouldn't have interrupted you."

"The point," said Delina, "is that the creatures we are . . . and perhaps most especially the *male* creatures . . . seem unable to set violence aside. But human beings who have never eaten mouth-food . . . who have *never* had to say to themselves, 'This substance in my mouth was once a living creature like me, until it was caught and killed and cooked for me to eat' . . . Sarajane, they won't just be the *same* creatures eating a different diet."

Sarajane stared at her, eyes wide, understanding dawning on her face.

"Exactly!" Delina was jubilant, running over with delight, her annoyance completely forgotten. "Exactly! When the fish crawled up onto the land, dearlove, think what they *gave up* . . . what they left behind. How dear the sea must have been to them. How bizarre the idea of air, instead. But they stayed, Sarajane. Little by little, they learned. And then they were no longer *fish*! They were something else that could not have been foreseen. Something new, Sarajane. Not modified *fish*, but something quite new."

"You are saying . . . evolution."

"Yes! Evolution. Exactly. It wouldn't have had to be audiosynthesis, Sarajane—any change of sufficient *scope* would have done it. Nazareth might have suggested any number of things."

"For instance?"

"She might have said, 'Delina Meloren, find a way to make all human beings three-legged.' Right? That would have been a change of the right kind, of the right scope. But this one was something we could manage!"

"How did she ever *think* of it?" Sarajane marveled, and then caught herself hastily. "Job's beard," she said, "I'll be the one who's being suckered here, if I'm not careful! I mean: how did *you* ever bring that idea up out of your innermost mind, Delina Meloren, and put just that idea into your hallucination? How?"

Delina looked away from her and spoke carefully to the wall. "Don't you think it's odd, Sarajane, given that it was my own idea, that I didn't understand what I was telling myself?"

Delina's first trip to the PICOTA domes had been delayed by her need for a travel pass validated by a Chornyak male. Although everything in the known universe had already shifted toward wild disorder, the system had still been running, the way the male praying mantis keeps right on thrusting at the female even though she has already bitten off his head. On that day Delina had still been inconvenienced by the fact that she might at any time be stopped by the Women's Security Unit and ordered to show her pass, and that if she didn't have one she could be held in a prizpod at the police station until an irritated Chornyak male came to pay her fine and take her home.

This time, the system had come to realize that its head had been bitten off. This time, the delay was caused only by the heaviness of her heart. Things were different; she just walked out the door of Chornyak Womanhouse and *went*.

Delina appreciated the new freedom as much as she had always resented having to carry the pass, but it was hard to be natural about it; she felt naked. She caught the first Green-16 robobus, pleased to find that, unlike the weather and many other things, the buses were still working; if they hadn't been, she'd been prepared to walk the whole way. And when the two sorters at the domes asked her for her pass she said simply, "I don't have one," and waited. They looked at her and at each other, shrugged, and took her once again to Will Bluecrane.

Who looked at her fiercely and said, "Do not tell me you are back again, Delina Chornyak!"

"I am back again, Grandfather," she said.

"Do not call me Grandfather."

"Yes, Chief Bluecrane."

Will sent the sorters away and motioned to Delina to sit down, remarking that she seemed to him to have improved not at all since her last visit, except for being drier.

"I'm sure I haven't improved," she agreed. "I rather expect I've gotten worse. Everything else has."

He nodded his head. "It's going to be worse still, you know."

"I know."

"And there is nothing we can do. Unfortunately. We can only hold on and try not to make matters worse."

Delina said nothing; you do not argue with old people.

"Why have you come back to trouble me again, Delina?" he asked her.

She dropped her eyes, staring at the back of her hands where they lay useless in her lap, wishing she dared take her crocheting out of her pack.

"This isn't going to be easy," she told him.

"Mmhmmm. Delina, do you plan on trying to convince me that we should see you through another vision quest? Because if you are, I tell you now: you can sit outside my door and die of hunger and thirst if you wish, you can fry in the sun and melt away entirely in the rain, but we will *not* give in to you on that one again."

"Of course not," said Delina. "Neither would I, in your place."

"That's not why you're here?"

"No, sir. It's not."

"Well, then! Are you in trouble? Have you kidnapped someone? Blown something up? Overthrown a government?"

When she didn't answer, he cleared his throat and said, "Perhaps I should send for my wife and have *her* come talk to you."

Delina looked up, then, and smiled at him. "No," she said, "I can talk to you—I *came* here to talk to you. I'm just not sure exactly how to start."

"Try the simplest method," he said. "The ancient one. Where you begin at the beginning, go on till you're through—within the boundaries of reason—and then stop. I will listen, whatever it is that's brought you back to the PICOTA. I am even happy to see you; I won't deny it, though I have no excuse for it at all."

Delina stood up, and he started to get up, too, looking puzzled, but she raised her hand to stop him. "No," she said. "Please don't get up; I'm all right. I just think I could do this much better if I went over there by the wall and looked at that holoprairie of yours while I talked."

"With your back to me."

"Yes."

"Coward!"

"Yes."

She crossed the room and stood in front of the holoprairie with its gently waving grains and flowers stretching away from her into the virtual distance, clasped her hands behind her, swallowed hard, and said, "Chief Bluecrane, I have come here to get a husband."

After a while, as the silence went on and on, she spoke again, and although her voice trembled, there was determination in it. "It's not such a bad bargain as all that," she said. "I have many useful skills. I'm not pretty, but I'm pleasant-looking enough not to hurt anyone's eyes; if I owned a decent dress I'd look just like any other woman. My back is crooked, but I'm healthy. I know how to carry on an interesting conversation . . . in a dozen different languages, if that matters to the PICOTA. And my wants are modest. I am a *very* hard worker, and there's no work I'm afraid of. A man could do worse."

"Stay there," Bluecrane said, behind her. "Stay right where you are."

He pressed the comstud on the edge of his desk and told the computer that answered to find his wife and send her to his office at once. "Wait, please," he said to Delina's back, "until Anne Walks Tall Bluecrane joins us."

Delina did as she was told, standing quietly in the holoprairie wind, until she heard the door open and the other woman said, "Will? You wanted me for something?" Then she turned to face them as the chief of the PICOTA told his wife, "This Chornyak female, who seems determined to plague us with her eccentricities, tells me that she's here looking for a husband. And she has followed up that declaration with a list of her alleged qualifications for the position of someone's—some Native American someone's—wife."

Anne looked at Delina, and back again at Will, obviously surprised. "She's not married, then?" she asked. "At her age?"

"I thought she was married, too," said Will. "It was one of the things that amazed me when she was here before . . . that her husband would let her take off like that. People have always called every woman from Chornyak Household 'Mrs. Chornyak,' married or not—I took it for granted that she was married."

"Now *you're* doing it!" Delina said in exasperation, before she thought.

"We are? What are we doing?"

"Talking about me as if I weren't here, or as if I were unconscious," she answered. And added, "I do wish I were unconscious."

"We shouldn't have been doing that," said Anne. "It's bad manners and we both know better. I apologize. But we were surprised."

"That I should want a husband? Or have the gall to ask for one?"

Delina was bluffing, but it seemed to her that she could hardly make things worse; she might just as well pretend she hadn't done anything outrageous.

"No, child," said Anne. "It was because we both are aware that no woman of the Lines is *allowed* to stay single—not once she's old enough to bear them children."

Delina looked past them toward the spot where the wall across from her began to curve upward and become the ceiling, and answered, "I'm single because I am barren. You see this spine of mine . . ." She traced its double curve in the air before her with one hand. "I carry the gene that causes it; I was sterilized at birth. And that's another advantage I can offer a husband, you perceive. No need to worry about my wanting to bring children into this poor flabbergasted world."

Anne Bluecrane went over to her, moving fast, and took her hands gently between her own. "Delina," she said, "do you mean to say that the linguists sterilize their children . . . their infants . . . if they're not perfect? Am I understanding you correctly?"

As if we were a Government Work project raising babies in test tubes for scientific experiments! she thought wearily; it got tiresome sometimes, dealing with all the myths that same government had so determinedly created. Aloud, she said, "No, not just if they're not perfect; we're allowed to be imperfect. Only if they are carrying a gene for something both unpleasant and incurable. Like this curvature of the spine . . . this scoliosis. In a case like that only. One injection, you perceive, and it puts an end to the prospect of passing the problem along to another generation. I understand that; I have always understood it, and approved. But that is why I have no husband . . . yet."

It was so still that she could hear Will Bluecrane breathing. She knew what they were thinking—that if she had been a boy-child, the sterilization would still have been done, but the *spine* would have been repaired. The infamous wicked Lingoes, with their well-known brutal abuse of their women and children. She could not let that pass.

"No," she said gently, "that's not how it was, nor how it is. The spinal reconstruction can't be done until the person is fully grown. When I reached that point I told them I didn't want it done, and they didn't force me. They *would* have done it, if I had not refused."

Anne Bluecrane caught her breath, and asked with honest bewilderment, "Why on earth?"

Delina remembered how she had felt in those days—mercifully

brief days—full of turmoil. She had been fierce. Wild. Running over with rage. Smoldering so inside that it had seemed to her she ought to die of the heat. Like anyone her age, she'd been convinced that she was the eternal center of everyone's focused attention, that she was awkward and ugly, that she did not and could not ever measure up to the standards coming at her, that the world revolved around a sinister plot to ruin her life, that none of these problems had ever existed for anyone but herself . . . all the usual things. But she'd had a very *severe* case of malignant adolescence, and she had been willing to suffer tremendously for the sake of punishing others. She had thought: *They don't like to look at me, twisted like this . . . well, damn them, they will just have to look at me whether they like it or* not, *the bigots! And the worse they hate it, the better for their character!*

And so she had pretended. Pretended she didn't care. Pretended she didn't want the straight back everyone else had. Pretended she liked the crooked one and preferred it. Pretended it didn't hurt. And had never had the courage to just open her mouth and say, "I've changed my mind, I'll have the new back now, please," not in all these years. Not after the extraordinary baroque scenes she'd staged, refusing.

"I did it for pride," she said, astonished to hear the words come out of her mouth, realizing that she had never before admitted it to anyone. "Wicked pride. And I have paid for it in full." *Pride. The deadliest of the seven sins that really matter.*

"And now," Will Bluecrane said, clearing his throat, "because your greatgrandmother says it must be done, you have come to ask for a husband from among the PICOTA. *Despite* your many and obvious flaws."

Delina bit her lip; he did remember, then, after all. She'd been afraid that he had forgotten.

"Yes, please," she said. "If one of your men will have me. I promise you: I will make a very good wife. I have no nonsense in my head about romance to cause him trouble. Our marriages have always been based on what is best for the Household and for the Line, and our husbands have always been chosen for us. My husband will find me sensible, and I will live wherever he likes now, or I will follow him wherever he wishes to go."

"You believe your men will let you do this?" Anne asked. "Are you sure?"

Delina sighed. "They don't care what we do anymore," she said. "They're trying to create an entire new economy from scratch, you perceive. They're trying to put things back as they were before we first began Interfacing our babies with the Aliens, with as few modifications as possible. They don't have time to care what we women do, not now. As long as I commit no criminal offense and am careful not to interrupt them, I can do as I please. More to the point, I expect . . . would one of *your* men be willing to marry a prideful Lingoe bitch in her thirties with a crooked back?"

The other woman cocked her head, and put her hands on Delina's shoulders, considering her, not hurrying. "Delina," she said carefully, "I'll take your word that your men have better things to do than to interfere in this; that's reasonable enough. And I will ignore the foolish question. We are wise enough here to understand what such an alliance would mean, and why it would be desirable. But there's one other thing. Delina, please think carefully before you answer me. You would have to come to us; no PICOTA man would go to live in the houses of the Lines. Tell me this—could you *bear* it? You have always lived surrounded by women; could you bear to live with only a man?"

"It has to be done," said Delina steadily, adding the pain in her heart to the other pain. "Someone must be first, and I am far more free than any other linguist woman. I have no children. No ties except ties of love. No duties, now that the interpreting booths are closed down and the Interfaces are empty. It will be hard, but it has to be me."

"You're sure?"

"If the PICOTA are willing, yes—I am absolutely sure."

Will Bluecrane did not dawdle once he'd made up his mind. He looked at Anne for approval, and when she nodded yes he sent for the sorters. "Take Delina Chornyak to a guest bedroom," he said, "and see that she has whatever she needs. She will be staying with us now for a while." He cleared his throat again, and added, "We have business to attend to. She and I; and the PICOTA."

It was Will Bluecrane, at the very end of his life, speaking from a bed where he lay in state on piled pillows while his relatives competed to wait on him and anticipate his smallest need, who declared the women an honorary tribe and gave the tribe its name. At first Delina, watching over him from the windowseat, thought he was joking, and she told him it was a pretty good joke, for an old man.

"It's no joke, you ignorant Anglo woman!" he shot back at her. "I am still Chief of the PICOTA, and if I choose to call all you women of the Lines who are married to us a tribe, no one can refuse me!"

That was absurd; he would need approval from the Tribal Councils for such an innovation, like anybody else. But Delina let it pass, and she listened, smiling, as he told her that from now on she was a member of the Meandering Water tribe.

"You tell them I said so, Delina Chornyak Bluecrane," he said huskily. "Because you linguist women don't go in a straight line from A to B to C. You go this way a while, and that way a while, and this way again, instead. And you go gently and quietly. But you *get* there, always! You meander, as water meanders, headed for the oceans . . . and then you arrive." He lay back on the pillows, breathless. "It's important," he said. "You tell them."

They won't believe me, she thought, but she said only, "I will do that, Grandfather; I promise." And cautiously, not wanting to tire him or to presume, she asked, "What does it mean . . . to be an honorary tribe of the PICOTA?"

"I don't know," he said. "There's never been one before. But I can tell you two things: It's an honor. A great honor. And with honors come *responsibilities*! No more loafing around. You tell them. And tell them that I want you and Henry with the Cherokees in Northwest Arkansas, where you can look after—" He stopped, gasping.

She wished he'd hush; it was so hard for him to talk. But Will would have been insulted at the idea that she thought he didn't have sense enough to make such decisions for himself. Nobody but Anne could tell him what to do, not even the healers. She held her peace, therefore, and waited for him to catch his breath.

"I've changed my mind," he said, in a little while.

"I'm not surprised."

"Not about the *tribe*."

"No?"

"No! That's done; I'm determined."

"What then, Grandfather Bluecrane?"

"I'm going to tell them about it myself," he said. "You'd get it all mixed up."

And then he closed his eyes, exhausted, and fell asleep.

PART TWO
WHAT THE SECOND TRANCER SAID

CHAPTER 6

Watch the children in church, taking Communion. The tiny bread-wafer is laid on the tongue; the mouth closes. And almost instantly, in the child's eyes, you see the ancient memory stirring. You can see that the tongue and the teeth, the tender inner surfaces of the mouth and throat, are all remembering: There was a time when the sensation and the taste of mouthfood were commonplace. Sister, you can see the old lust waking. And that is why the children must swallow the wafer and go straight into the choir to sing! That is why, at the four festivals of the seasons, whatever they may be called in a particular culture, everyone must take their bite of the festival bread and then break at once into song, and the louder the better.

When I think of that old lust, curled up somewhere in every one of us, I don't perceive it as snake or lizard or dragon, as one of the beautiful sleek swift coiled creatures. What stirs there in my mind's eye is an old, old cat . . . most probably a tom . . . covered with street scars, and wise in the cruel, sly ways of the alleys.

(Archives entry; Sister Jessamine Noumarque Shawnessey)

The Meander music school of Our Blessed Lady of the StarTangle sat close beside the basechurch, making the long end of an *L* around the pad where the skychapels landed for refueling and crew changes. It was a pretty little school, set down in deep woods in a spacious clearing; you could look out its windows and see the Ozark Mountains, low and blue in the distance. There'd been a town on the same site once, and that had conveniently provided the clearing; no one mourned it, no one even remembered it anymore, and all its buildings and artifacts had been taken away long ago. The new town that had grown up nearby was an old town now itself, and to the people of Meander, Arkansas, it was as if the school and church had always been there. Like all Star-Tangle music schools, this one was a rectangle of rooms, built round a central courtyard where the school orchestra and band, and all the choirs, could gather to practice.

The sisters kept the borders of the courtyard planted with blooming things . . . *practical* blooming things. Tall sturdy plantings of purple-flowered sage and chives. Rue with its bright yellow flowers and indestructible evergreen foliage. Fuzzy hoarhound; columns of blue-flowered chicory. Beds of crisp mint, with their roots firmly constrained by stones set on edge and sunk into the ground. That sort of blooming thing. Things that looked after themselves and went undisturbed through every kind of weather; things that not only looked and smelled wonderful but could be used for food and drink and medicine. Things that didn't notice when you took whole armloads of cuttings from them to send home with the small girls for their own gardens, after carefully showing the children how to get them to put out new roots and thrive.

"*Sing* to your gardens!" was always the final instruction, and the children obeyed. Every early morning or twilight of the year when the weather wasn't so foul it was actually a hazard, outside every house that had a girlchild, you could find a little girl with hands clasped behind her back and her feet securely planted to give her balance for big deep breaths, serenading the plants in the gardens. Sometimes, though not often enough, there was a boy-child, too. Even the children of Jefferson Household, free now from the interpreting booths, had leisure enough for such singing.

The mass-ed computers were wonderful for teaching children the basics, and the obligatory Homeroom sessions were satisfactory for teaching them how to interact with other human beings. But it took a school, in the old-fashioned sense of the word, to turn motley packs of kids into orchestras and bands and chamber music quartets and choirs. It took *groups*. You could learn to be a soloist from the computer. You could learn to sing or play along with a computer-generated group passably well. But there was always something missing. "The sum of the parts!" the sisters would say. "You can get all the parts going, on their own, with any old computer, but you can't get the *sum* of the parts!" For the sum, you needed all the young ones assembled together, pressed shoulder to shoulder in rows, lustily belting out the music, weaving a fabric of it strong enough to tie joy to and know that it would *hold*.

On this particular Monday morning the school's six classrooms were being scrubbed by the long arms of the cleaning servomech, snaking up through the ports in the floor from the basement, and the children were out in the courtyard in the sunshine that had followed the morning's thunderstorm. The courtyard itself had been scoured already, by the wind and the hail and the rain.

The glory that was the sum of the parts—carrying, today, one of Calendia's beloved "Consecrations of the Morning"—rose up toward the sky under the able direction of the music grammar teacher. And in the cubbyhole that served them as school office, the listening sisters were well satisfied.

"Just listen to that!" said Mother Superior Drussa Mbal, clapping her hands softly. "Calendia himself would be pleased!" She was right; the composer would have been both pleased and amazed. The current MGT from Jefferson Womanhouse, young though she was, had an almost magical knack for bringing music from the children that was pure bliss to listen to. She never had any trouble getting them to start practicing. She would give them the pitch, a clear true note ringing out like a bell in the courtyard, and they would respond instantly, singing their hearts out. The only problem she had was getting them to *stop* singing. They never wanted to quit, even when the sun was straight up overhead and it was indisputably time to quit. "We're not hungry, Miss Jefferson!" they would call out. "We don't want to go home!"

Their parents would have supported their claim that they weren't hungry. "She doesn't eat enough to keep a bird alive!" they would have told you. "He barely touches his food!" But none of the parents worried. Because the children grew, and they were as strong and healthy as anyone could have asked. When they were made to go home anyway, shooed away like so many flocks of birds, they would leave *still* singing, their voices drifting away on the wind as they got into family flyers or, if they lived near enough, went running off together down the road.

"I only wish," said Sister Septembra wistfully, "that the other MGT was as good." The teacher for the orchestra and band, that was. Sister Septembra had been a choir nun, but she had a great fondness for instruments, especially brass ones. Especially trumpets. She loved trumpets.

"But she *is* good," Sister Dolores Maria objected. "She does very well considering how few of the children want to play instruments instead of singing in the choirs."

Septembra sniffed. "She's not *topnotch!*"

"Septembra," said the Mother Drussa, "in my opinion, you say that only because she—quite properly—won't set up the brass choir you keep fussing for. With nine schools on her route, Sister, Cress Chornyak doesn't have time for brass choirs."

"Perhaps," said Septembra grudgingly. "But we *need* the brass choir, Mother."

"*You* need the brass choir, Sister; please be precise."

"We have so many brass choir music chiplets," observed Sister Dolores Maria, "that there's no space in the cupboards for anything *else*."

"It's not the same, Dolores Maria, it's not like *live* brass!" said Septembra. "You can hear the difference as well as I can."

"But we can't have *every* kind of musical group here, Sister! For heaven's sakes! We have no opera . . . no musical comedy ensemble . . . no raptyhop group . . . no *jug* band!"

The expression on Septembra's face at the idea that a jug band might be compared to her beloved trumpets sent the other nuns, even the Mother Superior with all the worries she had on her shoulders that day, into gales of helpless laughter. They laughed until Septembra gave in and laughed with them, wiping her eyes with the edge of her headdress. "All right!" she said. "I surrender! You're correct, you really are; Miss Chornyak does, in fact, manage to get very respectable music out of one trumpet, two flutes, a cello, and a couple of drums. And I cannot imagine how she can possibly see to the music for nine schools—when does she *sleep*? I don't give her nearly enough credit; I admit it."

"Very *good*, Sister!" said Mother Superior. "We are pleased to hear you say so at last."

"Are there StarTangle schools where more of the children want to play instruments?" asked Sister Kathra, who had been a silent observer until then. She was not a StarTangle nun; she was a visiting Carmelite sent to observe the way this small country school was run, to find an explanation for its choirs' reputation for excellence, and to pursue other familiar agendas.

"Of course," Dolores Maria answered. "Lots of them! The overpowering attraction for vocal music here is because Shawana Jefferson just plain *enchants* the children, and they all want to be part of the music *she* makes. It makes it hard on Cress Chornyak, I'm sure, though she never complains."

"I have never heard an MGT complain," said Mother Superior, and she looked at Septembra and Dolores Maria for confirmation. "Have you?" And when they shook their heads no, she said, "Well, then."

"Are they saints?" asked Sister Kathra, sounding cross. "Or what?"

"You never went to a music school, Sister? When you were a little girl?"

"My parents were against it," she said. "They had the idea that something else . . . something mysterious and dangerous . . . was really being taught in the music schools. That the MGTs had some secret agenda. You remember the sort of superstitions people used to have in those days, I'm sure."

"Well, the MGTs are *not* saints, thank goodness! Saints are wonderful at a distance, but nobody wants to *live* with one. It's just that the women of the Lines had such abominably hard lives in the past. All the records of that time were lost in the Greatwar, of course, but it's said that they literally worked from dawn to dark six days a week, and then were required to spend all of Sunday in church. That training is still with them; I don't think they even notice how heavy their schedules are."

"How could there possibly have been that much interpreting and translating to do?" the Carmelite protested. "It would have to have been makework . . . just invented to keep them busy at all costs. To maintain those silly myths about the linguists. Don't you think?"

"Oh, I'm sure you're right," said the Mother Superior, her eyes and face the very picture of candor. "But, of course, makework or no, it meant they had no time at all for themselves—and it's said they were put to work as young as nine years of age, Sister."

"More myths!" Sister Kathra scoffed. "That would never have been allowed."

"Well . . . it's hard to know what to believe, isn't it?" said Mother Drussa. "Whatever the facts may be, whatever the details, the women of the Lines seem to think what they do now is more vacation than work. And that is our great good fortune, because of course the more they delight in their teaching, the more the children learn and the better they learn it."

"And they do all the music teaching in your schools, by themselves." Sister Kathra sniffed. "Very commendable."

"They teach theory and performance. And we StarTangle sisters do rehearsals and coaching, and drill the students in scales and chords and exercises . . . that sort of thing."

"I see." Sister Kathra's face changed abruptly; she was suddenly all business. "It's time," she stated, "to start bringing in music teachers from outside the Lines. Really, Sisters. Surely it's time, and long past time!"

"The first time one of the linguist MGTs fails to give us satisfactory service," the Superior assured her, "we will certainly consider that alternative."

"It's already happening, obviously," said the Carmelite. "Your own sisters say the Jefferson teacher is pressed for time. And you've been sitting here, all of you, clucking over the burden that a nine-school route represents for one person. I *heard* you. Why won't you let us help?"

"My dear Sister Kathra," said Mother Drussa, and she reached over and touched the younger nun on her knee, apparently oblivious to the offended jerking away that resulted, "your Order, like any other, is entirely at liberty to set up music schools of your *own*. At any time. I don't understand the problem."

"Forgive me, Mother Drussa—you *do* understand! You know

very well that no one will send their children to music schools unless the MGT has been trained by a StarTangle teacher!"

"Then you Carmelites must try, don't you think, to develop a system of your own and build for it a reputation that is equal to ours?"

"But *why*?" Sister Kathra was genuinely annoyed, and having trouble hiding it. "The system you have . . . and have had for so many, many years . . . is superb. It accomplishes wonders, just as it is. Why should anyone need to devise a new music grammar curriculum from scratch?"

"It might be very valuable," observed Septembra thoughtfully. "Perhaps the women of the Lines have overlooked some major component . . . neglected some crucial element. Variety is healthy, after all. Your Order might add new breadth to the subject, Sister Kathra."

Sister Kathra closed her eyes for a moment before she spoke again, and said a swift prayer for patience and for tact. She wasn't getting anywhere, but then she hadn't really expected to; many had tried before her, over the years, with no better results.

"I do not understand," she said bitterly, "why those women must be given *all* the music teacher posts. It's not fair . . . there are so few careers for women, and so much teaching is terribly dreary stuff. Music is such *fun*. They're selfish, those women, keeping it all for themselves; they shouldn't be encouraged. We Carmelites could provide you with *excellent* MGTs, if you'd only give us an opportunity." And she said again, "It's not *fair*."

Mother Drussa sighed, and leaned her head toward Sister Kathra over steepled hands. "You know, my dear," she said, "you have a point. But the poor women of the Lines . . . if we took the music instruction away from them, what would they *do*? They have no training for anything else. Their men won't allow them to learn nursing, or any other sort of teaching except music grammar. They aren't permitted any social life. I'm sure you will agree with me that it would be dreadfully unkind to take away their only chance to get out of those underground buildings and see the outside world."

"We will petition your Motherhouse," Sister Kathra said grimly.

"Again?"

"Again. This year, and every year, until a more fair arrangement is negotiated."

"Well," said Mother Drussa, beaming at her, "we wish you the very best of luck in your efforts. As always." And she added, "We are more than willing to cooperate."

When Sister Kathra spoke again, her voice was strained. "I had forgotten," she said, her voice was rigid now as her back and shoulders, "that every nun of your Order is also a woman of the linguist Lines. I do apologize."

They assured her that it was perfectly all right, that they had taken no offense, that it was a mistake made every day, since no other religious Order had a family origin in the way that Our Lady of the StarTangle had. They were sure, they told her, that it would not always be that way, that the time would come when any girl-child with a vocation would be welcome.

And they insisted on getting her a footstool to put her feet up on, embroidered with blackberries and wild roses and Queen Anne's lace, and on her joining them over a pot of steaming tea and a plate of spicebread fresh from the oven.

Outside, the music of the children went on, abundant and splendid as the morning light.

In the orbiting offices of the US Department of Agriculture's Planetary Food Supply Division the statistics were feeding steadily into the databanks. This was as it should be; it went on twenty-four hours a day, seven days a week. But this morning an odd pattern was beginning to show up on the monitors. The comclerk who answered the alarm called her supervisor . . . the one with the funny name . . . to come check it out.

"Look at that, Miss Walks Tall!" she said. "What do you suppose it means?"

Lorena Walks Tall watched for a minute, and clucked her tongue. "It means," she said flatly, "that they've been sending up pasta again."

"But, ma'am . . ." The comclerk looked respectful, as she was paid to do, but she took the liberty of saying that personally, she could see no connection between pasta and the strange numbers on the monitor. Numbers that appeared to show a sudden unexplained increase in the planet's food supply.

"That's because there are a lot of things you don't pay attention to, Miss Barrett!" snapped the supervisor. "You must pay attention! Every time they serve us that GI pasta it sheds cheap flour dust, and every time they do that it gets in the circulating system—and every time *that* happens we get blips like this on the monitors! It's happened three times in the past six months. Pay attention!"

"Oh," said Miss Barrett, through the anesthetic fog that she determinedly kept set up between herself and the misery that went with full awareness. "I didn't know that."

"Of course you didn't," said Laura Walks Tall. "How could you know? You're not *qualified* to know such things, Miss Barrett; you are trained only to do data input."

And you *are trained only to be a flaming* bitch! thought the comclerk. *You make* no *sense; first you tell me pay attention, then you tell me I'm not* supposed *to know anything! No wonder they can't keep anybody in this job for more than a couple of years!* Aloud, she said only, "It shows too much food, Miss Walks Tall. What should I do?"

"Do nothing at all, Miss Barrett. Leave it to me; I've dealt with it before. Just put it out of your mind."

Jeanne Barrett sat patiently, waiting, while the supervisor went back into her desk. And sure enough . . . the figures on the screens flickered once as the adjustments were made, and returned to normal.

Miss Barrett nodded, satisfied, and went back to inputting data. She appreciated it very much that she could count on her supervisor to take care of things like this, so that she didn't have to try. She hated computers, and everything to do with computers. She hated the Department of Agriculture; she hated being in orbit. Next month, when she got married, just as soon as she finished training her replacement, she would say goodbye to all this with heartfelt joy. And it was her firm intention never to go near anything more complicated than her own comset and palmer again as long as she lived. She understood why it was always women who did this kind of work . . . it was so boring, no man would put up with it. But she didn't approve.

"A woman's place is in the *home*," she told the roomful of monitors. She wondered where Lorena Walks Tall lived; she wondered how anybody could bear to live with such a person. "In the *home*," she said again, forcefully. And none of them contradicted her.

CHAPTER 7

What is called "resonance medicine" by the women of the Lines is, of course, not medicine at all. When it works, it works only as a placebo, like "faith healing." But you need to be familiar with it in a rough way, because many of your patients will have gone to school to the music grammar teachers, and will have a sort of predisposition to believe anything a woman of the Lines tells them. Those women are trained in science and in rhetoric; they know how to wrap their nonsense in a scientific wrapper. They talk of "entrainment"—and it's true, the brain waves of a truly attentive listener do match themselves to the brain waves of a compelling speaker. That is: entrainment does in fact exist. Resonance exists; entrainment is one of its primary manifestations. When the women use those terms, they have science behind them. But their claim that the resonance healer can, by entrainment, cause the patient's brain to stop issuing destructive messages to the cells and replace them with the healthy messages that the healer's brain is issuing . . . now that, of course, is total nonsense. Fairy tales. Superstitious gibberish. And you can prove it to your patients easily. Just show them what passes for a medical text among the so-called resonance healers! Not one proper text exists, my friends—it's all poems *and cute little stories. One quick look will disabuse any educated patient, I promise you.*

(J. T. R. Phillip, MD, in "Current Frauds and Quackeries in American Medicine," a paper delivered at the annual meeting of the Virginia Medical Society)

Sister Naomi was a tall and bulky woman who ought to have cut her hair short; it took fourteen pins to fasten the heavy dark brown braids into a tidy crown around her head every morning so that she would take up no more than her allotted chunk of room aboard the sky chapel. She was well aware that the braids annoyed people; that was what made them worth her trouble and her time.

Skychapel Six had been giving her trouble of considerably greater significance this past week, and she was seriously considering cutting a few stops off her route and taking it back to Earth for repairs and refurbishing. Her crew was in disagreement about that, and they had had a more than lively discussion on the subject, spoiling an otherwise pleasant breakfast of basic Bach.

Sister Lauren had first called Naomi a coward to her face, and then spent ten minutes chastising herself for what she'd said. Naomi had declared that she would recover from the insult, and had gathered Lauren close and rubbed her back to demonstrate that there were no hard feelings. It had been a hard trip, and Lauren was so weary that Naomi was prepared to excuse almost anything she might say.

Sister Quilla, on the other hand, had made her usual calm and considered contribution. "Skychapels don't break down," she had said. "No skychapel ever has. Not one. They don't have *parts* enough, and they're not complicated enough. The problem is not danger but discomfort." And she had looked carefully past the other two women, pretending to be occupied with fastening back her skycoif, as she added that she didn't concern herself much about discomfort.

Sister Quilla had grown up in an inflatable plasticpod on the back streets of a tourist asteroid—named, absurdly, Fruited Plain—that specialized in rowdy parties and big drunken brawls; it had been established to preserve the peace of communities once plagued by such activities. The government of Fruited Plain saved money by shutting down services whenever the tourists were too far gone to care, without regard for what that might mean for its few hundred citizens in residence. This was deliberate policy, intended to *keep* the population to a few hundred; if it had been given any encouragement to grow, there wouldn't have been the necessary brawling and partying room. In the way of all governments, it found it necessary to maintain lights and water and toilets and so on in its official buildings and state residences; in the way of all governments, it didn't give one damn how ordinary people managed.

Sister Quilla had of necessity learned to get by with very little in the way of creature comforts, and she had breezed through training. It wasn't unusual for a novice of the Church of Our Lady of the StarTangle to need six months or more before she could break the habit of eating food; there had been novices who needed as long as a year. And there were many who failed, once they left the privacy of the cloister and had no choice but to eat mouthfood from time to time in public situations. Not Sister Quilla. "They thought it might be *harder* for me," she had told Naomi. "Sometimes it's like that, they said—people who've grown up on very short rations are truly obsessed with mouthfood. But my father had taught me not to care about it; for me, it was easy."

Sister Quilla's father had been born in a linguist Household; he understood what training *meant*. Like most men of the Lines, he had found the idea of a lifetime spent as an administrator for the women's string of music schools intolerable. Serving as an instructor of linguistics or foreign languages, either in government or in the private sector, hadn't appealed to him. Nor had he been willing to spend his life pretending that he was looking after one of the fortunes of the Lines, which had long ceased to need any direction other than that supplied by computers. He had drifted from world to world for years before settling down on Fruited Plain, where he could convince himself that he was only at a lengthy party . . . that pretty soon he'd be going back home to Earth again to *be* somebody.

Like Naomi, Sister Quilla never seemed to get tired, and that was one reason why Sister Lauren was so worn out right now—she insisted on trying to keep up with the other two women. She would outgrow that eventually, and Naomi would be greatly relieved when she did. It was far more trouble rescuing Sister Lauren from the messes she made when she went on working beyond the limits of her strength than it would have been just to do the work *for* her. It was even more trouble keeping her from realizing what was happening until after she was secure enough to laugh about it. But it was worth it, and it would be done. A skychapel crewmember who lacked the self-confidence to make decisions was dangerous.

Naomi was rubbing fretfully at her chin, wishing she could make up *her* mind, when the decision was taken out of her hands. The tiny comset screen on the panel before her lit up with the garish red of a distress call. Before she could ask, Quilla had the data for her; it was coming from a fieldchapel on Savannah, a planet too heavily populated to be on a skychapel route, but close enough to reach easily.

"You know anything about the place, Quilla?" Naomi asked.

"Only what the computer says . . . 'An unremarkable world of limited resources, settled by one hundred African American families of Earth origin; major industry, eucalyptus. One fieldchapel, staffed by Sister Cecily Mara Jefferson. No known plagues; no known predators not under full control. Government benign.'"

"Eucalyptus?"

"That's what it says. Shall I call up a bigger file?"

"No. Let's find out what Sister Cecily wants first."

She touched the comspot and waited for it to respond, sighed and touched it again when it ignored her, and then gave it the sharp blow with the heel of her hand that could ordinarily be relied on to get its attention.

"This is Skychapel Six," she said in Panglish, leaning over the mechanism to give its pickups every possible advantage. "We've seen your call and are near enough to reach you quickly. What's the problem?"

Nothing happened, and Naomi whacked the comspot again, hoping her message had been sent. It was no surprise to her, or to anyone, that the ancient machines were beginning to be unreliable; what *was* surprising was that no one had yet figured out how to repair them. Quilla was right that skychapels had very few parts, but wrong that it necessarily meant they weren't complicated; if there'd been more parts, human beings might have been able to figure out how they worked. On the other hand, if these small craft with their raindrop shape and bare-minimum fittings had been well understood, Motherchurch would never have been able to buy them from Pentagon surplus so cheaply, so there you were. Silver linings.

She had once heard a woman . . . a Noumarque Household woman, if she remembered correctly . . . say with apparent seriousness, "I think the chapels fly by faith alone." And nobody in the room had laughed.

Words were beginning to move across the small screen now, and she watched them closely, in case they were interrupted or began scrambling themselves. They were Láadan words: "Wil sha," the screen said. *Let there be harmony.* That meant the call was from Sister Cecily, which was a good sign. And then, "We have a man here who urgently needs surgery, and all our healthies stopped working weeks ago. I've ordered replacements, but they haven't arrived, and Motherhouse says ice is blocking takeoffs. Can you help?"

"As you know," Naomi said, in case the woman *didn't* know, "we don't carry healthies. But we can do simple surgery. If it's not simple, we can probably stabilize him enough to take him to a hospital. Turn on your landing beacon, Sister, and we'll join you . . . Give us maybe forty minutes. All right?"

"Very much so! And here goes the beacon, you perceive."

Either Sister Cecily was very economical with words or the comset was glitching again; it mattered only if she had been about ready to warn Naomi of some hazard on the landing pad. Naomi locked on to the beacon and headed the chapel toward Savannah; when she was close enough to tax the comset's power less, she'd check again. Just in case.

It was indeed simple surgery: a straightforward and simple cancer of the stomach. Naomi was able to handle it without calling on either Lauren or Quilla, even hampered by the primitive strings of tiny blinking lights that were the only medical instruments Sister Cecily had available for the purpose. And thirty-three minutes after landing, with the man turned over to the care of his obviously devoted family, she was able to join the other three women over their pot of tea and her own pot of coffee.

"All done," she said, "and no problems."

Sister Cecily smiled her thanks. "I know he's very grateful," she said. "I'd dealt with the pain, but there was nothing I could do about the fact that he *knew* what happens with a stomach cancer if you don't get rid of it. He was terrified."

"As anyone rational would have been," Naomi said.

"Thank you for seeing to it, Sister," said Cecily.

"Why on earth did he let it go so long?" Naomi asked. *And why did* you *let it go so long?*

"He didn't tell anybody."

"With cancer of the stomach?"

"Well . . . he didn't know that's what it was, of course. He's a potter, Naomi, and a very good one—a very *famous* one, and greatly loved. First there was a blue glaze he had in mind, and he couldn't get the shade exactly right. Then he got a commission for thirteen ceremonial bowls, one for each month of the year, and he wanted to finish that. And then . . . there was always something, you perceive. And when the time came that it could *not* be put off any longer, it had become an emergency."

Regulations required Naomi to ask Sister Cecily why she hadn't done the surgery herself; she intended to do it as soon as she could call her aside and ask her in privacy. But the obvious question hung unasked in the air, and she was glad when the woman volunteered the information without having to be asked.

"I tried," Cecily told them. "I did try. But every time I got close . . ." She paused, and took a deep breath, and tried again. "I've never been able to do it easily," she said, "and this was the first time I ever had to try it with a *male*. I had something wrong . . . something left out or misplaced; maybe I had added something that wasn't supposed to be in a male abdomen. I don't know what it was, but I couldn't get resonance."

Sister Quilla made a tsking sound with her tongue. "There's no excuse for that, Sister," she said severely.

"I know." Cecily looked miserable. Serene, as could be expected of a missionary nun well into middle age, but still miserable.

"Perhaps," said Naomi, "there *is* an excuse. Perhaps it was the fault of the *patient*, for example? Sister Quilla has a tendency to leap to conclusions and to make rude—not to mention unkind—comments based on inadequate evidence. It comes of not being well brought up." *And*, she thought, *of having no patience with those weaker than herself.* Naomi would have to remind Quilla again that not every woman she met had had her early advantages.

"I am so sorry," Quilla said at once; she was sharp-tongued and severe when she saw fault in someone who should have been doing better, but she had a warm and generous heart. "Naomi has put her finger on the problem with her usual precision; I had no right to say that. I'm sure you feel bad enough about this, Sister Cecily, without my blundering tongue laid on to make it worse—and no doubt, as Naomi says, you have a good reason."

"No," said Sister Cecily, shaking her head. "No, I don't. This is one of those times when there's no way to sugar coat the unpleasant facts. Ever since the last of our healthies quit on us, I have gotten up every morning and said to myself, 'Cecily Mara, today you will find time to study the anatomy of the male human being—*before* you need it. *Before* it's too late to refresh your memory!' And every night I have fallen into my bed regretting that I did not find that time. As Sister Quilla says, I have no excuse."

"And if we hadn't just happened to come along, Sister?" Lauren asked.

"Suppose you had not come along," Cecily answered. "And suppose not one of the three craft whose schedule is in my databanks for this week had come along either."

"Just suppose."

"I would have tried again. I would have been terrified of doing irreparable damage, but I would have tried; I wouldn't have just sat and watched Mr. Jordan die." She picked up the teapot, discovered that it was empty, and set it down again. "And," she said, "once I've seen you safely off, I will get out my anatomy holos and I will let *everything* else go until I've repaired my deficiencies. My word on it. Please add that to your report to Motherhouse."

Naomi nodded; she would do that most willingly. But it might not keep Our Lady of the StarTangle from replacing Sister Cecily here on Savannah and sending her somewhere even worse. However busy she was (and no missionary sister alone on a planet was anything but frantically busy), there *wasn't* an excuse for letting her grasp of anatomy slip so badly that she couldn't do basic resonance surgery with ease.

Since everyone present knew all that, she changed the subject. "Sister Cecily," she said, "some of this I understand, but not the part about ice interfering with takeoffs. We've been offplanet nearly ten months. Has something unusual happened?"

"Yes. Something very unusual." She stood up, picking up the empty teapot. "I'll make us some more tea," she said. And, "There's been no summer. Not anywhere on Earth."

"We had a bulletin about that," Quilla said. "But Earth hasn't had what *I* would call summer . . . not *real* summer . . . for years. We didn't pay much attention to the bulletin, I'm afraid."

"This time," Cecily told them from her kitchen, "it's not just that the summer is cooler than it used to be. It's nearly July, and it's still deep winter, with no sign of letting up. My sources said they'd intended to stop on Earth for cargo they'd contracted for, and they were warned away. If the report they gave me is accurate, all of Earth is bitter cold, and much of it is under two feet of solid ice."

This was serious. Naomi's palms were suddenly cold, as if they, too, had been in ice.

"And you couldn't get replacements for your healthies from one of the colonies?" she asked, keeping her voice steady. One thing at a time.

Cecily shook her head again. "I asked all over this territory and a good ways beyond," she said, "and nobody had any working healthies they could let me have. Not right now."

"They're all wearing out at once?"

Cecily nodded, tight-lipped, her eyes meeting Naomi's; the two women were almost exactly the same height. Naomi found it very pleasant not to have to look *down* at another woman, for once.

"What are people going to do if all the healthies stop working?" asked Lauren. "How are they going to take care of the sick if they don't have bedside healthies? There are almost no working medpods left, and the few that do work are reserved, every last one, for the government muckamucks."

Nobody suggested that the women of the Lines would have to take over with resonance medicine; nobody suggested that they would have to open medschools and train people in that skill. Just thinking about it was overwhelming; they were determined *not* to think about it.

"It will be a while, Sister Lauren," said Naomi firmly, "before that becomes a problem. They'll find a way to repair the healthies, before it turns into a crisis. Medpods are a different matter altogether—we have no idea how *they* work. But healthies, Sister, are only robots."

And Sister Cecily, sitting down again with the fresh pot of tea, agreed. Surely they could find a way to repair robots.

But they all knew what it meant—everyone's healthies faltering at the same time. It was called built-in obsolescence. It was against the law now, but when the current generation of the bedside tenders had been built there'd been no safeguards. Terrans would figure out how to build healthies and make them work properly; they weren't part of the inventory of mystery machines. But there'd be a run on them now, especially this far out.

"Are you going to be able to manage, Sister Cecily?" Naomi asked. "Think before you answer me, please. Because if this is really the famous Icehouse Effect they've been predicting on Earth for so many chilly decades, Motherhouse may have trouble getting anyone else out here to help you for a while. They'll need time to adjust to the conditions you're describing. If you think it's necessary, I'll leave one of my crew here with you as backup."

"Can you spare her, then?"

"No, I can't. Every skychapel flies short-staffed; ours is no exception. But we would get by; we're almost ready to head back home anyway. Don't try to be noble, Sister! If you can't handle this post alone, with your supply sources temporarily disrupted in ways none of us understand very well at this moment, you tell me so, and I'll leave Sister Quilla here to help."

Sister Cecily sat quietly, obviously thinking hard. Her eyes were heavily shadowed from the strain she'd been under, and the freckles stood out on her cheeks; it was clear that things were not easy on Savannah. But then, things were *never* easy at a missionary fieldchapel; nobody expected them to be. And after a moment, to Naomi's relief, the nun said, "No, you don't have to leave her . . . much as I admit that I would *love* it if you did. I can manage. I've been promised a healthy from Horsewhispering in a couple of weeks, if I can't get one anywhere else sooner . . . they have someone who'll be recovered enough to do without it by then. You needn't be worried about me, Sister Naomi. But I thank you for the offer—and for your help. I'm very grateful."

"You'll be all right, then?" Naomi observed Cecily closely and carefully, watching for telltale signs of mismatch in her bodyparl. She would be a woman with a *habit* of saying "I can manage; not to worry," put on every morning along with the cloth habit that all StarTangle sisters not working underground wore all their lives long. "Are you absolutely sure?"

"Yes! Yes, of course." She smiled at them, and the laughter in her eyes was more convincing than her words had been. "I'm really very capable, you know, or they wouldn't have left me here for twenty-three years all by myself. And I doubt they'll replace me, even after they see your report. They know my value, and they know I'll set things right—and *nobody* else wants a posting to Savannah, I assure you."

"Hmmph," said Naomi, and Cecily's eyebrows went up.

"Hmmph? Why hmmph?"

"I'm not going to recommend that they move you," said the pilot of Skychapel Six with her official hat on, "but I *am* going to recommend—in the strongest possible terms—that they send another nun out here to give you a hand. Twenty-three years by yourself, indeed! That's disgraceful."

Sister Cecily's smile deepened, and she chuckled softly; it was a pleasure to feel looked after for a moment, but it was a seduction she was prepared to resist. "I'm fond of the people here, Sister Naomi," she said, "and they're fond of me; we're very close. I'm not *alone*, after all, or under threat by gangs of thugboys, or facing a plague. Many sisters are not so lucky! I have a relatively peaceful posting, and good companions."

"You're saying what's expected of you, Sister," Naomi said, her voice stern, and her eyes alert for signals. "I am not impressed.

I know there's no one else from our Order here—is there even one woman of the Lines on Savannah?"

"No. There *was* one once, long ago, from Shawnessey Household—the first Shawnessey woman I'd ever met, in fact. We had a wonderful few months while she was just down the road. But she didn't stay. She was needed on some angelforsaken asteroid."

"Well, then!" said Naomi. "I'm sure the people of Savannah are wonderful human beings and a joy to be near, but it's not the same. They're not *family*, dearlove."

"And they don't speak Láadan," Lauren added, dotting the *i*.

"It's kind of you . . . Your intentions are kind, I mean," Cecily said earnestly. "But I must tell you: you can't *afford* to indulge me right now. Unless the things I've been hearing are terribly exaggerated, the troubles on Earth are going to distract Motherchurch from the question of whether I'm lonesome or not for a very long time. I won't get my hopes up."

"You think it's as bad as that?"

"I think it's as bad as that," Cecily said, nodding. "I think it is perhaps *worse* than that. Because the spacegypsies who told me about it consider me a sort of poor-little-thing. I know I don't *look* like a poor little thing, but that's their perception, maybe because after twenty-three years I still live in a bubblehut, with patches. I'm reasonably certain they made a serious effort to *under*state the problems, to keep me from worrying."

"When we left . . ." Naomi paused, and turned to Quilla to nudge her memory. "Quilla, do you remember?"

"I do. It was cold."

"But no ice."

"No. No ice. But you know, Naomi, there would come a time, if it just kept getting colder little by little, when suddenly there *would* be ice. It would be above freezing . . . and then, quite suddenly, there would be ice. That is the nature of water on Earth."

"Do you have any clear perception," Naomi asked the others slowly, thinking that she would have a good deal to say once they were home, about keeping spacechapel crews at least *roughly* briefed on what went on in the universe, "any clear perception of what it would *mean* for much of Earth . . . or even just a substantial portion of the landmass of Earth . . . to be under two feet of ice? Which has to mean, of course, that there are areas where the ice is even thicker than that?"

They had all read the predictions, in the bulletins and the newspapers and the popmags, year after year. The ones the government had kept saying were alarmist nonsense, even as each successive North American summer was just a little bit colder and the borders of the temperate zone where most crops were raised grew ever closer to one another. A temporary shift in weather patterns, the government had said. Nothing to be alarmed about. Just one more example of media scare tactics and sensationalism. And—in response to warnings from offplanet scientists who were observing the climate from very different vantage points—just one more example of the mischief the colonials delighted in creating for the mother planet they loathed. A mere blip on the chart of weather millennia, the government had insisted; any minute now, we'd be hearing about a Greenhouse Effect heading in the opposite direction.

But although they'd read the figures generated by the models, the women had no clear perception of what an ice-covered planet Earth would be like. It was impossible to imagine it. Impossible to plug the numbers into the imagination and make towns and cities and fields and lakes and mountains, all locked in ice, *real* in the mind's eye.

Sister Naomi stood up abruptly, heading for the hut's tiny kitchen area with the coffeepot and her cup to rinse them. Calling back over her shoulder as she went, "Come on! Quilla, Lauren— we'll cancel the stops we've got left. We're going *home. Now!*"

Sister Cecily had never wanted a missionary posting. She'd had her heart set on serving the Order of Our Lady of the StarTangle as a pilot, like Naomi. She had wanted to fly one of the seven skychapels, preferably on the most farflung route. She had trained for that, and she had done well. *Too* well. When Mother Superior had called her in to tell her the counselors' decision, she had not pretended otherwise. She had put her hands on Cecily's shoulders and looked up at her and said, "Sister, you are one of the finest pilot-candidates we've ever seen; no question! But your skill is matched by your passion for the task, and for the outermost regions of space. We've watched your fiz-status displays when you're piloting, Sister . . . the profile approaches that of sexual congress. We can't encourage that passion." And then she had put her arms around the stunned young woman and held her close, murmuring that she was sure Cecily understood, and that everyone was deeply sorry.

She had understood it, yes. Bitter as it was, embarrassing as it was to think that the senior sisters knew how her body would react to sexual passion, she had understood it perfectly, and she had not argued. It would not do; of course it would not do. You could not have the ecstasy of faith in competition with the ecstasy of flight.

That had been nearly a quarter century ago, and she had spent most of those years right here, looking out every morning and every evening over these same endless acres of cold, dry wasteland dotted with eucalyptus trees; presumably she would spend the next twenty-five years the same way.

"Mother," she had said, "could I try again? Someday?"

"Perhaps." The answer had been dry and crisp, like the cracked ground under her sandals on this bi-April morning. "When you are a very old woman, and less subject to . . . excesses. Perhaps."

The man approaching her now as she stood watching the skychapel leave, touching his cheeks with his fingertips in the traditional Savannah greeting-to-an-honored-elder, would have been astonished to learn that she lusted . . . that was the only accurate word for it . . . to be a skychapel pilot. Or that she was other than serenely contented with her lot. Even when Cecily had first arrived, only just turned a very naive twenty-four, he had perceived her as someone old and wise and free of *all* lusts. Cecily had tried to disabuse him of those notions, but then he had been awed by her humility, and that was far worse. The habit and headdress of the StarTangle nuns were carefully designed to evoke such reactions, and were backed up by appropriate body language; it all worked together to overrule many otherwise obvious perceptions.

She understood why it was important always to maintain the distant dignity of the church. Without that distance, its secrets could not have been protected; without that dignity, its nuns could not have lived safely in isolated offworld missionary posts. She did her part to maintain the posture, tolerating no slightest expression of disrespect and no familiarity. But she wished she could have managed to do it without her own person becoming all tangled up in it; she had a horrified distaste for being *revered*.

"Best evening, Luke," she said to the man, her hands safely clasped at her waist so that they wouldn't accidentally transmit some touch-message she had no intention of sending. "Aren't you early?"

"Maybe a little early, Sister," he answered. "I came to the end of the piece I've been weaving, and it was too late to set up the loom for a new one this day. When I saw your visitors leave, I thought I'd come on up and speak to you."

"The sisters came to help with the stomach cancer," she said. "We're lucky they were close by."

"Let's hope there will be no more emergencies until we can get more healthies; we wouldn't be that lucky twice, Sister."

She nodded, feeling the sharp jabs of guilt and knowing she deserved them, and asked, "What was the report, Luke?"

He frowned, and he stared at the ground as if words were written there, but written very faintly, requiring much effort to decipher. Cecily waited, smiling at this old friend encouragingly while he gathered his thoughts and shaped them to his liking.

"Sister Cecily," he said at last, "there's no food in the villages. I'm sorry to have to tell you that again; I wish we could do better." Over their heads the four-inch winterlocusts started up their mournful evening droning, a low, mellow note that would go on until the night was half gone. "I've polled everyone by comset, even the ones with infants, and they all say the same: there is *no* food."

Cecily had expected it; there hadn't been any food yesterday either, nor the day before that. There had been some knobby roots—the Savannan equivalent of potatoes—once or twice during the past month, and so far as she knew that was all. It would have made more sense to send someone to let her know when there *was* food.

"It's all right, Luke," she told him. "It doesn't matter. No doubt the Holy One has good reasons. We'll have a gathering tonight all the same, my friend—I have three new songs."

He smiled down at her, hearing her say that . . . he was much taller than she was, though she was nearly six feet tall herself . . . and he tapped his lower lip with one long forefinger to indicate his pleasure. Luke Stringbinder was fond of Sister Cecily's songs. He had a particular fondness for the A-minor ones.

"When the moons rise, then, Sister," he said, and she nodded her agreement as he made the intricate leave-taking gestures her role in his culture required of him. He turned then to go back along the narrow path of stones to the village of New Birmingham and the compound where he lived with his wife and son, and his son's wife, and his grandchild. And a recently arrived aunt, she thought, remembering that she hadn't yet gone to welcome that aunt and must put it on her schedule immediately.

If there had been food, people would have brought it on platters and in bowls to set out on the ground all around her bubblehut. They would have spent hours eating and talking; only when all the food was gone would they have turned to singing. People from other towns on Savannah would have joined in by comset, though for some of them the hour would have been inconvenient. She could remember evenings like that still, because Motherchurch had sent her here well ahead of the predicted famine.

There had been food enough during her first year. Often there had been more than enough. There had still been great fields of the dryness-loving grass that had given this asteroid its name; the cattle brought out here by settlers in better times as tiny flasks of embryos had already died, but there had still been goats. She'd had a lovely little brown nannygoat named Cocoa as a pet, that had followed her everywhere she went like the most devoted of dogs, carrying things for her in small saddlebags that Cecily had made herself from thick gray felt and stitched in brilliant patterns of blue and rose and yellow. The day had come when she'd had to send Cocoa to the slaughtering-woman in New Birmingham. It had been her duty to do that, and she'd done it; but it had broken her heart. Cecily still missed that little goat. And that, of course, is *attachment*. She was far from free of the tendency to attachment.

She watched Luke Stringbinder go, and thought about the moons; if she'd had a chapel to fly she would have visited each of them. Lolldory, the smallest and palest one; Quince, the bluest of the three; and bright Craw Moon, that hung in the sky like a round white melon. After so many generations, they had lost all the marks of manufacture; you could no longer tell that it hadn't been the Holy One's hand that hung them over Savannah to stabilize its orbit. Suppose the time came when she could not work any longer, she intended to ask the church to let her retire to Craw Moon. Luke would be long dead then, she suspected; perhaps one of his grandchildren would like to go with the creaking ancient nun she would be, to the black-rock moon, to live with her in a cave that was arched and ribbed with stone like the inside of a giant walnut shell. A cave that might as well have been *designed* for singing in, it was that perfect for the purpose.

Careful, Cecily! she told herself sternly. *Start lusting after that cave and you'll find yourself posted to Detroit!* But she chuckled softly, and Luke Stringbinder grinned back at her approvingly over his shoulder, waving the two-handed we-are-greatly-blessed-this-day wave, happy to hear her laughter. It was a joke; she could never go back to Old Earth, and she was sure no one there cared any longer about the unruly and varied passions of a sister who was still not broken to the yoke though she'd learned to *look* subdued enough. The missionaries of the StarTangle were too far away for anyone Terran to fret over, even in less troubled times.

She had known by the time she was five years old that she would join the Order. Standing in the hallway of Jefferson Womanhouse before a dozen women who were pretending to be mightily shocked, she had set her hands on her hips with her stickskinny arms akimbo and stamped her foot, declaring her intentions. "I will *not* get married!" she told them. "I will *not* have ten children! I am going to be a *nun*!"

In earlier times she could have stamped till she wore her toes away; it would have made no difference. The Head of Jefferson

Household would have selected a husband for her and chosen her wedding date, and she *would* have married. And she would have borne as many children for the Line as could decently be fit between puberty and menopause. Each one borne to go for hours daily into the Interface, separated from the current Alien-in-Residence by a barrier that kept back the AIRY's atmosphere but let its speech and bodyparl pass without hindrance; each one borne to match the Alien's brain waves by entrainment and acquire yet one more Alien language for the governments of Earth and of her colonies.

But the Aliens had been long gone and the Interfaces empty and cold; and at thirteen, as soon as she had finished the mass-ed curriculum, Cecily had gone to the StarTangle Motherhouse as a novice.

It had been easy for her. Linguist children, especially linguist girlchildren, were accustomed to communal life, to voluntary poverty, to hard work, and to obedience. As a Lingoe child she had had two tunics—one for work and one for formal occasions—plus a jumpsuit to be worn in the fields and orchards, and she had slept on a cot in an underground dormitory with dozens of other little girls. As a nun she had had twice that much clothing (and fancier!), and a room ten feet by nine feet that was hers alone and looked out on the gardens. She had found the convent downright luxurious. The conditions of the post here on Savannah—a post so primitive that Jefferson Household was paid yearly bonuses for her service there—had not bothered her at all.

Not being a pilot was what bothered her; not traveling. Staying always in one place. That had taught her what obedience *really* meant, and in her dreams, now and perhaps forever, she still flew a skychapel through the endless seas of space.

It's worth it, she told herself, meaning it with all her heart. *It has always been worth it.*

She turned and went into the bubblehut and called the computer link to the nearest Department of Agriculture satellite. It was time to turn in another report on the Savannah harvest. She would not be reporting only the eucalyptus that were the major product of this planet—and that *did* grow. Apparently they were as indifferent to conditions around them as the rocks were, and as astonishingly varied. She would be reporting sweet potatoes and yellow squash and several varieties of beans; corn had never grown here, but there had been an abundance of a plant very like corn, called pseudomaize, and she would report some of that. Grain . . . she would report grain. The figures she used would be based on formulas memorized before leaving Earth and worked in her head, the inner space of the mind being the only area relatively safe from possible surveillance. She would report total tons for the harvest on Savannah that were reasonable predictions from known conditions; she would report the harvest substantially down, far below what it had been even ten years ago. But the figures would show food *enough*. Food enough so that no DA official would feel inclined to send out relief ships or do flyover inspections or focus a satellite camera on Savannah. The computer would ask her: "Can you manage?" And she would reply that it would be a bit tight, but that she could.

And then, *even if there is an earthquake . . . a savannahquake?* . . . thought Sister Cecily, *I will get out the male anatomy holos and work with them until time for tonight's sing. No matter* what *happens! So that I will not be caught again failing in my duties.* The fact that she genuinely disliked doing resonance medicine, because there was nothing to *hold* . . . you could scarcely call the strings of tiny lights and bells, designed to help attract and hold the attention of the patient, medical *instruments*. Whatever she did, Cecily liked something in her hand to be used. Something that sawed, or cut, or pierced, or polished . . . something she could grip and turn and point. Something that she could *feel* doing its task. Even singing was like that for her; she could *feel* the sounds her mouth and tongue and throat were shaping as she released them.

But resonance . . . she understood it, but she could not feel it, and because of that she knew she would never understand it. Not *really* understand it, as she understood the flying of a skychapel or the digging of a well.

"*Never mind!*" she told herself sternly. "*You must try!*"

THE TRANCER IS TIRED . . .
WHAT'S ON THE SOAPS?

CHAPTER 8

Caroline hears the crying in the night; she knows that the women do weep for the ones who die. In the daytime she never sees or hears them cry, though she can feel the choked-back weeping when she is close to them and she can smell it on their breaths the same way you can smell snow coming. The women work tight-lipped and tightfaced, stumbling out of the bedrolls half-stunned long before dawn and setting themselves swiftly to the brutal work of keeping life going, stopping only seconds for a cup of tea swallowed on the run. There's been no coffee for a long time, and there's no more of the strong *black* tea that used to help so much; Caroline doesn't know what kind of leaves are in the tea now, only that the women warn her sharply not to drink it.

She melts ice and drinks water, first letting it percolate through the mats of charcoal at the bottom of the watertrough. "It doesn't get everything awful out of it," her mother tells her, "but it helps. Never drink water you haven't filtered, child."

"In the summertime we didn't filter it," her sister Chella has told her. "We didn't have to." Caroline is only nine; she doesn't remember a summertime. Their mother is on her way to the pits, so wrapped in quilts that she has no recognizable human shape; she is a walking bundle, and it cheers Caroline to look at the colors. "It costs no more," the women say, "to make the quilts beautiful." They don't use the old patterns that meant cutting and stitching flowers and garlands and stars, because they can't spare the time. But it takes no longer to use colored scraps. "Red's as quick as anything else," the women say, "and blue's no slower." In a world so white and so gray, the quilts bless the eye.

"Caroline," her mother calls back over her shoulder as she ducks into the exit tunnel, "you listen to your music! You hear me? Chella, you too! Both of you—mind you don't forget!"

Caroline and Chella watch her go, wishing she could stay with them at least until the shade of grayness that passes for light appears, knowing it's not possible. And then they hear her make a sudden sharp noise of distress, and the sound of the quilts brushing against the tunnel walls stops.

"Mama?" Chella goes to the tunnel entrance and opens the little talkdoor. Leaning over it, her lips close to the tiny slot, she calls, "Mama! Are you all right?"

The silence goes on a long time, and then, just as they are beginning to be afraid, the voice comes back at them, sorrowful and slow. "I'm all right," their mother answers. "I'm fine. But you girls stay out of the tunnel. I'll deal with it when I get back."

Chella swallows hard; behind her, Caroline begins to whimper with her fist stuffed into her mouth. *Another one. Another one that they will have to leave there.*

"Mama," Chella asks, talking fast because the cold air is pouring in through the slot, "Carrie and I know what to do! Let us try, okay? We can—"

"Chella Mary," says their mother, "please hush. It would be cruel; don't ask me."

Caroline opens her mouth and then shuts it again; Chella is already asking.

"Can't we come sit by him, then, Mama? So there's somebody with him till it's over?"

The girls wish they could see their mother's face. It's hard to know whether she's telling them everything or treating them like babies. But her voice is firm, and they hear the tone that means DO NOT ARGUE riding on every syllable.

"Dearloves," she says to them, "he wouldn't know you were here. I give you my word. He doesn't know he's dying all alone . . . he hasn't known anything for some hours now. Truly."

Caroline moans, and her stomach hurts her, but she understands. You do not risk one of the living, whose work is desperately needed, on slim possibilities. Such as the possibility that a man seemingly long unconscious might still be able to hear a word, feel a touch, take comfort in not being alone. You don't do that, because it is a stupid and criminal thing to do. You could die of the cold yourself, sitting there beside him in the silence, and then there would be *four* hands fewer to do the work. She understands; but that doesn't make it easier.

Chella is pulling at her sleeve. "Come on, Carrie-O," she's saying, trying to sound ordinary. "Music!"

"Chella?"

"Yes?"

"How many men are left now?"

"Don't be dumb, Caroline!"

"How many? I want to know!"

Chella shakes her head. "I don't know any more about it than you do—they don't tell me anything. *You* know that! They say there are even men still working, some places on Earth . . . but I don't know anything for sure."

"I don't believe you."

"Hush!"

"I don't *believe* you!"

"Believe what you like!" Chella snaps. "But come along."

"I *won't.*"

That startles the older child; she steps back and puts her hands on her hips. She looks just like their mother. "You will, too!" she says. "Mother has enough to worry about, without you worrying her more!"

"It's wrong," Caroline says sullenly, staring at the floor. "If we didn't use the power to run the comsets, we could heat one of the rooms—we could put pallets in there, Chella. We could get them warm again, so they wouldn't die. We could sing to them around the clock—we could take turns. We could—"

Chella is kneeling then in front of her sister, pulling the little girl close, wrapping her arms around her and laying her face against her hood, rocking her gently.

"Caroline, sweet Carrie," she says softly, fiercely, "come on! *Think!* If that would help, don't you think they'd do it? Carrie, you're talking about our mother, and everybody else's mothers, and all our grandmothers! Do you really think they'd use power to run the comsets if it wasn't something they *had* to do? Come on!"

"I don't know," says Caroline miserably. "How am I supposed to know?"

"You're not," Chella says firmly. She straightens Caroline up and backs off enough to look at her, her eyes level with the little girl's eyes. "You're not supposed to *know*, you're supposed to *trust*. You're supposed to take a good hard look at the way our mother and all the other women work from dawn to dark, just trying to keep us alive, just trying to keep this world going, and have brains enough to *trust* them! Caroline, they just plain don't have time to sit around and explain everything to us. Do you want the generators to stop because some stupid kids have to have explanations?"

"No."

It's a sullen answer; Caroline intends it to be sullen. It was a mean question.

"Are you going to go on like this all morning?" Chella asks, her brows drawn together and her lips narrowed. "Are you?"

When Caroline doesn't answer, Chella shakes her gently and reaches out to brush her hair back under the quilted border of the thick hood. "Caroline, darlin'," she murmurs, soothing, "everything the women know is being used. Every single thing. Everything they think is safe . . . everything that won't make the colding worse. And someday, when Earth starts to warm up again—"

"Will it warm up again, Chella? Will it?"

"When Earth begins warming up again," Chella goes on, steadily, "things will be different. People won't have to live like this. I promise. But right now, dearlove, we have to trust. And we have to help."

"Chella, listening to music isn't helping!"

"Listening to music while we melt water *is* helping. And we have an *awful* lot to do before Mama comes back! Caroline, please—be a good kid? The Icehouse Effect isn't *my* fault, and I breathe out warm air just like you do. Just keep on breathing out warm, Caroline, and the time will come when this is all over."

"Before I die, Chella?"

Chella lets her arms fall to her sides and stands up. "Probably not," she says, telling the truth as best she knows it. Lies are either laziness or incompetence, the women say. There is always some true thing you could say instead. "But perhaps before your grandchildren die."

Your grandchildren!

I will have children born of the frozen sperm of dead men, Caroline thinks, because it has all been explained to her many times. *And my children will have children the same way. Unless the little boys that are my children and my grandchildren can learn to stay alive in this terrible icy world.*

I am going to have fat *little boys for my children,* she thinks. Promising herself; promising those little boys. *The reason most of the women survive and most of the men die is the layer of fat that lies under the womanskin—I will make* sure *there is fat, thick and thick and* thick, *underneath my little boys' skins!*

She doesn't know how she will manage that, exactly. The women can't bury the ponics pits any deeper than they are now, and the yield from them is getting smaller and smaller all the time. Even with all of the mouthfood going to the male human beings, even with choirs on duty day and night for the ones that are willing—and still able—to listen, the men go right on dying. But Caroline is determined. She will have fat little boys who go out into the cold and come cheerfully back alive. She *will.*

In the center of the burrow Chella has turned the music on, and Caroline hurries. She knows this one, this ancient song, and she loves it dearly. Its name is "How Can I Keep From Singing?"

As the—

BORING!

CHANGE THE CHANNEL!

Marilisa is braiding light. She is getting better at it; better at selecting the strands, better at choosing her patterns, better even at the task of finding and undoing what has been badly done. She knows when she has done a braid well because it begins to chime. She has finished three of the chiming braids in this past month and coiled them into glowing wreaths; she has set them free and gloried to see them sail away from her toward the angels, still chiming. She is very proud of that. It takes great skill, and tremendous patience, but it is work she loves. If she could work at it without being interrupted, she is sure she would be expert, but her children prevent that. They are at her constantly.

"*Mama, don't you want your knitting?*" The daughter takes Marilisa's hands—breaking the strands of light, destroying the delicate sextuple pattern like someone stumbling, blind, through a spiderweb—and wraps her mother's fingers tightly round the knitting needles. "There *now, darling!* Now *you're all set!*"

Marilisa sighs . . . she will have to start all over again.

This isn't new, of course; she doesn't cry. She had given up crying about it by the time she finished at the multiversity, always having to work with the children around her, the intricate logical arguments she had to study interrupted every few minutes. She had considered herself fortunate when there were five minutes free of interruption.

Marilisa has always thought yearningly of those biographies of the great and the famous in which devoted children guard their parent, meeting visitors at the door with a hushed warning that the parent is *working* and must not be interrupted. In which the spouse sees to it that there is a separate room for the work to be done in, and sets a tray of food silently on the desk, tiptoeing away in order not to interfere with the work. In which the family is passionately proud of the work and sets aside all its own concerns to protect the one who does it. Her spouse, her children, had no such habits, nor any sign of them, and she knew why. If the work is treasured by the family, and the mother/wife is held precious, it happens; otherwise, no.

Marilisa had not had the knack of making herself precious. Her value had been that she was someone who knew where the clean clothes were. Under those circumstances her tears would only have added *more* delay, and she couldn't have afforded that.

The universal assumption that nothing she is doing could have any importance has always distressed her. But it annoys her far more now, when these children have children and grandchildren of their own . . . it seems to her that they should have acquired *some* sense over the course of a lifetime!

"*Mama, look at this pretty embroidery . . . you never finished it! Don't you want to do that tiny rose in the corner, Mama? Here . . . I'll help you start it!*"

"*Mama, you haven't played your dulcimer for months and months . . . it's not even in tune anymore. Don't you want it? Here . . . I'll put it in your lap, dear, and I'll find your picks for you. You just decide what song you'd most like to play, all right?*"

And to the doctor, when they've finally managed to tune him in on the comset after calling a dozen times . . . "*Look at her, Doctor, how she frowns! She's got to be in pain, to frown like that—Mother never frowned!*"

I frowned, Marilisa thinks. *I frowned all the time. I frowned when things didn't work. I frowned when something burned in the kitchen. I frowned when they fought over their toys and wouldn't clean their rooms. I frowned when they had fevers and spots. I frowned when I got Cs in the multiversity graduate courses—a graduate C is a graduate F, the professors told me sternly, shaking their fingers at me. Saying, "You're not going to make it, you know. You're a nice woman, but you're not PhD material!" I was forever frowning. What does the fool child mean, saying I never frowned? He never looked at me, I suppose.*

She frowns now when a pattern of the strands of light is becoming particularly complex, when her attention is needed . . . She is certainly not in any pain, and she has told them so over and over. They ignore it. They are not concerned with what she wants, but with what they are convinced she needs. Like her husband, who always bought her things he knew she needed, instead of the things she had asked him for. Marilisa had always wanted a nice drum, the kind you hold in your hand and strike with a synthowood-and-leather beater, and she had told him so over and over. And he had smiled and bought her yet another cashmere sweater. Of course, around the Christmas tree, with the children watching and the husband smiling, you cannot say, "But I told you I wanted a *drum*! A bhodran drum! Why did you buy me this stupid *sweater*?" No.

That would spoil the holiday. It wasn't necessary to ask that question, in any case; she knew what he would say back. He would say, "Darling, you *need* a new cashmere sweater; you don't need a bhodran drum."

Marilisa reaches for a lovely strand of light that floats toward her, that is a delicate color neither quite silver nor quite gold, with a luster like old pearls; she has never seen a strand quite like it before. She holds the braid she's working on carefully, gently, with her left hand, and begins adding the new strand. She holds her breath, too, because this will make it a seven-strand braid and she has never tried one of those. The light is so beautiful, wound in and out in the overlapping patterns—

"Doctor, it's awful to see her like this! Look at her—will you just look at her? She was always busy . . . always had work in her hands to do, even if she was sitting down for a minute. And now she just sits there staring at nothing, and her fingers . . . twisting like that . . . always twisting . . . Oh, Doctor, please . . . it's breaking our hearts. Can't you do something?"

If they come at her with the injection again, Marilisa thinks, she is going to lose her temper. It's ridiculous. She doesn't want to knit, or embroider, or play the dulcimer; she's tired of all those things. She wants to do *this*, this new craft, this lightbraiding. And she feels she has earned the right to spend her time as she wishes to spend it. *Why on earth can't they let her alone and go about their own affairs?* The injections make her sleepy, and they certainly serve no useful purpose.

"Mama, please, don't struggle like this—let us give you your shot, please, darling? It will make you feel better, Mama, really it will . . . it will let you rest, Mama! You're so tired, dear . . . please don't fight us like this!"

Marilisa is genuinely *annoyed*. She has spent a lifetime making allowances for them, reminding herself that they do what they do with the best of intentions, out of ignorance rather than malice, but it seems to her that there has to be a limit to it somewhere. She is not tired. She is not tired at all. She didn't need the cashmere sweaters; she doesn't need rest. In her frustration, her hands begin trembling and the braid of light slips out of her fingers. Not only the new strand, the one that reminds her of mother-of-pearl, but the sextuple braid she had been trying to fit it into. Both gone, swinging away from her, out of her reach. Furious, she shoves fiercely at her daughters and her son, and she hears them sighing the long heavy sighs of the overburdened. Damn them! How *dare* they! And she feels the icy spray of the drug on her bare throat.

She does cry, then. She *is* tired, then. She lets her head fall forward, and she cries.

They are saying, "Please don't cry, darling. Please. It's going to be all right, we promise you. Don't cry, sweetheart!"

Sweetheart. Sweetheart!

Who will deliver me from this? Marilisa wonders. *Isn't there anybody in charge?*

HISTORICAL ROMANCES???

AT THIS TIME OF DAY???

WHERE DID THIS COME FROM, FOR HEAVEN'S SAKES?

B O R I N G !

CHANGE THE CHANNEL!

Keekeen is four years old. She stands with her whole body flattened against the wall (she is so tiny that she can fit between the ribs that section the ceramic sphere's walls into narrow segments) and she watches the tornadoes. She particularly likes the way their tails seem to be crossing over each other, like kite tails; she particularly fancies the rare lavender ones.

"Nuvver one!" she says, clapping her hands against the transparent surface, dancing up and down on her toes. *"Nuvver* one, nuvver one!" On the horizon, stretching off toward the broad lakes, the tornadoes are playing, and she is quite right. Nuvver one, nuvver one. There are, in fact, six tornadoes to be seen between the house and the lakes.

The tornadoes of Horsewhispering are not like the tornadoes of

Old Earth. Terran tornadoes are called by misery that has reached a critical mass and is sending out a chord they respond to; they whirl down on a place suddenly, and they don't often visit it again. The tornadoes of Horsewhispering are more like the rain in a place where rain falls every day. Keekeen sees dozens of tornadoes every day, and it amazes her brothers that she doesn't get bored with them.

"Nuvver one!" shouts Keekeen. "Nuvver *big* one!" And then she shrieks, absolutely delighted, as the wallspider whips out a broad swath of porous membrane and lashes her to the nearest rib. She has time only to shout "*Got* Keekeen!" and feel the house roll over sharply as the tornado's tail dips groundward, and then the spider senses the end of contact, retracts the membrane, and sets her loose again, breathless and crowing, on the floor.

The intercom crackles and they hear their father ask, "You kids okay in there?"

"Yeah, Dad," says Brahklin, "we're fine. It didn't amount to anything." Beside him, Jordo nods his head, agreeing; Jordo leaves much of the talking to Brahklin and Keekeen.

"Just checking!" says the voice, and the chime rings for disconnect before they can leap in and ask him to bring something or other for dinner; their father is wise in their ways.

"Twice this week," says Jordo.

"I wish it would let up so we could go to Beridel for a while."

Jordo is silent; he doesn't like their grandmother's house, and if a couple of tornadoes a week will fend off the visit he's glad to have them.

"Hey, come on," Brahklin says, "don't you want to get out of here for a while?"

Jordo looks at his brother and shrugs his shoulders; against the wall, Keekeen cries "Nuvver one!" again. She is certainly no trouble to anybody, he thinks.

"Nah! I mean it, Jordo!" Brahklin persists. "You've *gotta* be tired of hanging around here all the time!"

"There's the virtuals," Jordo mutters.

"It's not the same!"

"Right. With the virtuals you don't get killed."

If his mother had been there, she would have seconded that. Two or three thousand people a year died traveling the surface of Horsewhispering in the ceramic spheres that slid along the travelgrids, dodging each other and whirling clouds; she was determined that her children would not become statistics, and she rarely allowed them to leave the house.

"But you *know* all the time they're not real, Jordo," Brahklin objects.

"Not if you cooperate."

"I cooperate."

"You don't. You fight them."

It's true. Brahklin is so determined not to be convinced by the computer's simulated realities that he talks to himself the whole time about their obvious flaws; there's no way his brain can perform its task of filling in the missing bits and pieces against such resistance.

"Well, you're a coward, Jordo," he says sullenly. "Mom and Dad don't want us to go anyway, and if you always say you'd rather stay here, I'll *never* get to go!"

Most of that is stupid, and Jordo ignores it; Brahklin hits him in the shoulder with one angry fist, and he ignores that, too. But it scares Keekeen into big-eyed silence. The little girl pops her thumb in her mouth and watches them warily, hugging the sphere's wall. She doesn't *think* Jordo will let Brahklin hit her, but she's not sure. Sometimes the boys bump into her, roughhousing; maybe Brahklin *might* hit her, and maybe Jordo wouldn't be able to stop him. She's just not sure. She is learning to pay careful attention to her brothers' body language, learning to spot the signals that mean they're angry. She is much more afraid of the two big boys than she is of the tornadoes, but she is going to have to protect *herself* from the boys.

"Hey, Keekeen!" Jordo says, grinning at her. "Hey! It's okay, littlest! Really."

Keekeen smiles at him, but she doesn't turn her back. Not yet. Brahklin has forgotten that he was angry. He asks, "How come you don't like Beridel, Jordo? There's a lot more room in a triplesphere, we can *do* stuff! Remember last time? Remember, we played basketball?"

"I remember."

"Well? Wasn't it better than the virtuals?"

"Yes."

"Well?"

"If you go to Beridel, you have to spend time with Grandmother," Jordo said.

"So?"

"So I don't like to listen to her."

"Oh. All the stuff about Earth."

"Right. It's embarrassing."

Their grandmother is deeply prejudiced against Earth and all things Terran. She calls the people of Earth "Terroes"; she says she'll be delighted if every last one of them gets wiped out by the Icehouse Effect. She was one of the staunchest supporters when the colonial governments decided to stop the expensive and seemingly futile rescue attempts, leaving Earth's citizens to die or survive on their own; she did not share the sorrow many people (including her own daughter and her son-in-law) felt about it. Their last visit, the one when they'd played basketball, had ended when their mother had stood up and told their grandmother that she was disgusting.

"You *gloat* over their suffering, Mother!" she had said, talking through her fingers that were clapped over her mouth. "That's *sick!*"

"They deserve to suffer," Grandmother Clark had retorted, her face twisted and ugly with contempt. "They're nothing but animals. The sooner they're all dead, the better for humankind. You are a sentimental woman, and you are exceedingly ignorant of history."

They had gone home that minute, right in the middle of the afternoon, at the most dangerous travel time of all.

"I don't care," their mother had said. "I couldn't have stayed there. I won't go back." And she had started to cry. "I am so ashamed of your grandmother!" she had said, almost whispering. "I am so sorry you heard her . . ."

"Jordo? Hey, Jordo Clown? Are you here, or what?"

Keekeen observes that the boys have forgotten all about her, and that neither one of them is angry anymore, and she relaxes; it's okay now for her to look out through the wall toward the lakes, where the windcreatures she loves are still to be seen, high in the air, sailing across the water in long swoops and banks and leaps. She turns around and pats the wall gently on the transparency stud, and her window grows larger. Now she can look out and down across the fields in three directions; only the far wall, the one her father would watch her through from his office, is still opaque.

"Nuvver one!" she says happily. "*Nuvver* nuvver one!"

ENOUGH . . . .

TURN IT OFF, PLEASE.

PART THREE
WHAT THE THIRD TRANCER SAID

CHAPTER 9

We thought, fools that we were, that it was all over. All the crime, all the violence, all the poverty, all the basic wickedness of humankind. During the two hundred years when we could end every frustration by simply moving on—to yet one more planet, yet one more asteroid—we thought we had it solved. In our arrogance we even set aside planets dedicated to specific varieties of wickedness, so that those who wished to devote their lives to evil had them as convenient havens shared only by others of like mind. But we had forgotten three important facts. That humans are not gods. That history always repeats itself, though it may take a very long time. And that the day would inevitably come when there were no more frontiers to move to and no more empty planets waiting for us. Nowhere left to ship those who disturbed the rest of us, to spare us the nuisance of having them among us. That time did come, has come; because there were so many of us to hurry it along, it came amazingly quickly. And now we have it all back again . . . and we have no more idea how to deal with it than our ancestors did. God help us all.

(Christopher Mbona Weatherford, "Introduction to the Taxonomy of Sin"; *Occasional Papers In Metatheology* 43:11, page 11)

The Vice President had always known, from his earliest childhood, that it was his destiny to save at least the nation, probably the planet and all its colonies, and perhaps the entire solar system. He had waited patiently to learn what form this exercise of his talents would take. Now, staring in amazement at his weeping, shuddering President, he realized that the moment had come at last. This was it. This was what he had been waiting for all his life.

He had to admit that it wasn't exactly as he'd thought it would be; he would have preferred something more dignified . . . something loftier. Saving some child, absolutely crucial to humanity, from a burning building, perhaps. Leading a battle charge that liberated a helpless people from a brutal dictator. That sort of thing. But the choice was not his to make, it was Almighty God's, and he was not about to argue with the Lord.

Still, he was taken aback by the image that had just been presented to him: the image of the *President*—this stodgy, conservative, solid, boring, aging family man, plodding along through his fifth term—coupling in erotic frenzy on the floor of the Oval Office with his equally stodgy secretary. It was hard to accept.

He knew it had to be true; the utter misery of the man across from him gave unequivocal testimony to that. But every time he tried to focus his mind's eye on it . . . especially as it would have looked from above to anyone who had happened to walk in on the scene . . . his mind's eyelids would snap firmly down and he could not bring himself to look. The President's rear end, bare to the breeze, his pants down around his ankles? Miss Brown's long narrow skirts thrown back, and her knobby knees parted to the same breeze?

It was too much; he couldn't face it. He would settle for just the words, written in decent black block letters on a tasteful white screen in his memory:

THIS MORNING, IN THE MIDDLE OF A LETTER THANK-
ING A MINOR AMBASSADOR TO A MINOR COLONY FOR
A MINOR FAVOR, MISS BROWN SUDDENLY STOOD UP
AND STRIPPED OFF HER JACKET, BARING MAGNIFICENT
BREASTS THE PRESIDENT HAD NEVER SUSPECTED SHE
HAD. AND THE NEXT THING HE KNEW, THEY WERE ON
THE FLOOR, ON THE PRICELESS RUG, IN FLAGRANTE.

It was sufficiently awful just like that; illustrations were not required.

President Dellwilder moaned again, and the Vice President forced himself not to say any of the things that came to mind. He had already asked how such a thing could possibly have happened, and had been told, "I don't know, Aron. As God is my witness, I do not know! One minute I was deep in thought, trying to select a perfect phrase, and the next minute I was deep in Miss Brown, right there on that rug! It happened that fast! I swear to *God*, Aron, I swear to you on my blessed mother's grave, I do not *know* how it happened!" The Vice President had had to fight an almost irresistible temptation to ask exactly *how* deep in Miss Brown. That temptation, and the way the snickering schoolboy question had very nearly come tripping right off his tongue, brought home to him how badly shocked he was. While he fought it, the President told him, without his having to ask, that it had all been over in seconds—that it had all been over, God be praised, before the discreet knock of the Secret Service man bringing their midmorning coffee.

"Oh, my dear God in Heaven, Aron!" the President lamented, his voice thick and clotted with pain. "What am I going to do? What am I going to tell my wife?" He caught the Vice President's startled glance, and he shook his head fiercely and corrected himself. "I'm losing my mind, Aron! Of *course* I'm not going to tell my wife! But what am I going to do?"

Somewhere off in the distance Aron Strabida heard the sound of trumpets high and clear, and they were playing a fanfare for *him*. He was profoundly aware of his surroundings, aware of all the trappings of this ancient room, one of the half dozen places on Earth not constructed entirely of synthetics. The rows of books— *real* books, not chiplets or fiches, but pages bound for the turning, in handsome covers. The huge desk, made of real wood, brought back from the Smithsonian's attics to replace the various monstrosities that had been briefly installed here during less sophisticated administrations, glowing in the light from the tall windows. The rich draperies, the magnificent rug, the paintings . . . the flags! The glorious flags, that were really there, their fabric frayed almost to a thinness you could see through, so that they, too, glowed in the light. It was like a museum; to go into this room was to step back into time. It was a room either loved or hated, depending on how you felt about government; it was a room so famous that even little children could describe it to you inch by inch. And the Vice

President was *there*; he was, as they say, only a heartbeat away from *sitting* at that desk.

And this was the President of the United States of America of Earth, asking *him* what to do! This was a man struggling with a skyful of planets run by what the Vice President would have described as an assortment of psychotics and sociopaths, each world trying to outdo all the others in the unspeakableness of its actions, each world looking toward this President. Not to actually *do* anything, of course. It had been centuries since an expectation of that kind would have made any sense. But they did look toward him to serve as a center to be rallied round or struggled against. Because the President and his office were symbols of such antiquity, symbols of the very heart of what it meant to be Terran, to be *of Earth*, even if your family's feet had not touched Earth's soil for a hundred years. Here was this man whose name was a household word to untold billions of people. This man around whom a carousel of civilizations, mired deep in the consequences of centuries of blunders, revolved. And he was saying: "Aron— what am I going to *do*?"

Aron wanted the moment to go on and on; he wanted to savor it, to make certain that every detail of it was etched permanently on his memory, so that he could return to it in recollection for the rest of his life. But he gathered himself together, aware that he must not hesitate any longer, that he must bring it to an end in spite of his reluctance to do so. He felt taller. Taller. Stronger. Wiser. It reinforced the old verse, he thought; the Lord did indeed move in mysterious ways, His wonders to perform. Who would ever have thought it? A mad passionate interlude, however brief, however sudden, between President Tobias Antonio Dellwilder and Miss Marthajean Brown? He could not think of anything *more* mysterious.

Aron drew himself up, threw back his shoulders, gave his hair one careful toss, and clasped his hands behind his back. "Mr. President," he said, hearing the trumpets again in the distance, "don't you worry about a thing. *I* will take care of it."

"You will?" The President's eyes were filled with tears, and his voice was quavering.

"Indeed I will," said Aron solemnly, intensely. "I want you to concentrate on forgetting that it ever happened. I want you to convince yourself that it *didn't* happen! You *must*, Mr. President. Worlds are counting on you; humankind cannot afford to have you distracted; humankind cannot spare you. Not now. Not with the intolerable crises we face at this moment in time. Put it out of your mind, Mr. President, once and for all. Tell yourself: *It did not happen!* And," he concluded, thinking that he was doing very well considering that he'd had no warning he would have to make a speech, much less a speech of such tremendous *significance*, hoping he would be able to remember it until he could transfer it to his private journal, "*I* will take care of *everything!*"

"God bless you, Aron," said Dellwilder. "God bless you."

"Thank you, Mr. President!"

And the Vice President, glowing with the awareness that his moment of greatness was upon him and that he was living up to its demands, laid one reassuring hand on his trembling chief's shoulder, gave him a smart salute that seemed called for by the occasion, and went off to secure his destiny.

When he looked back on that moment later, he did it wistfully. He wished—not idly, but with all his heart—that something could have happened right then, right then when he was at the peak of his entire existence. A stroke. A heart attack. An assassin's chem-dart. Anything that would have let him exit his life *like that*, splendid and confident and with the President of the United States of Earth looking after him in gratitude and admiration.

It hadn't happened that way. It has been downhill all the way from there. Despite his care. Despite his *meticulous* care! He had gone to Miss Brown's apartpod on an errand no one could have questioned, his docpouch conspicuous on his hip, all his movements clocked in and fully accounted for by the security robots accompanying him. The poison he gave her had been his own, issued to him as part of the equipment of the Vice Presidency—a poison that was odorless and tasteless, that acted in seconds, and that could be traced only if the body were found in five minutes or less. He had waited fifteen minutes by the clock (going back

into the hall three times during that period to reassure the waiting robots of his safety) before he touched her, to be absolutely
sure. He had bathed Marthajean and dressed her, working quickly,
in her finest nightgown, a thing of some sumptuous shining fabric the color of jonquils, frothing with lace, as unexpected as the
breasts that turned out to be just as extraordinary as the President had said they were. He had laid Miss Brown in her bed on
spotless sheets and arranged her hair; he had turned down the
coverlet to her waist and settled her clasped hands upon it. He
had left a vacuous little dignified suicide note on her computer:
"I am growing old, and I can see that I will never marry; I cannot
bear to go on like this, all alone, into the twilight of my life," it
had read.

And then he had stepped back and surveyed his handiwork,
making certain that Miss Brown looked as elegant as she would
have wanted to look had her death, in fact, been truly her own
idea. And he had gone over the apartpod one centimeter at a time,
making certain that there was *no* trace of his actions. No finger-
prints. No heatprints. *Nothing.* Only after he'd gone over it all,
and gone over it yet one more time, using items in his kit of security gadgets that he'd never used before and never expected to use
again, did he let himself out and go back to the Capitol Building
to occupy himself with business until Miss Brown was found and
declared a suicide.

It wasn't fair that he had been tripped up by such a silly thing. It
took away from it all. It *spoiled* it. It made him feel like a fool. He
knew that if anyone found out he was the murderer, they would
say it was just the kind of silly mistake he *would* make. It broke
his heart; it tormented and offended him. It was not *right*.

He saw it in the newspapes first, before anyone came to tell
him. There was the hologram of Miss Brown, as she had been in
life . . . they were not so tasteless as to show her dead. (He was a
little sorry about that, because he'd gone to so much trouble with
the scene.) There was the account of the finding of the body, its
surroundings, the bare statement that a suicide note had been in

her hand, things like that. And then the sentence that sent him into his utility to vomit up his breakfast.

"No woman," they quoted the official from the Washington DC Police Department as saying, "*no* woman, would lay herself out like that, to be found dead, in her very best nightgown, with her face all made up and her hair all freshly done . . . and put her nightgown on WRONG SIDE OUT." It was murder, the official said, not suicide. And because she was who she was, with the security clearances she had, it had been turned over to the highest law enforcement agencies for investigation.

Wrong side out? He hadn't checked. He hadn't even thought of it. Why *would* he have thought of it? It wasn't the kind of thing a man *did* think of! It was a perfectly natural mistake, and he understood perfectly how it had happened.

But now it was his turn. Like the President. Like the President, who would no doubt be calling him any second, terrified, to say something like, "Aron, tell me, please tell me, that this is some terrible *coincidence!*"

Now *he* was the one who was going to have to say, "What am I going to *do?*"

The terror he had felt when it finally became clear to him that it had all gone wrong—and the fact that, unlike the President, he was a realist—made it easy for the men from the agency to convince him of what had to be done. Convincing the President was not so simple; it turned out to be one hell of a job. Dellwilder started by flat out forbidding it.

"In that case," Zlerigeau said calmly, holding the President's eyes with the black-eyed stare he was famous for, "we have no choice. In that case, what we have to do is agree with you that it's a dumb and naughty idea, promise not to do it, and do it anyway behind your back. But we also have to work out some kind of half-ass alternate plan that you *will* approve. And then we have to go to all the trouble and expense of carrying out *that* plan, *too*. It's a big waste of the taxpayers' money, Mr. President."

"But listen, Zlerigeau," Dellwilder pleaded, "I understand . . .

God knows I understand . . . that this is a matter where national security—"

"And international security," the Vice President put in. "And *interplanetary* security."

"All of that," Dellwilder agreed. "I understand . . . security has to be put ahead of normal considerations. But you're asking me to let some ordinary citizen, some completely innocent person going about his daily life, just doing the best he can . . . you're asking me to let you arrest and convict him for this murder. A murder that he had nothing . . . *nothing!* . . . to do with. Zlerigeau, that's evil. That's *real, world-class evil*. That's repugnant to me. That can't be a thing that I have to agree to."

"Well," Jay Zlerigeau said, "I'm with you about the evil and the repugnant. But that's not the point. I tell you, if good and evil were relevant here, we'd just take in the Vice President and charge *him*—with first-degree murder and terminal stupidity."

"The Vice President is not responsible for this mess," said the President wearily, while Aron bit his lip and put every bit of his energy into not showing how scared he was.

"The hell he's not."

"Jay, it was me, not the Vice President, who went mad and ravished my own secretary—poor, sweet, hardworking, respectable Miss Brown—right there on the rug in the Oval Office. That was me, not the Vice President. I still can't believe it, but it was *me*."

"And it was the Vice President," the agency man snorted, "who decided Miss Brown had to leave this tearsvale—which was the correct decision, no question about it—and then decided he'd just take care of that himself, instead of calling us in and letting *us* do it. Mr. President, *my* staff knows that women, dead or alive, don't wear their nighties wrong side out."

"If the Vice President had called you?"

"We would have sent somebody . . . somebody professional, who knew what he was doing . . . and Miss Brown would have had an accident in her utility or tripped and fallen off her balcony or some such mild thing and we would not be sitting here facing this mess today. Why the *hell* didn't he call us?" He smacked his fist into his palm. "You *see* why we raise hell about using robots for

Secret Service bodyguards? This is just *exactly* the kind of thing we mean, Mr. President! This *would not* have happened if he'd had human agents with him instead of coffeepots!"

President Dellwilder said nothing about this issue; it was an old argument, and one that was settled by the budget, not by his personal preferences. There was enough money to put human security around the President himself, and that was all there was. He frowned at Zlerigeau, shaking his head slowly from side to side, and asked: "Are you saying that even if we'd called you in, an innocent person would have had to die?"

"Well . . . only *one* innocent person, Mr. President. As things stand now, it has to be *two* innocent persons. Your secretary, deleted by Vice President Muddle-fingers—"

The President spoke through clenched teeth. "Show some respect for the office, man!"

"—and a selected Fall Guy. And I don't *have* any respect for the office, the primary qualification for which, so far as I can tell, is the absence of either backbone or brains."

Tobias Dellwilder, who was called Toby by nobody, dropped his head into his hands and groaned aloud, saying, "You're not helping, Jay. You're not helping at all. This belligerent attitude toward poor Aron, who is as heartsick about this as I am . . . my God, he *killed* a woman in the mistaken belief that it was something he had to do to protect me! . . . it's only making matters worse. And you're spouting clichés . . . you know very well that we've had many distinguished Vice Presidents. This is no time for posturing, Jay; please cut it out. What we need is your *help*."

The man gave them both a long measuring look. The shattered Chief Executive, moaning through his hands like a lovesick teenage girl. The furious Vice Chief Executive, going alternately white and red with mingled terror and rage, without even the guts to stand up for himself. The look made it quite clear that Jay Zlerigeau didn't feel that the two of them together made one adult male.

There were lines the Vice President could have tossed off, if he'd been the line-tossing kind. About how much easier he would find it to murder a second time, and about how he was damn sure the agency chief didn't sleep in a nightgown. He choked them back, along with all the rest that occurred to him. He knew his role, and it didn't include taking the lead in a discussion when the President was present, unless he had been specifically ordered to do so. Let the man abuse him, let him insult him all he liked. Aron would remember him; and the day would come when he'd have an opportunity to demonstrate to him how deeply a man trapped in second place could hate.

"I *am* helping," Zlerigeau said flatly, finally. "I am telling you that there's only one thing to do. Just as we cannot afford to have the public know that the President of the United States of Earth had a toss with his secretary in the middle of a letter—your Veep was right about *that*, Mr. President!—we cannot afford to have the public know that the *Vice* President of the United States of Earth has murdered somebody, however incompetently. Because the victim of his incompetence was private secretary to the President, however, it can't be one of those cases you just let wither away unsolved. The public will insist on knowing who did it, and on making the criminal pay for the crime. And the only way out of this . . . thanks to the Vice President's bungling, because it *could* have been avoided . . . is to tap somebody who has no link with the Administration, no link with Washington . . . somebody off the wall. Some otherwise harmless tourist, or burglar, or druggo."

"And then?"

"And then, Mr. President, we'll haul his ass into court and we'll provide a couple tons of manufactured evidence and get him convicted of murder one, and we'll see that he fries—figuratively speaking, of course—and that will be the end of it. With any luck at all. *And* if your Veep stays out of it from now on. You will stay out of it, Mr. Vice President? For the sake of the nation? And so that you'll only have the blood of two innocents on your hands?"

"Right!" Aron snapped. "You can *count* on it! And I have no blood on my hands!"

He waited to be asked to explain that; he was proud of the justification he had ready. But the agent only snorted again, like an animal at a trough, and neither of them asked him anything.

"I can't approve this," said the President.

"Okay."

"You'll do it anyway?"

"Yes. Or you could order somebody to delete *me,* Mr. President, to keep me from it, and then you could try to deal with the consequences of *that* move."

"Jay," the President asked, the bewilderment in his voice obviously real, obviously painful, "why do all the answers to all the hard questions depend on some innocent person dying?"

"Because that goes with the territory, Mr. President. As long as people can't be trusted to keep secrets . . . and they can't, you know . . . people have to die to keep the worlds going around. It's always been that way; it always will be that way. Do you want me to explain it all to you again, Mr. President? I have plenty of time. That is, since the real murderer has nothing to fear and our Mr. Fall Guy doesn't know he's been picked, nobody's going to try to get away. We have all the time in the world. Shall I go over it again?"

"No."

Zlerigeau sighed. "That's progress," he said. "How do we choose this person?" It was almost a whisper.

"What, Mr. President?"

"I asked you . . . how do we choose this person? This 'Mr. Fall Guy?'"

"You don't have to worry about that, sir. Leave that to us."

"I want to know."

"Okay." Zlerigeau shrugged. "We try not to waste an opportunity of this kind, because they come along rarely. We have a list . . . with people on it who, for one reason or another, it would be useful to have removed. If we can find somebody on that list who's obscure enough . . . somebody with no Washington connections . . . somebody that doesn't have a powerful family or friends . . . we'll choose him. Or her. If nobody on the list qualifies right now, we'll go in and haul somebody in off the street—literally. Checking very carefully to be sure he's not one of your derelicts with a wealthy daddy in the background. And you can be sure, Mr. President, that we won't choose somebody with a wife and six little kids. There's plenty of single trash out there, lots of them miserable enough to welcome a fatal injection just to get the last meal that goes with it, believe me."

The Vice President thought his chief might throw up. He looked like he was going to throw up. But it didn't happen. The President swallowed hard, and he drew a long deep breath in the silence. And then he said, in a voice that trembled, "I have just one condition."

"Tell me," said Zlerigeau.

"This person . . . this Joe Fall Guy, with no wife and no kids . . . he doesn't get the death penalty. He gets life with no parole. Or he gets the back wards at St. Elizabeth's, with no parole, and enough drugs to keep his mouth shut forever. I don't care. But he doesn't die."

"Mr. Dellwilder . . . Mr. President . . . that's a very serious mistake. It leaves loose ends, sir—it would be so much better to just remove the man. Look . . . when the United States goes to war, it has to kill people. This is no different. This is the war for peace and security, sir. This is the war to keep the whole solar system from falling apart. However much the colonies claim to despise Earth one and all, if Earth fell apart they would suffer trauma difficult to repair. Without Earth to hate, they'd fight each other, you know—we all know that's what would happen, and it has to be prevented. It's a *just* war, Mr. President, and the death of Joe Fall Guy is just an unavoidable side effect."

"No," said the President. "I mean it. No."

"Then I'm sorry to have to tell you," said Zlerigeau, "that I will have to go back to the office and create a Plan B where Joe Fall Guy trips and falls off a balcony at St. Elizabeth's. Accidentally."

Zlerigeau leaned back in his chair with his arms folded behind his head, and he looked at the wall to give Dellwilder some space. The President sat staring at him, rubbing his cheeks with both hands, his eyes bitter and despairing, while the other two men waited. The Vice President could hear a bird singing outside the safepod window . . . it was saying "*A*-F-Of-*L! A*-F-Of-*L!*" The Vice President knew that bird; it had a mate whose song sounded exactly like water going down a drain.

"Get out of here," the President said at last, and he shoved his chair back from the table and got up and went to look out the window. He had both hands clasped behind his back in the classic pose of the man on whose head the crown has grown too heavy. "Get out of here," he said again, dully. "Go do your filthy work . . . for which I, the Almighty forgive me, am entirely responsible. But get out. I don't want to look at you anymore tonight."

And he added, "Actually I don't want to look at *either* of you ever again, as long as I live. But I have to, don't I?"

"Yes, Mr. President, you do," Zlerigeau answered, on his way out the door; he didn't take it personally.

As for the Vice President, he didn't say anything; after the agent was gone, he left, too, in silence. He was deeply hurt. *Deeply.* It was true that he had killed Miss Brown, but like Zlerigeau had said, it was no different from a soldier killing an enemy in wartime. He had done it to save the President, and to save the country, and to save all the civilized worlds. The fact that he'd made a little mistake didn't change any of that. It seemed to him that Dellwilder owed him—*not* "the office," by damn, but *him*, personally!—a little more respect than just being thrown out harshly into the dreary afternoon.

He left. Oh, yes, he left. But he would remember this. And God willing, the day would come when he could make *Dellwilder* pay, too.

CHAPTER 10

When Jay told him about it, Benny just sat there, staring at him, for a long minute and a half. Until Zlerigeau said, "I know, Benny. But so help me God and all the attending angels, I am telling you the truth. It happened just like I said."

"Aw, hell," Benny said. "Nah."

"Yes. Just like I said."

"Jay," said Benny, "the fate of the free universe is in the hands of these two dipshits. Isn't that the way they tell it?"

"Well . . . they leave out the 'dipshit' part; they say, 'in the hands of these two great and noble statesmen.' But yeah; sure. In their capable hands."

"How come we're still alive? How come the worlds still stay in their orbits? How come *anything works*?"

Zlerigeau chuckled. "God loves us, Benny," he said. "That's the only possible answer."

"The President lays his secretary on the damn Oval Office rug, in broad daylight. The President tells the *Veep*, that little boy who can't find the utility alone, about his adventure. The Veep proceeds to kill the secretary, all by himself, using his magic potion for high muckamucks. With Marthajean Brown's best nightgown on her wrong side out, so he gets caught. And I'm supposed to believe all this."

"That's how it started."

"And then . . . and *then*, the decision is to go out and handpick a fellow just a tad too close to figuring out something it would be very inconvenient for the public to know, and charge him with the Veep's murder. That part I understand."

"Right. That was next."

"And then, out of nowhere at all, Cleo St. Andrews, famous lady guitar picker—"

"Guitarist, Benny. Guitarist."

"All right—Cleo St. Andrews, famous lady guitarist—sashays into the front office of the federal lockup and announces that she can't live with the guilt of seeing an innocent man pay for her crime and insists that *she* killed Marthajean Brown!"

"That's it. You've got it. Stop right there."

"Awww . . ." Benny said again.

"So help me."

"Jay, it sounds like an effing opera."

"You know about opera, Benny?"

"I do. How could I go around posing as an unemployed multiversity prof if I didn't?"

"It often happens that life imitates art, you see. And this is one of those times."

"Sweet saints on a stick."

"I know, Benny. And maybe it will make you feel just a little bit better to know that I *told* the two gentlemen exactly how pathetic all this is, and how they fit into the picture. The idea being to convince them not to do anything else, or repeat any of what they've already done. It may not hold them, Benedict, but I did make the effort."

"And now they want you to clean this up. With the assistance of your stable of minions."

"If we would be so kind, yes."

Benedict Mondorro leaned forward in the desk's guest slot, suddenly serious. "Jay, suppose just for a minute we forget how unspeakably stupid this whole thing is. Tell me what you think is going on."

"I don't know what's going on. I wish I did."

"Give me your best guess."

"Well . . . what I *don't* think is going on is that Miss St. Andrews is acting on her own."

"Okay. And?"

"If I could believe she was on her own, just one of those

confessor nuts that turns up looking for publicity after any crime that makes the newspapes, this would be easy. Nobody knows about her yet. We'd just take her out, bury the story, and hang Joe Fall Guy. Figuratively speaking. But if she was on her own, there's no way she could know the things she knows. And since that's true, we don't know how many dominoes there are stacked up behind her, Benny. We delete her, up steps the next, belly to the bar . . . delete *that* one, it happens again. People would get very suspicious, very fast. The lid would blow off. We can't afford to test those waters—we have to assume that Cleo St. Andrews is part of something bigger." He sighed. "A plot to bring down the government and destabilize the inhabited universe, for example."

"Jay . . ."

"Yeah?"

"While you're lecturing, would you please explain how it happens that the President and Vice President of the United States are *always* incompetent? I mean, lo these past two or three centuries? How can that be?"

"Give it a little thought, Benny. Would anybody with a brain be willing to take either of those jobs? Think about it."

"There was John Mark Leverance."

"Yeah. That's once. But he didn't understand how things worked, Benny. He thought Presidents were allowed to fix things. He didn't last long."

Benny thought about it, and then he nodded his head. "Okay. What else have we got?"

"Nothing else. We don't know anything . . . at all . . . about what brings St. Andrews into this. But she knows too much, Benny. Lots and lots of stuff that didn't appear—and never will appear—in the newspapes, or on the threedies."

Benny frowned at him. "There couldn't have been *much* else, Zlerigeau," he said slowly. "The murder wasn't that complicated."

"I don't mean she only knew things about the murder," the other man said quietly. "No. She knew about the little incident on the Oval Office carpet, Benny."

Benny's mouth puckered, like he was going to whistle, and then instead he blew one little puff after another of astonished breath.

"You see, Benny. *That's* the problem. How could she know?"

"Maybe the Vice President told her?"

"Benny, the man is a pane of glass. If he'd told anybody, I would know. And the President sure as hell didn't tell her."

"Maybe Miss Brown told her?"

"Maybe. If I could be sure of that, like I said, this would be easy. But we have a pretty good account of everything Marthajean Brown said and did after the shenanigans . . . and there's not a lot of time to be accounted for. She could have called somebody, but we find no record of that anyplace. Like anybody in government, she thinks her computer is secure; like anybody in government, the agency knows every breath she draws. There was no call."

"Maybe she saw St. Andrews in the hall at the White House, or on the street, and said, 'Hey, Cleo, the President just deflowered me . . . or whatever . . . and I'm going home to cry!'"

"Maybe. Like I said. But we've accounted for the movements of both women, and we don't find them in the same place in that time period. If they'd run into each other anywhere, Benny, I think we'd know."

"It could have been just a few seconds, Jay—it could have happened."

"I can't afford to take a chance on it, Benny. There's no evidence of any contact, of any kind. So I have to think that maybe somebody put Marthajean up to this, and I have to think that there may be a whole *platoon* of people who know all about it. Which leads to the obvious and inconvenient conclusion: we can't afford to just get rid of St. Andrews."

"Is that her real name? St. Andrews, I mean?"

"No. Her name was . . . wait a minute, let me check the file. Oh, yeah. She began her life as Alice Mary Brown. No relation to Marthajean Brown."

"You sure of that last part?"

"We're sure. Marthajean Brown was a Kumeyaay Indian; Alice Mary Brown is Cherokee. And no relation."

"Both of them Indians, though?"

"Benny, there are millions of Indians. We're both Anglos, you and I—does that mean anything?"

"No. But it has to be checked out."

"We checked it. By the time St. Andrews had been booked for fifteen minutes—with the effing booking officer bleating, 'But a *woman* wouldn't have put on Miss Brown's nightgown wrong side out *either!*'—we'd run her through every computer on the planet, and cross-checked for contact with Marthajean Brown. You've got to remember, friend—Miss Brown was the President's personal secretary. We already knew everything about Miss Brown from the day she hatched, or she wouldn't have been able to hold that position. I even know what brand of underwear she wore, and how many pairs she had. Those two never saw each other, never met. They might have turned up at the same diplomatic cocktail party once in a while, that kind of thing, but they didn't *know* one another. Not in childhood; not later."

Benny didn't say anything. He had his own methods for checking things out, and they weren't the government's ways. That was one of the reasons they needed him.

"You'll find all the relevant files on your computer, Benny," said Zlerigeau. "Anything else you need?"

Benny shook his head. And then he said wistfully, "Oh, hell . . . oh, for the good old days. When everybody that wouldn't play nice could just be politely persuaded to ship out to the colonies."

"Mmhmm."

"It must have been wonderful. No crime. No poverty. No wars. No *trouble*, Jay, unless you decided of your own free will to settle on a planet dedicated to your particular favorite variety of trouble. It must have been paradise."

"Maybe so, Benny. But it's over. There's not one world out there that's not running over with the unfortunate products of human *mating*. Some of them lovely people, certainly. About half of them miserable. About a fourth of them miserable enough to take it out on the rest of us. Paradise was nice while it lasted . . .

maybe . . . I go by what I see on the threedies. Now it's long gone, and there's nowhere left to go. Not anymore."

The two men sat there together, in the kind of silence that's not empty because it has the thoughts of two longtime friends to fill it.

Finally, Benny sighed and said, "Okay, Jay. Tomorrow soon enough?"

"Sorry, Benny. Fate of the universe, and all that."

"I see. Right now. I suppose we have to start with Cleo St. Andrews Alice Mary Brown."

"Yes. We start with the lady, Benny."

"Damn women . . . Talk about the *good* old days! You know what I want back? I want the days when all the ladies were legally minors and they didn't open their *mouths* till a man gave them permission!"

Zlerigau grinned at him—they were in complete agreement on that issue. But he didn't mention that; he didn't have to, because Benny already knew how he felt.

"Like I said, Benny . . . we start with the lady."

Benedict Mondorro wasn't one of your elegant glamourboy secret agents with the private label on his whiskey and the handmade suits and all that crap. Mondorro came from ordinary people, and he was proud to keep their ways; even with the unemployed professor cover, he stayed a common man. But he was one of the best—maybe *the* best. It wasn't easy work. In the 2400s, when secret agents were about half machine . . . all high ceramics and fibers and virus metals, so they were damn near invulnerable to ordinary problems, it was maybe easier . . . it must have been easier. It wasn't like that anymore.

There wasn't enough money now to do it for *all* agents, and it was hard to do it for some and not for others; that was one reason, and it was valid. But the real reason was techsickness. The human beings of Earth, having had a chance to learn what a taste for machines can do—and coming painfully up out of the Icehouse Effect those machines created, with only a third of the population left—had acquired a taste for doing without machines whenever possible. Not to go back to living primitive; only the Primmoes, the fanatics, went that far. But Terrans tried hard to keep the techlevel down. Benedict was strictly biological except where he'd actually been *repaired*.

And he didn't have anything against women. He'd married one once, and he still had her at home. Her name was Annalaura, and what got to Benedict about her was this face she had. He'd known that the face wasn't really important in a woman; it's the body that matters, and the behavior. But there'd been something about her face he couldn't get out of his mind. Annalaura looked out at you with great huge eyes like a little kid's eyes, through clouds of dark brown hair, like she was hiding in there. The first time he saw her, all he wanted to do was get both hands deep into that hair, and kind of wind it all around him; he wanted to hide in there *with* her. It looked warm in there, and safe. And he'd found himself unable to do without her. She was older now, and her face was soon going to need its third set of cosmetic injections, but the eyes and the hair had not changed. Except that the hair was longer; Benny had never let her cut the hair. No, he firmly believed that it had been an error to give women adult status again, but he was *tolerant* about them.

Sometimes they had advantages men would have liked to have—like the way they had survived the Icehouse Effect, all that fat under their skin bringing them sailing through it while the men died like pathetic flies all around them. It seemed to Mondorro that that couldn't have been chance; it had to have meant something. It was, he thought, a warning of some kind. Maybe a warning to be kinder to the women. They could have let all of the men die except for a few specimens kept at stud, and they had not done that; they had, in fact, worked doggedly to save as many as possible, often at considerable sacrifice to themselves. He kept that in mind; and he did try.

But he hated it when he had to deal with them while he was *working*. Everything took five times as long. You ask a man a question, you just get the answer, and it takes maybe two minutes. You ask a woman a question, *your* hair grows while she goes around and around and around . . . eventually she answers, if you know what you're doing, but it takes forever. He and Jay would try to shove St. Andrews down the path at a reasonable pace . . . they would ask her only the absolute *minimum* number of questions and they would encourage her to be brief, so they could get on with it. And still it would take them forever to get through the crap to the information they needed.

But she had an excuse. The excuse of *being* a woman. The President and the Vice President—they had no excuses.

THE TRANCER IS TIRED . . .
WHAT'S ON THE SOAPS?

CHAPTER 11

Being a child, on Birog, is not easy. Miktok Fitzgerald is aware of this. She is the first to admit that she dreams . . . of winning a Goldenpurse . . . of moving her family to one of the high-security condoroids. Like any other normal person, she would like to live in luxury inside high walls, with a staff of robots making damn *sure* life is gracious. Miktok would even settle for a two-bedroom apartpod, one of the ones on the top floor, that have a balcony fashioned from the building's roof; she has slept in a livingroom wall-niche so many years. A real bed, in a room that was hers alone . . . she would settle for that, and be grateful.

But she tells the twins it could be a lot worse. "You could be on Gehenna," she reminds them, "serving as targets for the teenagers in the Games. You could be on Polytrix, working in the mines they won't send robots into because robots are too valuable to risk that way. You could have been born on *Eden*, you know—your father's grandmother was a Square Corner Fundamentalist, and if she'd had her way that's *exactly* where you'd be!"

This is a lie; Miktok knows nothing at all about their father's family. For all she knows, Flesser Fitzgerald sprang fullgrown from the stinking pavement of the alley where the twins were conceived. But it's quite safe to tell Martha and Tommy the lie, since they know no more about him than she does. Miktok has found the fabled fundamentalist greatgrandmother extremely useful over the years. "And you could be stuck in one of our famous swarming filthy cities, instead of here in Jerrenton," she goes on. "You could be living in Birog *City*. *Remember* that!"

"I'd rather . . . *lots* rather . . . be in Birog City!" Martha snaps at her. Martha is naked except for two strategically placed blue silk scarves; that saves on clothes and helps them get by. She is as scrawny as a killbird chick, and as ugly. Miktok is grateful for that ugliness, which will perhaps protect her daughter just a little, and she nourishes it carefully. The little girl's face is screwed up into a freckled knot; her hands are shoved deep into the tangled mop of carrot-red hair. This is a conversation they've had a hundred times, and Martha is only nine. Miktok wonders how many thousands of times she will have to go through it before the twins either give up and accept the fact that they are, like it or not, Birogians—and suburbanites—or figure out some way to go off into the various worlds and seek their fortunes.

"If we lived in Birog City, at least there'd be something to do!" Martha wails, pounding her fists on her flat little chest, which offers no resonance at all for the pounding. It sounds like cheap sandals on a plastic walk. "At least we could go *out* sometimes instead of spending our whole lives inside a stupid apartpod!" And it is true. The twins have been outside only half a dozen times in the seven years they've lived here. But that is the way things are. For everybody except the very wealthy.

Miktok doesn't understand why they aren't used to it. If you have always stayed inside, why would you want to go *out*side? It seems to her that the twins should feel the same way about being outdoors as about being at the bottom of the sea . . . it should be the Dread Unknown for them.

"Sure," Miktok says, narrowing her eyes at Martha, measuring the frantic body and words and deciding that it's the usual act and not something new to be worried about. Miktok remembers quite well what it was like to "go out" in Birog City; of the elevenpack she ran with, she is the only one who survived their goings-out. "Sure you could go out! And you might live to be fourteen, if you were very, very lucky."

"This," Tommy announces dramatically, stepping right in front of his sister to claim Miktok's attention, flinging his arms wide to indicate the broad scope of his description, "is not *life*. This is not *living*. We'd rather die young and know we've *lived*!" The scarf wrapped carelessly around Tommy's loins . . . can a nine-year-old boy have loins? . . . is a deep yellow color, like butter. What is ugly in Martha is dangerously attractive in Tommy; redheaded boys are all the rage on Birog this year. And he is as aware of that as Miktok is. He plans to be a threedy star when he grows up.

Miktok stares at them, frustrated, ready to smack them both (although she would not really do that, but she is ready to *think* about doing it). The two of them. Born during a silly fad of naming your kids for ancient Terran politicians and their families . . . she is sorry now that her children are Thomas Jefferson Fitzgerald and Martha Washington Fitzgerald. She is sick of watching the threedies about the first Thomas Jefferson and the first Martha Washington, pious and frugal and wise and *forever going outside*; the twins play them over and over and over again till Miktok could scream. Why couldn't she have given them ordinary names like Clarm and Geyra . . . or Miktok and Flesser?

Flesser. Beloved. His arms burning, the fire licking along the edges of his hands, looking at her with such surprise, such complete astonishment, because he had been sure the place was safe . . . Flesser ordering her to leave him there, because she is pregnant. Flesser shoving her, using the insides of his bent wrists, where the flames haven't caught yet. Miktok still cannot think about Flesser without pain, and that makes her voice sharp.

"You don't know how lucky you are, you rotten little beasts!" she hisses. "And you're *twins*, too! You always have somebody around to talk to and do things with, somebody you get along with! Two weeks in the Birog City streets would make *you* into fundamentalists, praising God for the miracles of good luck you've been gifted with—if you *lasted* two weeks! Shame on you! Stop complaining! Go watch the threedies!"

Martha sighs deeply, and smooths back her hair from the high white forehead Miktok will not soften with bangs with both small hands. "Mothers who really *love* their children," she offers, "don't always dump them by the *com*set to watch the stupid threedies!"

"Oh," says Miktok. "Really. Well, Martha Washington, what *do* mothers do? Mothers that really love their kids, I mean, as opposed to mothers like me."

Martha has no idea, of course. She's never been around any other mothers, and she has brains enough to know that the ones she sees in the school *three*dies on the mass-ed programs are fantasy mothers. She has to settle for her most snobbish expression, the one that says she is far too refined and intellectual even to stoop to discussing the subject. She has her hands firmly planted on what will one day be her hips.

Tommy breaks in then, before Miktok can tell her daughter what she thinks of her performance.

"Mother," he says, "you know what T.O. says about the threedies?"

T.O. is Tommy's APCP—his Assigned Peer Call-Partner. Thirty minutes a day on the phone with T.O. is supposed to help socialize them both. Like Tommy, T.O. is nine; unlike Tommy, he has a father resident, living in his home. Miktok hates T.O. He is a whiny and cruel little boy, fiercely dedicated to making every call an occasion for reducing Thomas to tears. But the government has paired the boys off and there is nothing she can do about it. She has filled out an application for APCP reassignment every month for the past three years. They go into the comset and come straight back stamped DENIED, every single time.

"What?" she asks. "What does T.O. say?"

"He says the Galaxy Twelve series is *true* stuff, Mama!"

"Don't call me 'mama.'"

"Mother, I mean. He says the government just doesn't want us to *know*!"

"Galaxy Twelve?"

"Yeah."

"The one where the giant aliens fly over Washington flapping their flaming wings? The one where—"

"Wait!" Thomas protested. "T.O.'s not stupid. I mean, you can see where they've seamed in the special effects and stuff. But he says that the boring parts . . . all the stuff where you've got the Aliens behind a big window, and you've got a linguist in a terpreter booth, and they talk about—"

"*In*terpreter booth, Tommo!" says Martha. She is still

sneering, but she aims it at her brother this time. "'Terpreter'
booth! *Hon*estly!"

Tommy turns on her and demands to know if she can explain
what a terpreter booth *is*, and Martha admits at once that she can't,
but points out that she can at least pronounce it. It's clear to Miktok that they're going to occupy each other for a while with this,
which will save her from having to tell them again not to believe
everything they hear.

It seems to Miktok that these two children of hers, whose
sophistication sometimes frightens her, ought to be able to set
aside the rantings and ravings of T.O. Delareska, but it's a rare
week when she escapes a hushed account of his latest wild imag-
inings. Martha has no APCP, there being an adult female in the
house to serve her as a role model, and Miktok is glad of that. One
uncontrollable source of input into her home is more than enough.

She thinks she is going to be able to get back to her housework
. . . she has to figure out some way to make two chops serve three
people for their dinner, and there is something awful growing on
the bathroom floor again that she has to call the extension service
for advice about. But Tommy surprises her. He cuts off his argument with his sister, patting Martha distractedly on the back by
way of apology, and insists on knowing Miktok's opinion about
what T.O. says. After all, he says, there really *were* linguists; they
appear in the mass-ed history course several times. Maybe there
really were Aliens, too. Maybe—

"Tommy," says Miktok gently, "you know better. You *know*
those are science fiction threedies. You *know* there were never
really Aliens living on Earth!" She hopes. It makes her skin creep,
just hearing about it. And of course she *has* heard the rumors,
just like T.O.'s parents have heard them, and apparently discussed
them in front of their child. Miktok has a sudden happy thought. If
T.O.'s parents are the kind of kookoes that believe in Aliens coming to Earth and a government cover-up and all the rest of that,
then maybe there's a chance she *can* get a new Assigned Peer for
Tommy! This is well worth investigating.

"Tommy, honey," she says, holding his eyes with hers, putting her hands on his shoulders to show him she's serious, "tell me. Tell me *exactly* what T.O. says. And how he says he *knows* all these interesting things."

Tommy pulls away from her, incensed at being treated like a child, and—

BORING!

CHANGE CHANNELS!

The judge is sick at heart; his long thin fingers travel aimlessly over his splendid robes with their narrow purple and lavender stripes, now touching his chest, now a shoulder, now moving down over an arm . . . they are like skinny insects moving. The judge seems to be unaware of what his fingers are doing.

He hasn't eaten this morning, nor will he eat this day; he never eats on torture days. It seems to him unspeakably obscene that anyone could cause another human to suffer agony and, on the same day, feed himself. He will take a little water; nothing more.

In another ten minutes it will be time for him to go into the little cubicle where the torture takes place. And it will be like it always is. He will sit down beside the table where the prisoner lies waiting for him. The prisoner will be motionless because of the net of energy fields that restrains him, but his *eyes* will be moving; their eyes are always dancing, frantic, trying to get away for the sake of the terrified body. The judge will sit down beside the prisoner and he will say the prayer he always says: "Merciful Lord, guide me in this work, and guide this man that he may profit by it, Amen." And then he will give the prisoner the injections.

There are two injections. The first paralyzes the vocal tract, so that there will be no screams, no moans, not even whimpering, during the torture. The second administers one hour of the fiercest pain this young world's scientists can devise; it is, they tell him, a whole-body pain. Unlike traditional tortures, which tend to focus on one body part or perhaps two or three, there is no part of the prisoner's body that does not feel the unrelenting agony. Except, of course, the heart. The prisoner's heart is given a constant mix of other drugs during the session, to exempt it from the pain and keep it beating, even as the prisoner's body and mind beg only for it to stop and grant the peace of death.

The judge will not do what he longs to do after he has given the injections. Unlike other judges who have filled this post, he will not get up and go away and come back in an hour, when the torture is over. He will sit beside the prisoner for the entire hour, holding the man's hand, tears pouring down over his cheeks and falling from time to time on the man's suffering flesh, and he will explain.

"My friend," he will say, as it goes on and on and the *eyes* talk to him about what it is like to lie silent and motionless through pain like that, "I want you to understand why this is being done to you. I want you to know that this pain has purpose.

"You were brought here to this place," he will say, while the prisoner tries to die, and fails, "because you have tortured another human being. This procedure, this process that you are undergoing now, is administered *only* to torturers. Please understand that.

"There are those who would tell you that you are an evil man," he will say, "and that this is a suitable *punishment* for such evil. I want you to know that it is not punishment at all. If I wanted only to punish you, this is not what I would do. I know that you are not evil, my friend. And I know that when you understand what torture *is*, when you truly know how it feels to suffer the kind of pain that you inflict on others, you *will not do* it. Not ever again. I understand that.

"The point of this procedure," he will say, "is to show you what it is like, so that you *will* understand. There is no other way, no other way but this terrible one that breaks my heart, that breaks all our hearts, to make you understand. We know that. Because everything else has been tried, since the beginning of time, and the torturers have gone out and been torturers still."

And he will say to the prisoner: "Please know, my friend, that I would love you if I could. It is my own shortcoming that a man who is a torturer is a man I am unable to love. But although I cannot love you, I can feel regard for you. I can feel sympathy for you. I can wish a better life for you. And when this is over, I can rejoice that you will go away from this place a *different* man—a man to whom the idea of torture is as unthinkable as it is to any normal human being.

"You will be cured," the judge will say, as he always says. "It will all be over. You will once again be a member of the human race."

The judge is so squeamish about others' pain that he cannot bear to visit a friend in a hospital. He thinks sometimes of the dolorics, who are born unable to shut out pain from any living creature, born to a life of total isolation inside a shielded psi-bubble, or to the life of total filth that falls to the painprostitutes of Gehenna. He can think of nothing more terrible; he is sure he would go mad, in their place. He has tried all his adult life, but it remains incomprehensible to him: how *could* any human being be indifferent to another human being's agony, or, most repulsive of all, *enjoy* another human being's agony? It is the Mystery of All Mysteries; it always has been.

With some mysterious things there is at least a thread of meaning that can be grasped. If only by the grace of metaphor, there is a way to say, "I could not do that myself, but I can *understand* how someone could do it." Not with torture. Torture is different. There are no metaphors for torture.

When one of the judge's sons had been injured in a flyer crash and required various repairs, he could not go to the beloved boy's side; he had to send his wife. He sat home and waited, motionless as a prisoner in a restraint net, until she came to tell him that the pain was over. No one will ever know what it is like for him, administering the injections to these prisoners and staying with them through the torment, until it is over. No one. Only his knowledge that it means they will not hurt other people anymore gives him the strength it takes.

And he knows very well that if it were not for the first injection—the one that imposes silence—even that knowledge would not be enough. Not if the prisoner could give voice to the pain. He gives thanks for the first injection. And for the fact that, so far, he has never gone into the torture room and found a prisoner there who was a woman. Perhaps that will never happen; there is no record of it ever happening on this world; he prays that it will never happen.

He will go into the cubicle this morning and do what must be done, as he always has; it will be like it always is. He knows that no man *could* commit torture if he knew what his victim was feeling; it is just a matter of making it absolutely clear. It is a process of education, nothing more, and it must be done.

Except that this time it is *not* like it always is.

This time, when he leans over the prisoner to administer the two drugs, it is not the same. Because this time he recognizes the man who lies there with only his eyes trying desperately to run away from the agony that is coming. This man has been on the torture table before, has had the injections before . . . the judge remembers this man.

The judge sets down his instruments without a word. For a moment he looks into the terrified eyes, and then he turns his back and walks away.

There is another cubicle in this facility of the Justice Department. The cubicle has no floor, and no proper door; it has a small square panel that covers an opening shaped to receive the tidy bundles of daily trash. A fat human being would not be able to fit through the opening, but the judge is thin. With almost no trouble at all, he slides the panel back and climbs into the opening. He makes not one sound, although he has had no injection to paralyze his vocal tract, as he falls toward the vaporizer.

HORRIBLE!

WHERE DO THEY GET THIS STUFF?

CHANGE THE CHANNEL!

The great paddlewheel that turns at the rear of the riverboat is made of a silvery filament as strong as steel. The wheel is taller than a house, and the lacy circle it spreads against the background of space is lovely to see. It is, of course, as ridiculous as it is beautiful, and as useless as the lacy ornaments that loop and festoon the railings and posts and windows. The seas of space offer the wheel nothing to push against. It is the drive hidden in the boat's belly that moves the craft toward its various destinations. This has its advantages.

If the paddlewheel had to be functional, there would be many constraints on its shape and size and design. Since it need not be, it can be made as intricate and as splendid as the owner chooses, and the only constraint is that it must not be made in such a way that it becomes a sail and *interferes* with the drive. (There is also the constraint that the riverboat's owner must have money enough to pay for it; but that comes from a different class of constraints.)

On board the *Delta Princess*, Charlotte Elizabeth Buckley Cantrell is thoroughly annoyed by the way her children are behaving, and she does not scruple to tell them so. "Law!" she says. "I declare, I am tempted to throw youall over the side and let you drift off forever and ever *more!*"

"Now, Mama!" chides her oldest daughter, who makes a commendable effort to look after the rest of the brood. She smiles at Charlotte Elizabeth from behind a small white fan trimmed with pink rosebuds and a blue satin pleated ribbon. "It's not so bad as all that."

"It *is* as bad as all that!" Charlotte Elizabeth insists. "You've been at that maddening game of tag for half an hour now, and I can abide it *no* longer—I feel like I'm locked up with a pack of monkeys and hyenas! Surely you can find something more genteel to *do?*"

There are five of the children, four girls and one boy, as is customary. (If the number of pirates keeps growing, there will have to be more boys, but not for the Cantrells; they have completed their obligations.) They stand there looking at her and at each other, back and forth, shrugging their shoulders and sighing elaborate sighs. Truth be told, they haven't been enjoying their game either;

they are still small, but they're too old to find pleasure for very long in chasing each other around the furniture and in and out the doors of the saloon. The idea is that if they keep it up long enough it will provoke their mother out of her morning routine and entice her to spend a little time amusing them. One and all, they adore their mother. They love their father, too, when he is around, but that's not often and never for long; a fortune the size of the Cantrells' requires great and constant effort not only to create but to maintain.

Charlotte Elizabeth is fussing at them again, reminding them that they know very well she has household accounts to deal with that morning. *Must* they pester her? Can they not find something to amuse themselves with? Just because they have no lessons to do today, must they inflict themselves on her like five persistent rashes? She stands up and shakes her finger at them, setting her crinolines swishing against the polished wooden floor, setting the long ringlets of her red hair swinging. "Mercy!" she says. "Where did I go *wrong?*"

They push the littlest girl forward, knowing their mother has a hard time resisting her, and Cassie Jennifer Cantrell pulls her thumb out of her mouth long enough to look up at her mother and say, "Mama, tell us a story! Please?"

"A story! On a Saturday morning, with all I have to do?" Charlotte Elizabeth shakes her head in astonishment, asking, "Whatever are you *thinking* of, child?" She is pretending, but it is in many ways true; managing a spacegypsy household the size of hers is no small task, even with the dozen new houserobots Jason Cantrell has added to her staff this past year.

But the child is not impressed. "Please, Mama, darlin'!" she pleads, and she lays her little face, surrounded by coppery curls gathered high at the back of her head just as her mother's are, against Charlotte Elizabeth's ample skirts. "Pretty please?"

"What story did you have in mind, sweetness?" asks Charlotte Elizabeth tenderly; she is weakening. She always does, and the children know that.

"About the Ozarques!" says Cassie Jennifer. "The Ozarques, Mama, and the little Quindaws! Please, Mama."

"The Quindaw, Cassie Jennifer. One Quindaw, two Quindaw, many Quindaw—however many."

"Yes, Mama," the child says, looking up at her. "About the Ozarques, Mama, and the little Quindaw that live on persimmons! Oh, please."

"Wouldn't you rather watch the comset, littlest?" the woman asks, and she looks at the others as well. "Are you sure youall really want to just listen to me talk? You could be watching that show you like so much, the one about the two-headed whateveritis with the silver tentacles . . . wouldn't you far rather do *that*?"

They shake their heads, grinning at her, and she sighs and surrenders; the sooner she gets it over with, the sooner she can get back to the matter of the disgraceful sums they've been spending on groceries since she replaced the cook last month. She has just told the children to sit down around her on the floor by her chair, when Jason Cantrell appears in the saloon door.

"Madam?" he says, and Charlotte Elizabeth draws herself up, dignity dropping over her like a shawl, to answer him.

"Good morning, Jason," she says. "It's a pleasure to see you; we thought you were still on the *Gallant Belle*, my dear."

Jason grimaces just for an instant, and then his handsome face clears; no one who wasn't paying close attention would have seen the brief expression that signals his courteous distaste for the Cloverhasty family and their ostentatious *Gallant Belle*. "I'm not staying," he tells them, "I've got to go make another attempt to get some sense into their heads over there. I just stopped to speak to the pilot, and I thought I'd bid youall good morning before I left."

"Good morning, Papa!" all the children say together like a chorus, and he goodmornings them back.

Young Edward, encumbered by two sisters younger and two older, but still the *boy* among them, with the privileges that go with being the boy, steps toward his father. "Mama was just about to tell us a story about the Ozarques and the Quindaw, Papa," he says. "But I would surely rather go along with you instead, sir, if you'll have me."

"Hmmmmmmm." The man frowns, careful to look as if he is really thinking it over, and then he shakes his head. "I'm sorry, son," he says. "Not this time." That is what he almost always says, and almost always will say. Until Edward is twelve years old and can begin to learn how a man of the spacegypsies orders his life and looks after his family. The boy nods; he was expecting it, but it's always worth asking. Just on the off chance.

"Well, don't let me keep you," Jason says fondly, putting the broad-brimmed hat he has been holding in his hand back on his head, touching the sword at his hip to be sure it's properly placed. "Children!" he says. "Madam." And he touches the brim of the hat and strides away down the deck, shouting for the dinghy to be brought to the side for him.

In the saloon, Charlotte Elizabeth settles the children around her and says, cautioning them, "Just one story, mind—I *must* get those accounts done this morning!" And then she begins.

"Once upon a time, long long ago, on the Planet Earth, long before it turned to mostly ice and then—praise be!—warmed up again, there was an Ozarque who lived in a limestone cave scrubbed clean as a whistle just outside a town named Meander, Arkansas. Outside the cave there was a thicket of persimmon trees, and under the persimmons there lived so many Quindaw that the Ozarque had stopped trying to count them. But on *this* day . . ."

HOW CAN PEOPLE *WATCH* SUCH STUFF???!!

TURN IT *OFF*!

CHAPTER 12

There was no real need for the two agents to actually visit Cleo St. Andrews in the prizpod. The entire preliminary interrogation could have been done—and would, ordinarily, have been done—by comset. But the President of the United States had insisted.

"I want you *there*," he had said, rubbing his fingertips together in the nervous habit he had acquired since the day of the murder. "I want you both there with her, physically. So that you can see every smallest twitch of her face and body. Hear every tiniest nuance of her voice. I want you in the best possible situation . . . I don't want you to miss *any*thing."

They had tried explaining that it had been at least a hundred years since computer observation had been in any way less efficient and effective than in-presence observation, but their words had no effect on the Chief Executive.

"I don't believe it," the President said flatly. "In fact, I know it to be false."

"Mr. President—"

"I know it to be *false*, I tell you! Why do you think I bother doing any of *my* work face-to-face? It's not because I don't have infinite access to the best technology! It's because again and again the most important things I learn don't come from any of the senses that computers—even the very newest and fanciest computers—have. They come from a *feeling* I get, a feeling I get only when I am in the same room with somebody. Computers don't get feelings, gentlemen. You go to Miss St. Andrews's apartment, you go *into* the prizpod, you sit down there with her, and you talk to her. Face-to-face—in the old-fashioned way."

Zlerigeau said nothing at all, wearing a face that said he was courteously thinking it over; and when he thought time enough had gone by he nodded his head slowly, as if he had come to a conclusion after careful consideration. "You may be right," he admitted. "I don't like to say that, Mr. President, because our justice system would collapse if we had to deal with all prisoners in-presence. But there's something to what you're saying."

And we're working on it, he thought, but he didn't say it aloud. It was better for the President not to know what was going on in the Cetacean Project in El Centro . . . until they were *certain.* Certain that computers modified to be more like the brain of a whale than the brain of a human being (in some sense he understood not at all, but clearly it was not anatomical) would, as the President had said, "get feelings." It would be a while before the prototype could be properly tested; no point raising premature hopes and then being obliged to frustrate them.

"We'll go right now," he had said, standing up, signaling with his eyes to Benny Mondorro that the meeting was over unless the President brought up something else to talk about.

"And report back. Immediately!"

"Yes, sir. By sometime this afternoon, if you've got a free spot in your schedule."

"I'll find one," said Tobias Dellwilder, his voice weary and grim and determined. "I'll cancel something, if necessary. Call it 4:30 p.m.?"

"We'll be here."

"And one more thing."

"Yes, Mr. President?"

"Keep one more thing in mind. Don't ever forget it for a second. *Remember,* gentlemen, that Cleo St. Andrews was born a woman of the linguist Lines."

Gently, because it was wisest, Zlerigeau said, "Sir, that doesn't make any difference."

"The hell it doesn't! Those women are witches . . . magicians . . . whatever. They can do uncanny things . . . they *know* things."

The Vice President, sitting by the window, was nodding solemnly, and he put in his penny-and-a-half's worth. "That's what people say," he announced. His face took on his Grave Matter expression. (It was one-third of his entire facial inventory: Grave Matter, I-LIKE-That!, and Vacant.) "I've heard that all my life."

Zlerigeau shrugged. "Once upon a time, perhaps," he said, "it may have had some truth to it. Long, long ago. Today those women are like any other women. I've dealt with them all *my* life, and I assure you, they're a little better educated than the average person, but otherwise just your typical middle-class woman. *Nevertheless*, since you've specified it, we will keep that fact especially in mind. You can count on us to make sure that—"

"Jay," the Vice President interrupted, "why do they teach music theory?"

"What?"

"Why do the women of the Lines teach music theory?"

The President made an irritated noise deep in his throat and turned his head to glare at Aron Strabida; he had abandoned some of the attitude of public deference toward the Vice President that had been his habit in the past. But Zlerigeau answered the question.

"They're used to working," he said. "The Lingoe women have always worked; they apparently aren't happy staying home. And music theory is closer to linguistic theory than . . . oh, say, geography would be. It makes perfectly good sense."

"Hmmmmm," said the Vice President, shifting from Grave Matter Face to Vacant Face. He had no interest in either music theory or linguistic theory. He had less than no interest in geography. So many planets . . . so many asteroids. So many *names*.

In the prizpod that had been inflated to fill her livingroom and bathroom, the two agents watched Cleo warily, through narrowed eyes. They had taken the time to review the threedy of her booking interrogation, done first by computer and then by allegedly skilled lawpers. They had watched and listened with amazement as she first sent the computers into nonsense loops—a baby trick, but not one the average criminal suspect had on tap—and then led the hastily substituted human questioners down one garden path after another. So that instead of skilled personnel finding out what the hell she was up to, the threedies had recorded blissed-out interrogators telling the woman long rambling stories about their childhoods. While she murmured at them about how *fascinating* it all was.

Jay Zlerigeau had reluctantly decided that the President might have been justified in his warning for this one *particular* woman of the Lines, and he had set up his plans to take that into account. He was sure this first meeting was going to be just a walkthrough; he had told the interrodoctor to stand by for a call. He opened by stating the facts. Just the facts. Ma'am.

"We've watched your earlier interrogation sessions, Miss St. Andrews," he said, "and we're grateful to you for bringing to our attention a gap in our training that we didn't know existed. I promise you: our next generation of lawpers will know how to deal with the strategy you used. And I promise you also: it won't work on me, or on my associate."

She cocked her head, smiled a charming smile, and told them how admirable that was; even in the shapeless beige prisonshift, even with her hair clipped almost to the scalp, she had elegance and style. Jay had assumed she would waste time insisting that she didn't know what they were talking about; he was relieved when she gave that option a pass, but he didn't like the fact that he'd made the wrong prediction. The new curriculum module for dealing with people like her, should they have the misfortune to have to do it again sometime, had been named "Southern Lady Unit."

"What we want to know," he said, settling in, doing his best to ignore the constant high nasal whine of the mechanism that kept them from suffocating inside the thick gray plastic, "is just this one thing. We want to know *why* you did what you did." He was careful. Not "why you killed Miss Brown." Not "why you are *pretending* that you killed Miss Brown." Just "why you did what you did."

"Well, gentlemen," she answered—and he realized that she was truly lovely, and set the observation firmly aside—"I did it because I had no choice."

"More, please."

She looked them right in the eye, something he disliked in any woman not presenting him with an open sexual invitation. Her expression was as serene and open as if she'd been entertaining them in a drawing room instead of a prizpod that should have brought her down a peg or two. And she said something she had not said before to any of her questioners, mechanical or human.

"When Marthajean Brown seduced Tobias Dellwilder," she said, "when she put herself in the position of being someone who is able to blackmail the President of the United States of Earth, she *betrayed* us. She put our cause at risk. *Intolerable* risk! We are opposed to violence, Mr. Zlerigau, but in a situation like this one there was no choice at all. We had to remove her."

Zlerigau sat up straighter in the sitniche, and he sensed his partner tensing beside him. The President would have been feeling smug if he'd been there; they were definitely getting a feeling.

"'We'?" It hung in the canned air. The infuriating whine grew louder, and one of the prizpod mechanisms set up a series of thumps and clicks; it sounded like someone old and weak and sick with a disgusting disease, coughing. "We?" he said again. "Us? *Our* cause?"

"Exactly," she said. "Yes indeed."

"Miss St. Andrews," said Benny; "who is this 'we'? This 'us'?"

She clucked her tongue . . . *Tsk!* . . . and smiled at him. "Now, you know I won't tell you that!" she said. "Why do you ask? Why *do* you ask that, really? On what basis . . ." She leaned toward them, her long slender fingers slowly stroking the sides of her throat, her eyes growing wide and bright, the pupils of her eyes growing larger. "On what basis does an investigator decide that it's useful to ask a question when he knows in advance that the prisoner won't answer it? Do you learn that as a strategy? Has it proved to be something worth doing? I would have thought—"

Jay nudged Benny sharply with his knee, cutting off the words that were about to be spoken and shame them both, and then cut off *her* words, too, as sharply as he knew how. "Miss St. Andrews! *Don't* try that with us. Drop it. You're wasting your time."

"Oh," she said softly, almost sadly. Letting her hands fall to her chest, where they lay crossed, with the long delicate fingers (that he could well imagine on the fingerboard of the classical guitar) spread wide. Letting her head drop toward the crossed hands, turned away, her eyes downcast, her lower lip trembling.

That would be Injured Innocence, Jay thought, *and perhaps a little touch of Guiltstricken Maiden Regretting Her Errors. It was all so* obvious! *How could his own lawpers, trained by him personally, have fallen for her crude tricks, telegraphed every step of the way?* It was such an unimpressive and amateurish and pathetic performance that he almost felt sorry for her; she'd be fluttering her eyelashes at them next, and wiping away a tiny tear.

"I am so sorry," she went on, looking first at Jay and then at Benny. "I'm sure you both know that I have only one intention, and that it is to cooperate fully with the police. After all, gentlemen—I came into your station of my own free will. I *confessed*, without even being asked. Why would a woman do that, with all the terrible consequences it entails, if she didn't want to cooperate?"

"That's easy! She would do it because—"

Zlerigau stopped short. She had him! She'd done it. In spite of the hour spent studying the threedy, analyzing her techniques, he had opened his fool mouth and been ready to launch into one of the monologues he'd watched the lawpers deliver. He consoled himself with the fact that he'd noticed what was happening immediately, and stopped. The study hadn't been wasted.

"You *will* tell us who you are associated with," he assured her. "Right now you think you won't. But you will."

"We have ways of making you talk?" She played it straight; she didn't add the trite accent.

"We do. *Legal* ways."

"Well, then, for heaven's sakes, let's get on with it!" Her eyes crinkled at the corners with tiny laugh lines, and her voice held no hint of the sarcasm he *knew* had to be behind her words. "Since I don't seem to be able to meet your standards on my own, let's get me some help; bring on your thumbscrews, or whatever."

Jay was angry with her; it was time to get past this obligatory stuff and get the real interrogation started. He set his teeth and jerked his head at Benny, who fired the closing questions: one, two, three.

"Who, precisely, did Marthajean Brown betray, Miss St. Andrews?"

"I won't tell you that."

"What is the 'cause' she endangered?"

"I won't tell you that."

"And why won't you?"

"I won't tell you that."

Jay sighed, and stood up. This was silly. It was boring. It was insulting. She was in *serious* trouble. She was locked up in an effing prizpod. And she sat there beaming at them, the perfect hostess, all charm and gracious living, so *terribly* sorry to have to refuse them anything, like the Queen of the effing May! Who the hell did she think she was? He'd had all of it he intended to tolerate.

"Come on, Benny," he mumbled, and then, "We'll just step outside and get the thumbscrews, Cleo, and we'll be right back. We have a couple of forms to fill out."

"I understand, officer."

"I'm sure you do."

"And I wish you the very best of luck in your endeavors."

Outside the prizpod, on the apartment's small balcony overlooking the street, Benny shuddered and took a great gulp of the air. It was polluted, but at least it was fresh. "I hated that," he said. "Kind of like being inside . . . oh, one of those bubbles in seaweed, maybe. You know? The kind kids like to pop? Those slick gray walls . . . I know they don't feel slimy, but they look like they would. Everything on the other side all distorted and blurry. And the *noise*. Think about being shut up in one of those for years at a time."

"Easy to avoid," Jay told him. "Just don't do any crimes."

"She hasn't done any, and *she's* in one."

Zlerigau ignored that, and entered into his wrist computer the codes that would summon the interrodoctor and remind him to bring along all the necessary forms.

"I'm not going to like *this*, either," Benny pointed out.

"I suppose you won't; you've always been a sucker for pretty women, Benny. But it's got to be done. Hell, you saw her—she was just playing with us. Just having *fun*, at our expense. We could have gone on doing that silly number for days, without ever getting anywhere useful!"

"Yeah, I noticed that."

"Well? Would you *prefer* thumbscrews?"

Benny shook his head. Of course he wouldn't. The mindtrap was painless; the woman would feel absolutely nothing, and would not even remember the experience. Still, he wished there was some way he could stay out here and let the other two men go on with the unsavory process without him. She looked too much like Annalaura. Even dressed as she was, even shorn very nearly bald as she was, she had Annalaura's heart-shaped face, and the same huge eyes, and the same soft low-pitched voice. When she talked, he could imagine easily that it was his wife's voice he heard. It was one thing watching a mindtrap fitted to some big hulking thug that had raped a little old lady or murdered some kid; this was going to be different.

"You know what I'd like to do to the Vice-effing-President?" he asked the world at large.

"You're wrong, Benny," said Zlerigau. "That poor no-neuron just happened to stumble into the middle of some kind of enormous mess—which Cleo Baby is going to tell us about. Sooner or later, it would have come out, and the longer it took the more likely it was to be a real catastrophe. The Veep just speeded things up a little."

"Yeah, but if it had been some other set of circumstances we might have been mindtrapping a *man* instead of . . . a lady."

Jay chuckled. Benedict Mondorro was one of the best. One of the *very* best. But it was lucky for the population he served that ninety-seven percent of all crime was committed by males.

They didn't get back to report to the President that afternoon after all, and the memo that presented Dellwilder with their reasons had made the President's face go suddenly white and old. It was late in the following day before the report was made, and Jay Zlerigau made it alone, Benny's security clearance having run out only four hours into the investigation. And Jay arrived at the Oval Office in bad shape; he'd had to call on the agency doctor twice for stimulants to keep him from falling asleep in the marathon of meetings that had followed Cleo St. Andrews's confession.

Meetings during which very serious consideration had been given to the contingency plan in which the Vice President is permanently removed from the scene. But a thorough look at the files on the man who would replace a deceased Aron Strabida had revealed numerous problems; in the end, it had been decided that a brief illness would suffice. Strabida was now resting comfortably in a luxury medsuite in Virginia where he could do no harm, sedated but still available at a moment's notice, with Benny keeping him company; Zlerigau fiercely envied them both.

"Well, Jay?" The President was abrupt; it was appropriate. "Let's have it." And then, as the silence continued, "Well? Are you here to report or *not*? I accept your reasons for this delay, and I've been patient, but enough is enough."

"Mr. President," Jay answered, trying to choose, each time he spoke one, the *perfect* word, "It's a cliché—but it's the only way to put it: I don't know how to begin. Much less how to go on with it."

"I'll help you," said the President curtly. "You couldn't get the woman to cooperate. You applied a mindtrap. You—"

"We didn't have to apply it, sir. We only had to *show* it to her. She wasn't especially brave; she caved in immediately when she saw it." It was the only small bit of satisfaction available to him, and he savored it; he would always treasure his memory of the terror in Cleo's eyes and her abrupt collapse from elegant rhetoric into frantic pleading. He only wished he'd made her plead a little longer; if he'd known what was coming, he would have made it harder on her. A *lot* harder.

"All right," the President conceded. "Fine. Revise it, then. You showed her a mindtrap, she quit resisting you and told you everything she knew, and now you are here to tell *me* everything she knew. I see no problem about how to begin except your dawdling. Begin at the beginning of what she said; go on to the end. Nothing could be simpler."

"Nothing about this report is going to be simple," Jay said grimly. "I'm damned near unable to say the necessary words—and you're not going to believe them when I do say them."

"Does that change anything? Will it make any of the words you're about to say to me *different* words?"

"No, sir."

"Then get *on* with it! What did she say to you that was so important that it brought . . ." The President stopped; there were names you did not say aloud, even in the Oval Office. "That made those meetings necessary. What, exactly, did she say? In three or four sentences, please. I'm not interested in a display of your rhetorical skills."

"All right, Mr. President. I'll try. But I must warn you—with all due respect, sir—to let me just say them straight through. Interrupting will only confuse me."

The President's fists struck the top of his desk, but he said nothing. He glared at his most senior and trusted agent, and he waited in silence.

Jay collected his thoughts for a moment, and then he said, "Here we go; one two three four. ONE: Cleo St. Andrews confessed to us that the women of the Lines—*all* of them, sir!—have for centuries been running a secret conspiracy that stretches throughout the entire solar system. TWO: That a serious federal investigation of the murder of Marthajean Brown—not a woman of the Lines, but related to them through the PICOTA, and a coconspirator—would have put that conspiracy at risk. THREE: That St. Andrews confessed to the murder in an effort to forestall such an investigation. And FOUR: That her confession was an impulsive act, not cleared with any of her colleagues, and a mistake, since she has brought about all by herself the very disaster she was willing to sacrifice her life to prevent." He paused and took a deep breath. "There you are, Mr. President; four sentences."

The silence went on and on; Jay was in no way surprised by that. He had expected it.

"Nothing that . . . extravagantly absurd," declared the President, finally, "could possibly be true."

"I'm sorry to have to disagree, sir. The fact is, nothing that

179

extravagantly absurd could possibly be *false*. Nobody could make *up* anything that absurd. In spite of every rational consideration, it's as true as it is true that I sit here before you now."

"Perhaps you are a simulacrum, Zlerigau."

"And perhaps *you* are, Mr. President. It's equally likely."

I could be *a simulacrum*, he thought. Certainly he was not the same man who had sat here and talked to the President with such serene self-confidence about Plan A and Plan B a few days ago. He was a man in some kind of shock, he was reasonably sure. The world he knew had been a rug under his feet. Giving him purchase. Letting his feet and his brain know everything was all right. And then that rug had been pulled out from under him.

"What kind of . . ." Dellwilder choked on the words, and then got them out, half-strangled, ". . . secret conspiracy?"

Zlerigau knew he had no choice. *Spit it out*, he told himself. *Just spit it out and wait for the storm to break over you.*

"Mr. President, those unspeakable Lingoe bitches have found a way to wipe out hunger." He saw the President's mouth open; he brought both hands up sharply, cutting off the interruption. "Pretending to be music teachers, Mr. President, they have taught a large percentage of the citizens of this planet—and sizable percentages, we're not yet sure precisely how large, of the citizens in the colonies—how to live by substituting music for *food*." He swallowed hard, and finished, "They call it *audiosynthesis*, Mr. President."

There. He'd said it. He braced himself, and the President didn't disappoint him.

Tobias Dellwilder cried out; it was the sound of a man pushed past endurance. "God *damn* it, Jay!" he shouted. "You would have to be part of a conspiracy yourself—a conspiracy to drive me *mad*—to stand there in my face and spout such *shit*! I've been walking the floor of this office, waiting for somebody to tell me— to tell *me*, the President of the United States of Earth!—what the hell was going on. Trying to maintain some kind of appearances. And when you finally get here you tell me a thing like that! Have you gone completely out of your *mind*?"

"I know how you feel, sir," said Jay helplessly. "I don't blame you a bit. I've heard all of this now several times, from several different persons. I *know* it to be the truth. But let me tell you, sir, I don't *believe* it. I've seen the figures . . . I've read the reports . . . I still react to it exactly as you are reacting now. I cannot make myself look at it as anything but the ravings of someone demented. Demented. And not very bright. Nevertheless, Mr. President, nevertheless—it is God's truth."

And he added, softly, "Remember, sir—it was *you* who told me solemnly that the Lingoe bitches could do magic. That they were witches. Remember? And you were absolutely *right*."

"Jay!"

The President leaned over the desk, then realized that he couldn't reach across it and came striding out from behind it to grip Zlerigau by both forearms. "You listen to me!" he shouted, as the agent tried, and failed, to pull away. "There cannot be a conspiracy, a conspiracy that size, to do *good*!"

That surprised Zlerigau; it wasn't on his list. He had been prepared for the reactions everyone else had had. *Human beings living and thriving without food? Impossible! An interplanetary conspiracy of women kept secret for centuries? Fairy tales! Come on! Smirk, smirk . . . snicker, snicker.* Dellwilder's reaction was a new one.

"I don't understand you, sir," he said slowly, disengaging himself as courteously as he could; the man holding him was, after all, the President. He couldn't just slap his hands away and shove his face in, as he would have done with anybody else. "You're going to have to help me out with that one."

"Jay," said Tobias Dellwilder, stepping back two paces, his arms falling to his sides, "all of human society, all of human culture, rests on the knowledge we have . . . oh, we don't *admit* it, of course, but we all have it . . . that human beings are only capable of really buckling down and working together in groups when their goals are *evil*. They'll do it for money or power or conquest . . . they'll do it to be famous, to get themselves on the threedies and the newspapes . . . But a conspiracy to *feed everybody*? No, Jay. That's not possible. That is a thing that could not happen."

Jay realized he had been holding his breath while Dellwilder babbled; he let it go now with a long sigh. Behind the drugs they'd pumped into him he could feel the hooks of the exhaustion that was clinging to him, waiting to be turned loose. And he wasn't sure exactly how to handle this. Like Benedict Mondorro, he was monumentally unimpressed by the series of men who had held the office of US President over the past several centuries; no really *top* man would touch the office. On the other hand, it remained one of the most important positions, in symbolic terms, that a man could fill. You didn't like to think that the President was really *stupid*. It was a tremendous relief to him when he saw Dellwilder's face change and realized that the man had suddenly understood.

"Dear Christ, Jay!" breathed the President. He had used more curses, taken the Almighty's name in vain more times, during this one conversation, than Zlerigau had heard him do in all the years he'd known him. "I've got it all wrong."

"Yes, Mr. President."

"I've got it backwards. Let's assume, just for one minute, just for the purpose of discussion, that this idea—feeding people with music—isn't a fantasy. That it's not like telling kids about the Easter Bunny. Let's say that, as you appear to be telling me, it's actually true. In that case, Jay, my God, whoever controls that process has the *ultimate power*! *That's* why they did it—not for *good*, of course not! They did it for *power*!"

Whoever controls that process? How? How do you control it? Jay thought. Aloud, he said, "Almost sir."

"Almost? Why almost?"

"They tell me that finding a way to substitute something for *water* would be, as you put it, the *ultimate* power. But this comes very, very close."

"Jay, it would mean . . . Wait. Do we know what it would mean?"

"No." Zlerigau coughed, his throat raw from the drugs and from all the useless talking. "No. Nor did those goddamn *women*. We asked them, 'Did you have *any* idea what you were *doing*? What would *happen* if you did it?' And they admitted that they'd had no idea at all. 'We knew it would change things,' they said. It would *change* things! But they went right ahead, ignorant as shit, tampering with the very heart of all human life. *Women! Damn them!*" There were tears in his eyes, he realized; he didn't care. "Can you believe it, Dellwilder? The Lingoe men—they didn't know . . . they didn't know *anything!*"

"Never mind that," Dellwilder said. "I can believe that; it doesn't even surprise me. Are you telling me that the group you've been meeting with—the best people *alive*—are as ignorant as that pack of witches? Is that what you're saying?"

"No. In a *way*, we know what it means. In broad general terms. The computers are running the specifics right now." He didn't tell the President what the women had said about that: "*Every time you put a new variable into the model the computer gives you a radically different output . . . and there are literally* millions *of appropriate variables.*" Instead, he said, "We know one thing for sure. We know that if audiosynthesis is as widespread as the women claim, what it means is just plain the end of the world. The end of *this* world, sir. All of human life from the beginning of time, all of culture, all of economics, everything, has revolved around the need for food. Take that away . . . you don't have human life any longer."

"What *do* you have?"

"I don't know, Mr. President. I don't think anybody does . . . maybe the Lingoe bitches do."

The President had been standing all this time; he sat down suddenly, like something deflating.

Jay knew how his mind must be racing, how the questions would be flooding him, how the implications would be pouring in, each with its *own* wave of questions. There was nothing he could do to help, except by giving Dellwilder the files he had brought, where the information was set down in a manner that allowed you to move from item to item at your own pace instead of just being buried in it.

He set the chiplet down beside the other man, saying, "Here are the reports from the meetings, Mr. President, with statistics and rough extrapolations . . . that kind of thing. It's all preliminary, of course, but it organizes the chaos a little. There's also a file on there from the women . . . something they gave us when we confronted them with Cleo St. Andrews's confession. And there's a file that will absolutely amaze you . . ."

"More than I'm already amazed . . . that's not possible."

"It's a different kind of amazement. It's the record of the financial transactions these women have carried on all these many hundreds of years."

"Jay, it's only been decades since they were given their adult status back. They can't have done that much financially."

The agent looked at him, and smiled. "Think," he said. "If you were part of a large group that every week received sums of money to buy food, but you didn't *need* any food except just a little for purposes of deception. And every week—for centuries, Mr. President—you put almost all of that money into investments and projects of your own choosing. If you let the invested money sit and draw compound interest. If the projects you chose were the worst and most destructive kinds of social ones . . . like supplying millions and millions of meals for people in famine areas that you hadn't yet been able to get to with your training in not *needing* food. Like blanketing the solar system with supplies of vaccines and medicines, all from an 'anonymous' donor, assumed to be male. Like buying up businesses that trade in weapons, Mr. President, and simply shutting them down, letting them sit idle, with phony excuses. Like—" He stopped. "I'm sorry. It's all on the chiplet, sir. For you to examine at your own convenience."

Dellwilder looked utterly stunned; he sagged, and then he shook himself, a wet dog of a man, and went around the desk to sit down in his chair.

"You are prepared to tell me," he said to Jay, "to *swear* to me, that this audiosynthesis business is a valid concept. That our top people agree that it is."

"Yes, I am. Mad as it seems, I am." And he added, "The women say, and *our* people agree, that it isn't even anything new. It's been lying around since the first writing system, but the only people who ever used it were religious fanatics. Nobody ever paid any attention."

"It's like photosynthesis, for plants. It's *free*."

"Yes, sir."

"Zlerigau . . ."

"Yes, sir." He knew what was coming next.

"It's got to be *stopped*!" the President shouted at him. "It can't have gotten very far. Not really very far. God knows everybody *I* know still eats food, three times a day! We've got to stamp this out. Advertising campaigns solar system wide, on all the comsets, to make people crazy about food . . . the look of it, the smell and the taste of it. Scientific reports about what audiosynthesis *really* does to the human body!" He was sitting up straight now, beginning to look once again like the symbol that he embodied. Taking *charge*. The leader of the free universe, in action again. "I want spectacular fakes, Jay! Studies proving that audiosynthesis dissolves bone. Fries blood. Turns you into a fungus. I don't care how ridiculous the conclusions are, just as long as they're scary enough. And I want—"

He stopped, suddenly, with an exclamation of pain, and covered his face with his hands.

"*Gets* to you, doesn't it?" Jay said, no longer caring whether he sounded sufficiently respectful. The stimulants were wearing off, and he could feel himself sliding. Sliding down into the darkness of truly not giving a *damn*. About anything.

"You know, Dellwilder," he went on, dreamily, "I would have sworn that I was *not* somebody who wanted to see babies starving and women weeping over their skeletal little bodies. I thought I was a decent man. Suppose you'd said to me, 'Hey, we just found out that we can end hunger forever, for all human beings, everywhere in the inhabited universe!' I would have *sworn* I was a man you could have counted on to rejoice about that. And it turns out that that's not *true*. It turns out that if fixing it so babies don't starve means my life has to be changed into something I don't recognize, I'm willing to let them starve. I'm *eager*."

The look on the President's face told him that the President felt the same way about it. That it was no longer possible for the President to know, either, what was *good* and what was *evil*, because it all ran together for him now the way it did for Jay.

"It has to be stopped," the President said again. "Now. Right *now*. It cannot, must not, be allowed to go on for even one more day. No matter what has to be done. No matter who has to be removed. It has to be *stopped*!" Dellwilder was shaking all over; if Jay hadn't been in even worse shape, he would have hit the alarm that brought the White House doctor in here at a run.

"They're working on it, Mr. President," he said softly, just before the drugs ran out at last and he slipped into unconsciousness. "Round the clock. They're working on it."

CHAPTER 13

*We were greatly worried at that time about the men—about how
to give them a sense of Being that wasn't tied to how strong (or
how rich, or how cruel) they were. We talked endlessly of finding
them a new metaphor—not Warrior, not King, not Giant, not Wild
Man, not Iron Man, not Owner of Most Toys—and of finding a way
to insert that metaphor into the culture for them. We did this; and
we listened courteously to the arguments of those among us who
said we were wasting our time, that the only appropriate thing
to do with regard to men was to step back and let them destroy
themselves.*

*This was before the Icehouse Effect gripped Earth in its teeth
and shook us like a big dog shakes a kitten. This was before we
saw how human men . . . most human men . . . were so helpless
before the cold that the only metaphor we could find for them was
Lost Child. When that happened, we set all such matters aside and
concerned ourselves only with seeing to it that as many human
males as possible survived. In that terrible time we no longer
listened to the Abandoners. We said to them only, "Don't start."
And they held their peace, because anything else would have been
indecent.*

(Archive entry; Belle-Charlotte Adiness St. Syrus)

FROM THE ARCHIVES OF: Chornyak Barren House
ENTRY OF: Ruth Aquina Chornyak Adiness

We knew many years before the murder of Marthajean Brown
that the Audiosynthesis Project had spread far enough to guarantee that it could not be stopped. Even if the governments banned

all musical performances and made it a federal offense to own any device that provides music. Even if they found a way to monitor "consumption" of music and levy taxes on every citizen, based on personal totals. Even if they jailed parents who refused to feed mouthfood to their children. Even if they set up programs to constantly torment those learning audiosynthesis with multisensory holograms of mouthfood. Even if they managed to create epidemics of deafness by deviant medicine and outlawed the surgery that allows the deaf to hear when hearing is their preference. Even if they did worse things.

The Holy One knows, governments are skilled at finding things so profoundly evil that they startle the rational mind; nevertheless, we were sure they could not win this round. We were certain that even though they might be able to stamp out audiosynthesis in limited areas, for limited periods of time, they could not do so on any general basis. It isn't possible to observe every person, at every moment. Sounds are easy to hide, and they don't have to be *loud* to be nourishing. Nor is it possible to stop evolution by force. We had learned by then that no one who had had the opportunity to live by sound alone for a year or two would ever willingly go back to mouthfood again. Not once the habit was broken.

Not even those who, like most people who grew up eating food, still felt the lust of the mouth. In spite of that lust, they came to have so strong a distaste for mouthfood that they almost could not bring themselves to eat it; so much of it was, they realized, *dead flesh*. The dead flesh of animals. Usually, something that had been alive had to be dead, to provide them with mouthfood, and they knew it. Except for foods that did not require killing . . . fruit, for example, that could be picked and still leave the plant thriving . . . the feeling was much like the distaste people have always felt for eating human flesh. (Think only of how much intense training it takes for our MGTs to be able to manage, since they must take sometimes music, sometimes mouthfood, as the situation requires! It's not easy.)

At that point, after we were quite certain that it was safe to stop hiding the Project, we added an arbitrary fifty years to the secrecy—just in case. Just to hedge all bets. Experience has taught us to allow that kind of margin. Because even when you think you have set down every conceivable circumstance that might occur to hamper you in what you're doing, even when you're certain you've analyzed every item and found ways to deal with it, outsiders will surprise you by adding a dozen items to your list that you failed to think of. It comes of living in among the trees where you cannot see the forest.

During those extra fifty years, we tackled the question that we had always dreaded (and that was the logical extrapolation of Delina Chornyak Bluecrane's original question, "Who do we tell?"):

How do we turn this loose?

How were we to make it public? What was the best way to tell the populations of every human world that no one ever needs to go hungry again? That it was no longer necessary to earn money in order to eat? How were we to make audiosynthesis training universal? How could we get people—people who had abundant food supplies available to tempt them—past the difficult early stages? How were we to soften the shock and betrayal that our past and present students would feel when they understood why they so rarely felt any need to do more than toy politely with their food? We had *lied* to them, day after day, for as long as they had known us; they would be justified in feeling outraged, and they might never be able to forgive us.

And then there was the hardest question of all: what would *happen* once the information was out? What would happen when the rich and the powerful realized that much of their advantage over the rest of humanity had been to a substantial degree *canceled*? There was no way, no way at all, to answer that one. No matter how many times we ran our computer models, hoping for resolution, they only confirmed our human fears, agreeing with us that almost anything was possible.

We knew there was the very real possibility that the women of the Lines would be slaughtered in the first waves of rage, those waves that would be the birth pangs of the first race of human beings to take its sustenance from sound rather than from flesh. Birth pangs are good in the long run; women who are weary to death of hauling babies about in the womb long for them. But they are brutal and messy and painful and, once begun, unstoppable. We were too many to hide, and no match for the forces that could be brought against us. There was no way to make *sure* it wouldn't happen, as there is no way to be sure you won't die at the tip of a lightning bolt. We had accepted that; but we thought we ought to be able to find ways to make it very unlikely. The strategy we chose was the one that has so often been our mainstay:

> *Don't tell them; let them "discover" it for themselves.*
> *So they feel that it is their knowledge, gained by their*
> *efforts, and won by their skill at overcoming your*
> *puny attempts to prevent them.*

We were satisfied with that plan; we decided upon it by consensus and we were agreed that it was best. We didn't stop there. We constructed more than thirty substrategies for implementing it, to be distributed among the women of the Lines. In the linguist Households; in the churches and chapels of Our Lady of the Star-Tangle; and among the linguist women of the Meandering Water tribe, most of whom were living with PICOTA husbands and families. We worked it all out in detail.

And *that* was where we got stuck.

I have no idea how long we might have stayed like that, smack against the cliff face and unwilling to budge. We were so afraid! So full of what-ifs. What if we had miscalculated and should have added ten more years of secrecy, or twenty, or a hundred and twenty?

What if we didn't do the "allow discovery" process with sufficient skill, and people learned that that was what we were up to, before enough time had gone by so that they could forgive us for it?

What *if*?

We were just plain scared. We had always been scared, because it had always been possible that we'd be caught. But that was a *chronic* sort of fear. Background noise. This fear was not chronic but acute. This was not "I might die one of these days if things go wrong" but "I might very well die tomorrow before nine-thirty." This was *different*.

We are ordinary human women, with the same fondness for our own skins that other human beings have. We dithered and dawdled and procrastinated and waited "just one more week" over and over and over again. I admit, and we would all admit, that we were scared useless. Perhaps we would *never* have told, if left to our own devices? It's a terrible thought, and I won't try to imagine the results of such a course of action—or inaction—but I won't try to deny that it might have been our choice.

However, as often happens, we were saved by a fanatic. Cleo St. Andrews saw the news story about the murder of the President's secretary. She recognized it as the perfect opportunity to raise the suspicion of a conspiracy of women and bring an investigation down upon us. And she marched straight into the Washington, DC, police station and—as flamboyantly as possible—confessed to the murder. Just like that! Without any consultation. Without any discussion. She knew . . . of *course* she knew . . . what would happen if she called a needlework circle meeting and proposed the idea: she'd be overruled. She didn't chance it. Just thought, *At last! The perfect opportunity!* and off she went to seize it. Only fanatics behave like that. We must always be grateful that they exist, infuriating though they surely are, as catalysts to overcome our understandable human hesitations.

Cleo's failure to let any of us in on her plan did have one compelling advantage to set against its abruptness and lack of careful consideration. It made our confusion and our fear when the police came knocking at our door (with the men of the Lines right behind them demanding an explanation, of course!) convincing. It was absolutely genuine. Nobody had to put on an act. Nothing that had happened to us since the terrible day when the Aliens first abandoned humankind had come upon us with such suddenness and such crushing force. That may have saved us much suffering in the initial turmoil; for *sure* it saved us the agony of having to make a decision for or against her plan. We owe her more than we can say—for getting us past the hook we were dangling on; for leaving all of us innocent of responsibility; for taking all the potential guilt upon herself.

> To the women yet to be born . . .
> Ruth Aquina Chornyak Adiness

CHAPTER 14

The women of the Lines might have been willing to go in person to the UNE satellite; nobody asked them. It might have been possible to ensure their safety; the issue was not raised.

The United Asian Alliance had been particularly strident on the subject. "These so-called women have destroyed our worlds!" the head of the delegation had hissed in his meticulous Panglish, with his hands curled like claws, palms up, before his face. "Human beings, gentlemen, could not *do* what *they* have done. We were right to call the linguists evil; we were right to treat them as pariahs. Our error was in backing down and accepting them into the human community as we did. You *see* how they have repaid us! They have made *rubble* of our lives! They have bitten out our living hearts and spat them onto the bare *ground*! I will not stay in a room where such devils are permitted to roam free!"

"It was only the *female* linguists," said the member from New Ireland. "It's unfair to blame the Households of the Lines in their entirety for a wickedness that is confined to their women."

Ahmling Medde Sang made a rude noise, and the curled fingers tightened into fists. "You believe that?" he shouted. "You believe that women, all on their own, could have devised a plan like this and carried it out, over *centuries*? More fool you, if you believe that!" He shook both fists frantically; it was clear that his anger overwhelmed him.

As it overwhelmed them all. If there had been a way to make ending hunger a criminal act under the law of any nation, the women of the Lines would have been locked away by now; if it had been up to Medde Sang, they would have all been *hanged*, every last one of them, and there were many who agreed with him. He went on, speaking more softly now, the anguish building in his voice, saying, "I tell you there was a *man*—some one man of a vileness impossible to imagine, driven only by an all-consuming lust for *power*—running that pack of females!"

"He lived hundreds of years, Medde Sang?"

"This is no matter for jokes—do not insult us with your attempts at *humor*! There was a man, and he passed the task on to someone in the next generation, and so on down through all the years until this day; that is as obvious to you as it is to me. We may never know who he is . . . who he was . . . it fills me with awe that he has been able to remain hidden . . . but he has to exist. I agree that with the situation as it is, hunting him down would be a stupid waste of resources; I agree, let him go anonymous into history. It's the only rational course to follow. *However . . .*" He held up one finger to mark the importance of his words, "How*e*ver, the women of the Lines were his puppets, and they did their foul work at his bidding! If they come into this hall, gentlemen, I leave—and all my delegation *with* me!"

The shouts of "And so do I!" "And that goes for us, too!" made the consensus amply clear. On the dais at the front of the crescent-shaped room the UNE's chairman had raised both his hands in a gesture of surrender. "All right," he said. "Very well. I understand. And I will advise the Lines that their delegation is ordered to appear . . . a small delegation, carefully chosen . . . tomorrow morning, by comset only."

He didn't try to gavel them into silence, or to control the hubbub in any way. Like the rest of them, the outrage he felt burned in his heart and mind like a live coal. The dilemma was impossible either to bear or to escape. *The end of hunger for all mankind has arrived; I should rejoice. Celebrations are in order. The end of my life has arrived; my heart is broken; I can only mourn.*

In a random silence, he heard the voice of a delegate from the United States fiercely declaring that this is what happens when you make it illegal for men to beat their wives, and he made a note. No adult male finds it necessary to use *physical* force to control women; it was time the man was replaced and sent for

medical observation. He would advise the head of the US delegation to see to it, and this time he would not agree to diplomatic
postponements.

In response to the UNE's order, the women of the Lines put
together a delegation of five, one for each of the traditional colors
of humankind.

For the whites they chose Amalie Noumarque Chornyak,
because she was tall and imposing and gifted with a presence
that could hush whole roomfuls of the unruly. In case something
went wrong, they chose Noukhane Lin Verdi, with her month-old
daughter, Mary Leaf, to represent the yellow peoples. Noukhane
was their most brilliant and skilled spontaneous strategist, and the
baby was a superb prop. Sharowa Ndal Adiness, whose voice was
so compelling that you could not keep from hanging on her every
word no matter *what* she might be saying, was there to represent
and honor the blacks. The browns had Judith Lopez St. Syrus,
chosen for her grace of bearing and her beauty. And Cheris Shan-
nontry Bluecrane, a woman of the Meandering Water Tribe, stood
for the red peoples.

"Your role, Cheris," they told her, "is to feed the eye. Beads,
please. Feathers. Bells. Whatnot. The rest of us will be in our usual
plain tunics; we need you for bird of plumage."

"Among the birds," Cheris reminded them, "it is ordinarily the
male who is spectacular to look at."

"Moot point, Cheris, since there *are* no males of your tribe. We
want you absolutely *splendid*, please."

There had been much hilarity in the Womanhouses when the
committee announced its selections after their hasty meeting.
"Perceive," someone had said, "there's nobody to represent the
greens! You've left them out!" What passed for water on the
pseudo-planet Hoos had turned its population the color of young
grass; it wasn't unreasonable to say that there was now a race of
greens who were more *truly* green than any human beings had
ever been truly red or white or yellow.

Why not a representative for all the *tall* peoples of humankind?
Why not someone for all the *fat* ones? Ona Chornyak suggested

that she herself go along to stand for all *left-handed* humans. At Chornyak Womanhouse the game of suggestions went on, growing more and more raucous, until Noukhane began tapping her fingertips together in front of her face and peering at them over the steepling.

"Well, Noukhane?" Ona challenged her. "None of this is any sillier than what you're actually proposing. Red and black and white and yellow and brown? With Cheris as Token Exotic? It's absurd! You know what it reminds me of? Those doll-of-the-month clubs they huckster on the shopping threedies!"

"There is a reason," said Noukhane. "There are *two* reasons."

"And they are?"

"One woman per alleged human color is something the members of the UNE . . . and the men of the Lines . . . will accept without question. It will keep them from wondering why we chose this particular one and not that particular one; it will keep them from perceiving plots and stratagems."

"Ah. And the other reason?"

"And," said Noukhane, "it will serve as a symbol."

"Of what?"

"Of traditionalism. They say that we've ended human life; this says that we remember and honor it still, and from its deepest and most ancient roots."

"But why should we say *that*?"

"For that matter," put in another, "why should we do this at all?"

"We've been over it a dozen times," Noukhane reminded them. "You know we have. And it was decided: nothing can be gained by seeming to oppose the United Nations of Earth, and nothing will be lost by seeming to accommodate them."

"No skin off our noses?"

"Exactly. We want to *distract* them from this flap about 'an interplanetary secret conspiracy of women,' not *focus* them on it by making them lose face."

"It *is* an interplanetary conspiracy of women," Ona pointed out, "and until now, it always *has* been secret!"

"Yes—but the sooner they forget that, the better."

"They want to lecture us," said Noukhane's mother. "You are providing them with the opportunity. A public scolding, you perceive."

Noukhane laughed. "A ceremony honoring us for heroism is too much to expect," she said.

The five women sat courteously listening through the speeches, in each of which they were rebuked one more time for not having gone *immediately* to male scientists with Delina Chornyak Bluecrane's rediscovery of audiosynthesis and were sternly advised that by their egotistical and childish behavior they had held back the process inexcusably and condemned millions of human beings to hunger that could have been prevented.

They understood that these things had to be said. The members' constituents, watching the proceedings on their comsets, would have rioted worldwide if they had not been said. *You do not interrupt an adult temper tantrum; the raver will only begin again at the beginning and go on longer.* The baby tucked into Noukhane's ample sleeve was lulled by the droning; she slept quietly the entire time.

The crucial message was then delivered by the President of the United States of Earth himself. In person. He had insisted on it. He began by running through a few accusatory paragraphs from the script the other speakers had been using, watching the women carefully. It was incomprehensible to him that they could simply sit there, as serene as if he were reciting nursery rhymes at them. He had prepared carefully for this, eager to the depths of his heart for the opportunity to pillory them, relishing the fact that the UNE had the power to make them just sit there and *take* it, no matter how brutally they were attacked. He had been trembling with the anticipation of watching them squirm under the lash of his tongue; he had been prepared, when they tried to speak in their own defense, to come back at them in a way that made them look like what they were: Unspeakably filthy Judases. Betrayers of all humankind. He had had a whole litany of such phrases ready to be fired at them. He had been ready to reduce them to hysteria, he had hardly been able to wait to get at them and bring that off. How could they just sit there smiling at him, without even a flicker of response in their eyes? It was intolerable.

And then suddenly understanding dawned on him, and he relaxed. *They're* drugged, he realized. *Of course. It had been a mistake, letting them attend only by comset; if they'd had to come in person they would have been checked for drugs and given anti-dotes on the spot.* But it was too late to change that now, and he was wasting his time; they were protected by their chemicals against anything he could say. Because that was how it was, he cut short his prepared words and went straight to the list of demands, pausing only to send the assembly a brief clarifying message before he began speaking.

"This," he said to the women then, worn out now both by his passion and by his disappointment, "is what you will do—and I *warn* you: we will tolerate no argument.

> *"You will immediately send your best MGTs to the US Department of Education, where they will assist on a crash basis in the development of a Panglish cur-riculum series for the mass-ed computers—to teach audiosynthesis to all the children of the inhabited universe.*
>
> *"You will immediately send other MGTs to every gov-ernment agency of Earth to train its officials in audio-synthesis and assist in the development of inexpensive threedy courses for adults."*

"We've got to have a better name for it," the President said crossly, interrupting himself. "You can't expect us to go around saying 'audiosynthesis'! We have our best people working on that."

> *"You will immediately send women of the Lines, skilled in audiosynthesis, out to designated posts in the colonies—to counsel and comfort the populations as they make the transition from mouthfood to music.*

"And you will immediately turn over to us the Archives of the Barren Houses and the Womanhouses, so that the useful information they contain about all these matters can be entered into the government computers of every human nation and shared with their populations."

The President would have liked to end with something like "And may you burn forever in the depths of hell," but that wouldn't have looked or sounded presidential; he settled for "And may God have mercy on your souls."

He'd said nothing about appropriating the wealth that the women of the Lines had accumulated over the centuries; because its source had been the *men* of the Lines, there seemed to be no way to do that legally. But it pleased him to know that taxes and penalties of enormous size could legally be assessed against those vast fortunes, and that the invoices were being drawn up by the computers at that very moment.

The farmers of Earth and the agrirobot companies were demanding compensation on the grounds that audiosynthesis was going to put them out of business; similar claims were pouring in from every profession and business involved in the production and preparation and serving and advertising and distribution of food. Because there could be no end to this chain of demands, because every segment of the economy directly affected by audiosynthesis was intricately linked to every other segment, it was clear that the only possible solution was a total prohibition of *all* claims. That decision would be announced by the State Department as soon as the world's people had had a few days to recover from their current state of shock. And it delighted Tobias Dellwilder that the funds necessary to ease the inevitable suffering during the years of transition would then be under the direct control of the government of the United States of America. Not all of the members of the assembly would share his opinions about that, of course, and on the colonial worlds that counted on Terran consumers the temporary return to colonialism was going to create interplanetary turmoil. But the President, despite his fear of what was to come, was looking forward to managing all that money.

When they saw that the speech was over, the men of the UNE delegations sat motionless in the silence that follows any catharsis. The note that had been flashed to them from Tobias Dellwilder's wrist computer—"THESE WOMEN HAVE ALL BEEN DRUGGED!"—had made everything clear. It had deprived them of the pleasure they would have taken in watching the Lingoe bitches suffer a little, but it had comforted them, too. If the women hadn't known what was coming, and feared it, they wouldn't have resorted to drugs. There was some satisfaction in knowing that at least they had been *afraid*.

Now the delegates—

OUT OF THE NIGHT, OUT OF THE RAGING BLIZZARD, CAME A MAN IN A BLACK CAPE, CARRYING A DYING WOMAN IN HIS ARMS. "HELP!" HE SHOUTED, THE SNOW SWIRLING AROUND HIM IN THE DOORWAY, "I—"

???

THE TRANCER MOANS SOFTLY . . . "I CAN'T HELP IT," SHE SAYS. "I AM SO SORRY. I KNOW IT'S ALL SCRAMBLED AND ROUGH . . . I'LL TRY AGAIN."

THIS IS THE FOREST PRIMEVAL. THE MURMURING PINES AND THE HEMLOCKS, BEARDED WITH MOSS AND IN GARMENTS GREEN, INDISTINCT IN THE TWILIGHT—

????

"WAIT," SAYS THE TRANCER. "PLEASE. WAIT. I AM HAVING A VERY HARD TIME. FORGIVE ME; I THANK YOU FOR YOUR PATIENCE. NOW . . ."

The delegates waited only to hear what terms and conditions the women would try to establish, wondering whether, in their drugged condition, they *would* try. The men were prepared to bring up a retroactive law against "the willful withholding of information critical to the survival of the human race" as a way of demonstrating who was in charge here. It turned out not to be necessary.

"We would be delighted," said Sharowa Ndal Adiness, her voice filling the room like molten gold flowing warm and thick over black marble. "I speak for all of us, and for all the members of the Households of the Lines, when I tell you so."

And she *was* delighted; she spoke the truth. The seniors in the Barren Houses had been almost perfectly accurate in their predictions of what would be demanded; it had only been a bit simpler than they had expected. Nothing had gone wrong in this command appearance; no confrontations had had to be dealt with; boredom had been the only unpleasantness. And the edited copy of the Archives was at this very minute sitting on the desk in the Oval Office at the White House, waiting for the President's return. It was all very satisfactory.

"We will be very pleased to comply," she assured the delegates, inclining her head a measured fraction of an inch, "and to cooperate with you in every way possible."

Just like that?

The chairman of the UNE cleared his throat and asked, cautiously, if there wasn't something more the distinguished ladies wished to say, but Sharowa only smiled again. In Noukhane's sleeve the baby responded to a skilled bounce or two by growing restless, and Sharowa reached over to take Mary Leaf from Noukhane. "You are referring," she said, cradling the baby before her in her arms, rocking it gently, her attention clearly on the child and not on the assembly, "to the formal *details*. For that information, gentleman, I refer you to Thomas Barlow Chornyak of Chornyak Household." She looked up from the baby briefly, saying, "And now I am sure that you have no further need for us.

Good afternoon to you, gentlemen!" And the image of the five women and the child disappeared from the dais.

The delegates gave one long collective sigh and moved immediately to excited discussion among themselves, falling into the usual political groups and subgroups, while the chairman pounded the gavel for order without effect, also as usual. They would have preferred carte blanche for "the formal details," of course, but they had known that to be unrealistic. The linguist men no longer had any special power, but they had been trained to *remember* having it; they would relish this opportunity to be in control again, however briefly. The delegates understood that, and would have felt the same way if the situation had been reversed. What mattered was knowing that things could move forward now—that the negotiations would not have to be carried on, infuriatingly, with a bunch of women.

It was a tremendous relief to them. Women don't know how the game is played.

The Interplanetary Women's Congress had an elegant office in San Antonio, opening on the old River Walk, a place of fountains and tiles and plants and tasteful pieces of art. They had an even fancier office in Geneva, overlooking the lake. But when the PICOTA envoy Banyon Jordacha went to apologize on behalf of the tribes, he didn't go to either of those places; he went to headquarters.

He found Delina Jefferson sitting at a narrow worktable putting the final touches on an Ozark rainbow wreath. He waited a minute to be sure she'd seen him, and then he said, *"Nice!"* It was a fair comment; the wreath itself was a sturdy circle of Virginia creeper vine as thick as his thigh, and the God's-eye in the seven bands of rainbow color that filled its center glowed up at him. Delina cut no corners in the craft-work that filled her shop. No sloppy wreaths made by just winding vine around and around and fastening it off. No cheap yarns for the *ojos*. Nothing glued that should have been sewn or set with pegs or woven in; no imitations. Only the best of both materials and craft, always. Banyon respected that, and he decided that if the price was not completely beyond his means he would buy the rainbow wreath for his oldest sister's fiftieth birthday, coming up on him fast and not yet attended to.

"Banyon!" she said, sounding very pleased. "*Wil sha*, Banyon."

"Hello, Delina."

Banyon nodded at her, pleased to see her in his turn, wishing he weren't here on formal business—but then, of course, he wouldn't have been here at all. He didn't know Delina in person, but he'd been talking to her threedy image in councils much of his life; they were old friends.

"I'm glad you like the wreath," she said. "And I will give it to you for Nordranna's fiftieth birthday, if you think she would find it acceptable."

Banyon grinned in spite of his determination to stay solemn; now he was *really* pleased. "We'll discuss it," he said. He knew how much money the Traditional Holiday Crafts Shop earned for Delina in Meander, Arkansas, he knew how hard she worked, and he knew how many people depended on her. He'd take the rainbow wreath, but he'd buy its fair value in other goods.

"Coffee?"

"I'll help myself."

He went to the shelf where the coffeepot . . . made by Delina, he was sure, looking at it . . . sat steaming. He filled a mug, wrapping both hands around it for the warmth it gave him, and went to pull up a battered rocker across from her.

"Delina, I've come with a message from the PICOTA," he said, after he'd tried the excellent coffee and given it the minute of quiet appreciation it merited.

She glanced up from her work and smiled at him. "Are they throwing me out?" she asked.

"No."

"I'm glad of that!" She laughed, and tied off an end of emerald green yarn. "It would be awkward to be chief of the Meandering Water and have to manage without the PICOTA."

He knew she was waiting for him to get on with it, but it was hard. He didn't recall ever before having to carry a message that was a formal *apology*.

"Can I help?"

Banyon shook his head.

"Then I will wait," she said, and went back to her work.

He looked around the room, enjoying the array of beautiful objects that were both good to see and good to use. She set her prices too low, he saw; he would talk to her about that. Or perhaps he wouldn't. It depended on how this went.

Finally, he took a deep breath, and said it straight out. "Delina Bluecrane Jefferson," he said, "on behalf of all the tribes of the PICOTA, I come to offer you our apology."

She sat bolt upright and stared at him, and he could see that she was truly astonished.

"I can't have heard you right," she said.

"Sorry," he went on, in a strained voice. "We . . . the PICOTA . . . are deeply sorry for what we have done. And we would be grateful if you would carry that word for us to the women of the Lines."

"But Banyon—whatever in all the world *have* the PICOTA done?"

"We didn't intend to do it," he said, fixing his eyes on the floor.

"You didn't."

"No." He cleared his throat. "It wasn't planned."

"Go on."

"Putting Marthajean Brown into the Oval Office was planned," he said, keeping his voice clear and steady. "Before ever she was born, they say, that was planned. Making a classical guitarist of Alice Mary Brown . . . Cleo St. Andrews . . . so that she could move easily among the powerful all over this planet; *that* was planned. The idea was that Marthajean would be in a position to influence the President of the United States of Earth, should that prove necessary, and that Cleo would be a source of very useful information from many places we could not otherwise have gone."

He looked up, saw the stony face he was expecting to see, and looked at the floor again. He drank some more coffee, and continued.

"What was *not* planned," he said, "was the deaths." His chest hurt him, and his throat; it was pain he knew was well-deserved. "We never intended Marthajean Brown to die; the murder was not planned. We never meant Cleo St. Andrews to die; it wasn't the PICOTA that tampered with the life-support mechanisms in her prizpod."

"Oh, Banyon . . ." He heard the long sigh, and knew it was safe to look at her; their eyes spoke, and his own eyes filled with tears.

"We are so sorry," he said. "It went terribly wrong, somehow."

"Do you know what happened?"

"We know what *must* have happened. We know part of it."

Delina got up, setting the finished wreath aside, and went after a cup of coffee for herself. "Please," she said. "Tell me what you know—and tell me what you only suspect. Cleo was very dear to us, you perceive, and Marthajean Brown would have been dear to us, too, if we'd known her."

He began with the seduction of the President, which had been the PICOTA's idea, well aware of how strongly she would disapprove of *that*, looking carefully past her at the wall. "We know that took place," he said, "because she sent a signal to her aunt, as had been agreed upon. We know Cleo was told about it, because we passed the information on to her ourselves. And then we *don't* know exactly what happened next . . . but we think we know what it has to have been. The *President* must have told somebody."

"Who?"

He shook his head. "I doubt we'll ever know that," he said. "But somebody who then either took it upon himself to kill Marthajean . . . or had authority enough to order her killed. To guarantee her silence. And to prevent exactly the sort of influence over Dellwilder that we were after."

"Perhaps it was the President himself that gave the order."

"No," said Banyon firmly. "We know him better than that. He couldn't have killed her *or* ordered her killed. But there was someone, someone he trusted enough to tell, who *was* able to do it."

"Poor Cleo. Poor dead Cleo. Poor Miss Brown."

"Yes."

"Banyon Jordacha, look at me."

He did, and when she had his full attention she said, "The PICOTA *should* be sorry! And they should be ashamed of their bungling!"

"Yes. Yes, we know that. That's why I'm here. But you see, it never occurred to us that Tobias Dellwilder would *tell*. We knew he would be sick with guilt . . . he had the usual mixed-up ideas about such things. We thought guilt would keep him silent, and keep him beholden to Marthajean. We believed that might some-day prevent the sort of disasters that Presidents are so fond of causing."

"And then Cleo leapt into the middle of it."

"We had been telling you," he said softly, "for many years, and Cleo had been telling you on our behalf, that it was time to make the Audiosynthesis Project public. She didn't consult us *either*, Delina. And once she made her move, there was nothing we could do to save her."

Delina turned her head away so that he would not have to watch her weep, and said, "I don't understand why they had to *kill* her!"

"Well . . ." Banyon took a long breath. "It is possible, I suppose, that when the prizpod failed it really *was* an accident."

She said nothing, and he was glad; there was nothing more to say. And there were only two more things he had to do before he could go home.

First: he would settle the matter of the rainbow wreath, for his sister's birthday gift; he would let the question of what Delina charged for her work wait until some other, more suitable, time and place.

And then he must go, in person again, to the Cetacean Project in El Centro. The PICOTA had another message for him to deliver. Like the message he had given Delina, this one was to be passed on to another ultimate destination. But there was a difference.

If he'd had to, Banyon could have gone to some of the senior women of the Lines and apologized to them directly, instead of asking Delina to do it. He wouldn't have liked doing it that way. It would have been a violation of customs that he respected. But he could have *done* it. Contacting the Council of the Consortium was not at all the same thing; only the whales knew how that was done. There was no way he could have contacted the Aliens on his own.

He had to go ask the whales to tell the Alien consortium that the end of the plague of human violence had begun. That it might take a long time, because so many of the human males were going to fight it every step of the way, but that praise be—as the women would have said—it had at long long last *begun*.

APPENDIX
SELECTIONS FROM THE TEACHING MATERIALS
OF THE MEANDERING WATER TRIBE

CANTICLE OF THE ANIMALS

What does the owl say to me,
as it watches?
    The owl says:
    "Daughter,
    your wings are folded under your breastbone;
    Daughter, your wings are hidden.
    If you do not feel them try to move,
    you are not paying attention."
Blessed be the wary owl for the lessons it teaches.

What does the fish say to me,
as it flickers?
    The fish says:
    "Daughter,
    you had gills when you were in the womb;
    Daughter, you come from the water.
    If you no longer remember how to swim,
    you are not paying attention."
Blessed be the slender fish for the lessons it teaches.

What does the cow say to me,
as it stands?
    The cow says:
    "Daughter,
    I make food from the grasses;
    Daughter, you and I are makers of food.

If you cannot perceive how beautiful we are,
you are not paying attention."
Blessed be the broad cow for the lessons it teaches.

What does the dog say to me,
as it waits?
    The dog says:
    "Daughter,
    there is a wilderness in you;
    Daughter, your body's skin covers tangled thickets.
    If you cannot smell them on the wind,
    you are not paying attention."
Blessed be the steadfast dog for the lessons it teaches.

What does the lizard say to me,
as it leaves?
    The lizard says:
    "Daughter,
    you know how to live in a desert;
    Daughter, you know where the drops of water are.
    If you have lost the track of your own wisdom,
    you are not paying attention."
Blessed be the quick lizard for the lessons it teaches.

What does the tiger say to me,   *(This verse is discarded where*
as it lies curled?   *audiosynthesis is known.)*
    The tiger says,
    "Daughter,
    you do not run your kill to ground;
    Daughter, your kill comes cut and wrapped and packaged.
    If you have forgotten that all life kills to eat,
    you are not paying attention."
Blessed be the fierce tiger for the lessons it teaches.

What does the snake say to me,
as it slides by?

The snake says:
"Daughter,
if you hoard poison, it will multiply;
Daughter, never turn your hand to venom.
If you have not noticed that my forked tongue speaks truth,
you are not paying attention."
Blessed be the shining snake for the lessons it teaches.

What does the beetle say to me,
as it scuttles?
　　The beetle says:
　　"Daughter,
　　I remind you to tend to the small things;
　　Daughter, power is not only the property of the large.
　　If you cannot see me from the corner of your eye,
　　you are not paying attention."
Blessed be the antlered beetle for the lessons it teaches.

What does the spider say to me,
as it weaves?
　　The spider says:
　　"Daughter,
　　your fingers are skillful;
　　Daughter, you know how the web shines in the light.
　　If you feel that there's nothing left to spin with,
　　you are not paying attention."
Blessed be the busy spider for the lessons it teaches.

What does the heron say to me,
as it wades?
　　The heron says:
　　"Daughter,
　　Notice my elegant bent wing;
　　Daughter, I would have you join me in my dance.
　　If you and I dance together, we will dance glory,
　　and we will pay attention."

Blessed be the tall heron for the lessons it teaches.

<NOTE: HERE ADD VERSES FOR THE ANIMALS OF THE
PEOPLE WITH WHOM YOU ARE WORKING.>

What do all the animals say to me,
as they go about in the world?
    The animals say:
    "Daughter,
    you have us for the holy book;
    we move by our principles, in the innocence of our time.
    You will learn from us,
    if you pay attention."
Blessed be all the beloved animals,
for the lessons they teach.

THE INSTRUCTIONS THAT CAME WITH US

Behold the hollow in the rock,
and the clear water rising,
bearing one red leaf;
this is the spring and the source.
    When there is water enough and water to spare,
    the bright leaf trembles on the surface,
    and the first drop rises;
    the spring returns its substance to the air

Behold the cloud in the sky,
and the dark edge spreading,
folding the white under;
this is the spring and the source.
    When there is water enough and water to spare,
    the dark rim turns over like a hand,
    and the first drop falls;
    the sky returns its substance to the land.

Here is no first or second, here is no last.
Here no below nor above nor beginning nor end.
This is the unbroken wreath of living water,
land answering sky answering land.

Thus *lovingkindness* moves,
from the Holy One to the person and back again.
There is no first or second, there is no last.
There is no below nor above nor beginning nor end.
This is the unbroken wreath of lovingkindness;
love answering Love answering love.

TEACHING STORY THREE

Once, three wise men went to see an old woman.

The first wise man showed her his Housebuilding Machine. It was thirty-seven feet tall and twelve feet around and it shone golden in the sun and went rolling around in circles roaring like a lion. "Your, your, your!" said the old woman, and she clapped her hands. "What a fine big powerful expensive machine!"

The second wise man showed her *his* Housebuilding Machine. It was fifty-four feet tall and thirty feet around and it shone silver in the sun and went leaping round in rectangles shrieking like a hawk. "Your, your, your!" said the old woman, and she clapped her hands twice. "What a fine big powerful expensive machine!"

And the third wise man showed her *his* Housebuilding Machine. It was ninety-four feet tall and seventy-four feet around and it shone copper and crystal in the sun and stood spinning on its single foot howling like a hyena. "Your, your, your!" said the old woman, and she clapped her hands three times. "What a fine big powerful expensive machine!"

The wise men charged the old woman for looking at their machines, plus tax, and went away satisfied.

When they were gone, the old woman said, "My, my, my!"

And then she shaped in her mind a house that was exactly what she wanted and needed. And out in the around-her the Stuff said, "Oh, how beautiful! Let me come be that, too!" And the walls rose lovingly up and the roof curved lovingly over them, and the floors spread tenderly out to meet the walls, and the door and windows opened themselves wide to offer joyful welcome.

"Less fuss," said the old woman. And she went inside.

HEALING NOTE #11—CANCER

You who come to be healed—
your mind is out of tune;
it is sending out the wrong messages
to the little cellbodies.
  It tells them: Grow!
  It tells them: Multiply!
  It tells them: Be many—
there are not enough of you little ones!

Tune your mind to my mind now, and we will edit the message.

TEACHING STORY SEVEN

Once there were two wise and powerful men who owned many machines and properties and much information. And they happened to arrive at the same time on the same day at a single door.

The first man stood by the door and thought, forcefully: "Door—*close*." The second man stood by the door and thought forcefully: "Door—*open*." And the door, then, was well and truly Stuck.

Time went on, and the two men grew more and more miserable. They could have just gone home, but they didn't.

"Go home, you!" they said to each other.

"You first!"

"No, *you* first!"

After they were both dead as a doornail, the door began to dance, Opening and Closing, but it did the men no good at all; they stayed dead.

ANATOMY NOTE #13—THE SPINE

I am the spine of the body;
I am the back's bone.
I am no rigid rod; I meander.

I am the body's broad highroad
and its spacious canal.
In the service of the brain/mind,
the layered central womb of information,
I ease the body's swift messengers coming-and-going
on their rounds.
When I can, I make their paths smooth.

Person, hear me; I run respectfully through you.

TEACHING NOTE #44

"Only God can bring a thing to be by saying its name," they malesaid. "Only God."

But they themselves had said the words that brought these things (and countless more like them) into being:

The Mexican border.
Obesity.
National airspace.
Ugly women.
Borderline personality disorder.
Hypoestrogenemia.
The poverty line.
Attention deficit disorder.
Fibrocystic breast disease.
Retirement age.
Private lakes.
Hyperactive children.
War. And sometimes peace.

CANTICLE OF THE PEBBLES

My mouth is hungry for hot bread with butter;
foolish mouth, locked in Old Time!
I will give my mouth a scarlet pebble
warm from the sun.

My mouth is hungry for chocolate, melting;
foolish mouth, locked in Old Time!
I will give my mouth a pebble of rich dark brown
warm from my hand.

My mouth is hungry for fresh pineapple, tart on the tongue . . .
no, let me change that . . . for pineapple cooked with brown sugar.
Foolish mouth, locked in Old Time!
I will give my mouth a lemon-yellow pebble
cool from the creek.

*(Continue here with the list of beloved foods of the people you are
training; carry with you at all times your bag of beautiful stones.)*

The hungry mouth is locked tight in Old Time;
feeding it will not help.
Feed it, and you will access the even older time
when it hungered for raw meat and thirsted for blood.
Give the hungry mouth a pebble to hold,
against such Times.

Earthsong (1994) concludes Suzette Haden Elgin's Native Tongue series, drawing together the trilogy's disparate yet deeply interwoven narrative threads in a metaphor-based model of feminist revolution. The struggle to use language to combat violence, begun in *Native Tongue* (1984) and broadened in *The Judas Rose* (1987), turns in the final volume to an experiment in alternative nourishment that ends up literally *feeding* peace. Elgin's trilogy provides an imaginative commentary on the nature of human societies, the causes and consequences of violence, and the range of effective strategies for inculcating feminist principles in social practice. Originally, Elgin had intended the trilogy's third book to bear the title "The Meandering Water Tribe," not only in tribute to the all-female honorary Native American nation of that name (begun by Delina Chornyak) but because of Elgin's own conviction that feminist revolution proceeds most effectively by indirection:

> That title mattered to me because it expressed my conviction that a feminist revolution—the only kind that has any chance of succeeding—would have to meander toward its goal. Patriarchal revolutions (which always fail) go in a straight line, in a hurry; a feminist revolution would meander, slowly. The title mattered to me because water is so good a metaphor for a feminist force; it wears away resistance gently but inexorably, over time, and is almost impossible to withstand. Attempts to restrain water by force (with dams and dikes and levees, for example) eventually breed water disasters; it has to be channeled.[1]

While this title was rejected by the original publisher, the sense of productive and culturally rich indirection it connotes remains evident in Elgin's text. With its concluding volume, the Native Tongue trilogy takes a rather surprising detour from its initial focus on gendered linguistic practices and the social effects of linguistic change. In exploring possibilities for escape, both from the restrictions of human biology and the constraints of language, *Earthsong* envisions the creation of a *new* human being, tailored to the demands of feminist revolution. In its portrait of a human species that retreats from violence, no longer needs material nourishment, and grows able to communicate nonverbally, even nonlinguistically, *Earthsong* anticipates later visions of the "posthuman" explored in Octavia Butler's Xenogenesis trilogy and analyzed by feminist science studies scholars Donna Haraway and N. Katherine Hayles.

In order to see how *Earthsong* extends and complicates the themes of the previous two novels, however, we must first review what has already happened in the trilogy. In *Native Tongue*, the women of the Lines develop Láadan, a secret language created to express the perceptions and experiences of women, while the US government simultaneously tries and fails to acquire a nonhumanoid Alien language. When the women, pushed by rebellion leader Nazareth Chornyak Adiness, finally begin speaking and teaching Láadan among themselves and the girlchildren, it changes the fundamental gender relations of the participants. As Delina remembers, "After we women began speaking Láadan, and after our little girls began growing up speaking it, . . . we were *different*. So different that the men could no longer bear to have us with them for more than half an hour at a time . . . so different that they built the Womanhouses for us, to keep us separate" (74).

But it is not until *The Judas Rose* that the women of the Lines begin spreading Láadan, through a complicated network of religious institutions, to the larger Terran populace of women, resisting the systematic isolation of women and separation between Linguists and the general population. Through the Linguist women's own prayer services and the subversive work of non-Linguist women planted throughout the galaxy as Catholic nuns (made possible by Linguist nun Miriam Rose), the women make Láadan more broadly available while still resisting the religious authorities' attempts to make Láadan serve patriarchal goals by excising any suggestions of feminism or goddess-worship. At the same time, the US government is participating in a new race with other Terran nations to expand space colonies, efforts that are tightly controlled and monitored by the Aliens.

As *Earthsong* opens, we learn that the Láadan experiment apparently has failed (at least from the women's immediate perspective), the Aliens have abruptly withdrawn from the Earth, and Terran society has been plunged into deep ecological, social, and economic chaos. The Alien retreat is disastrous. It has left the Earth without renewable technologies (since the machines left behind by the Aliens will slowly fail) and without any resources or knowledge to repair those machines. Soon Earth enters the Icehouse Effect, which, coupled with the loss of Alien income, plunges the colonies into famine. Men are particularly vulnerable to cold and hunger. Intensive work by women, often led by women of the Lines, to save the lives of the men gives way to sperm banking and in vitro fertilization as the only recourse to prevent human extinction. Although the famine and ecological disaster are devastating to the entire human population, *audiosynthesis*, a technique of aural nourishment already spread by Linguist women through the Music Grammar Schools and by StarTangle missionaries through their ministries, prevents humanity's wholesale annihilation.

Desperate for guidance after the Alien abandonment, Delina Chornyak braves the objections of the women of her household and a number of Native Americans, and goes through a vision quest. She does so to contact Nazareth, who died on the very day that the Aliens departed. During their vision-quest conversation, Nazareth reveals to Delina that the Aliens abandoned Earth because of the incurable violence of human beings, and she counsels Delina that to end violence she must find a way to end hunger. Ultimately, this encounter prompts Delina to study and name audiosynthesis, a practice by which the human body is nourished with music, and the women of the Lines form an alliance with the PICOTA (an alliance of Native American peoples) to spread audiosynthesis secretly, just as they had spread Láadan. After many years, audiosynthesis is being used galaxy-wide, though the non-Linguists using it are unaware that they are doing anything other than making music. Hence, this renegade technique of human nutrition has become too well-entrenched to be squelched by Earth's patriarchal governments when it finally comes to light. Despite their innate resistance to any technology that will threaten the balance of power, the Terran male leaders are forced to install it as policy, bringing with its adoption the beginning of the end of violence.

While initially the first two books may seem only tangentially related to *Earthsong*'s stress on hunger and violence, a closer consideration reveals that all three books are joined by the essentially *linguistic* perspective they present on the challenges facing human society. The plot swerve in *Earthsong* turns on a homologue—aural/oral—and the principle, "'[based on linguistic science],' that changing any distinctive feature from the definition of humanness would transform the human being into a *different* creature . . . and that the *new* human might well be able to do without violence."[2] Elgin's science fiction premise—her *novum*, to borrow a term from Darko Suvin—is the discovery that human beings can nourish themselves without killing.[3] The act of substituting a nourishment that is *aural* for one that is *oral*, and in so doing substituting an act of artistic creation (music) for an act of violent destruction (the production of food through both agriculture and animal husbandry), enacts a revolutionary reconfiguration of one of the essential traits of a human being. In short, Elgin's novel turns Shakespeare's romantic proposition into a revolutionary answer to human violence: "If music be the food of love, play on."[4]

The Seeds of Change

In this final book in the Native Tongue trilogy, the themes of violence, revolution, gender, power, language, and religion culminate in a model for creating effective change. Elgin's Linguist women are patient, proceeding by indirection, working in parallel and nested organizations to catalyze change on a number of fronts:

medical, social, spiritual, and political. In short, the women incarnate in fiction the strategies required of feminists and social activists during the Reagan/Bush era of conservative backlash against the gains made by the various political movements of the 1960s onward, the context for *Earthsong*'s initial publication in 1994.

The contours of Terran society after the Aliens' departure reflect the gender dynamics of the Reagan/Bush era as well as humanity's unremitting violence, particularly the important and destructive connection that the Terran men perceive between political power and personal identity. Once the Aliens leave, the control and power wielded by the Linguist men lose their foundation; their linguistic skill with Alien languages is no longer valuable to the governments of Earth. As Chief Will Bluecrane remarks, "It must be like losing both your legs at once, with no warning—very disorienting" (18). With the much-vaunted power of the Lines no longer theirs, the men give way to often dissolute despair. Their options, after all, are to administer the Music Grammar Schools, teach linguistics or languages, or pretend to look after the fortunes of the Lines, none of which is challenging or fulfilling after having more or less run intergalactic trade (99). The women recognize that the men equate loss of power with loss of self, and they try "to give [the men] a sense of Being that wasn't tied to how strong (or how rich, or how cruel) they were" (187). In the end, though, the memory of power cannot be so easily eradicated; when the men of the Lines learn about the women's audiosynthesis project, they once again resume their former power struggles (184–85).

Although the Alien quarantine of Earth exposes the tenuous connection between possession of power and a sense of self most clearly in the men of the Lines, other male characters in the novel demonstrate this problematic connection as well. The Vice President, for example, "had always known, from his earliest childhood, that it was his destiny to save at least the nation, probably the planet and all its colonies, and perhaps the entire solar system" (133). The central role of violence in maintaining male power and dominance becomes clear when we realize that the Vice President considers killing the President's indiscreet secretary as forwarding, rather than undermining, the grand destiny he envisions for himself. Indeed, it is telling that he ruins himself not by trying to kill the secretary, but by botching the job. With that act, he hasn't just made a mistake, he has erased who he was meant to be: "He wished—not idly, but with all his heart—that something could have happened right then, right then when he was at the peak of his entire existence. A stroke. A heart attack. An assassin's chemdart. Anything that would have let him exit his life *like that*, splendid and confident and with the President of the United States of Earth looking after him in gratitude and admiration" (137).

The characteristically masculine habit of assuming a connection between selfhood and power that Elgin diagnoses and portrays in *Earthsong* leads those in political power to misread the women's motivations for discovering and circulating audiosynthesis. As the President argues, "All of human society, all of human culture, rests on the knowledge we have . . . that human beings are only capable of really buckling down and working together in groups when their goals are *evil*. They'll do it for money or power or conquest . . . they'll do it to be famous, to get themselves on the threedies and the newspapers. . . . But a conspiracy to *feed everybody*? No, Jay. That's not possible. That is a thing that could not happen" (181). The Linguist women have been prepared for this reaction; they expect the government to try to suppress audiosynthesis as a potential threat to the balance of power (60). Because power is central to the male self-image, any shift in this balance is met with sanctioned violence.

The response of US government staff to the sex- and murder-scandal that troubles the President reflects the patriarchal reflex toward violence as a solution. As Zlerigeau explains:

> Look . . . when the United States goes to war, it has to kill people. This is no different. This is the war for peace and security, sir. This is the war to keep the whole solar system from falling apart. However much the colonies claim to despise Earth one and all, if Earth fell apart they would suffer trauma difficult to repair. Without Earth to hate, they'd fight each other, you know—we all know that's what would happen, and it has to be prevented. It's a *just* war, Mr. President, and the death of Joe Fall Guy is just an unavoidable side effect. (144)

The irony of having a war for peace isn't lost on the reader. The death of Joe Fall Guy hinges on violence *as a way of life*, not simply a strategy to be used when necessary and then again avoided. Violence is so pervasive, in fact, that when it is resisted, it does not disappear; it merely gets displaced into a more deeply hidden plan. When the President disagrees with the plan to convict and execute a substitute for the murder of the secretary, Zlerigeau announces,

> In that case . . . we have no choice. In that case, what we have to do is agree with you that it's a dumb and naughty idea, promise not to do it, and do it anyway behind your back. But we also have to work out some kind of halfass alternate plan that you *will* approve. And then we have to go to all the trouble and expense of carrying out *that* plan, *too*. It's a big waste of the taxpayers' money, Mr. President. (139)

Because violence is the official response to any problem, it is also the official response to other violence. Torturers, for example, are systematically paralyzed and given an hour's experience of torture. However, violence functions ideologically here, masked under the sign of "rehabilitation." As the Judge tells the prisoner:

> There are those who would tell you that you are an evil man . . . and that this is a suitable *punishment* for such evil. I want you to know that it is not punishment at all. If I wanted only to punish you, this is not what I would do. I know that you are not evil, my friend. And I know that when you understand what torture *is*, when you truly know how it feels to suffer the kind of pain you inflict on others, you *will not do* it. Not ever again. I understand that. (163)

But it becomes painfully clear that the "education" fails to work as intended when a torturer appears in the prison, slotted to be tortured a *second* time. The Judge's disillusionment is so great that he kills himself (165). The book's critique of violence rests on exposing and undermining the idea that violence can ever produce anything other than violence: there could never be a war for peace because that war institutes the very violence that undermines peace.

When the system *does* acknowledge violence as problematic, segregation of the worst offenders is usually the primary strategy (hence our overflowing prisons system). In this world of the future, violence is also segregated in an attempt to ameliorate its effects on Earth. But what worked in the era of the first novel is here demonstrated to be a temporary solution at best. As a theologian in the novel remarks,

> We thought, fools that we were, that is was all over. All the crime, all the violence, all the poverty, all the basic wickedness of humankind. During the two hundred years when we could end every frustration by simply moving on—to one more planet, yet one more asteroid—we thought we had it solved. In our arrogance we even set aside planets dedicated to specific varieties of wickedness, so that those who wished to devote their lives to evil had them as convenient havens shared only by others of like mind. But we had forgotten three important facts. That humans are not gods. That history always repeats itself, though it may take a very long time. And that the day would inevitably come when there were no more frontiers to move to and no more empty planets waiting for us. Nowhere left to ship those who disturbed the rest of us, to spare us the nuisance of having them among us. (133)

As Delina mourns, "The problem, the terrible problem that human beings have always faced, is that it seemed as if violence were somehow part of the *definition* of being human. Getting rid of it . . . it's like getting rid of *lungs*, somehow" (74). Violence is not a trivial problem, then, and under patriarchy is as central to human life as the act of breathing: indeed, *Earthsong* indicts the very structure of human society and human interaction.

The novel does take care not to suggest that *all* violence should be eliminated. Sometimes, violence is a necessary part of positive change. When the women are preparing to let their audiosynthesis project be discovered, for example, they "knew there was the very real possibility that the women of the Lines would be slaughtered in the first waves of rage, those waves that would be the birth pangs of the first race of human beings to take its sustenance from sound rather than from flesh. Birth pangs are good in the long run;

women who are weary to death of hauling babies about in the womb long for them. But they are brutal and messy and painful and, once begun, unstoppable" (189–90). Violence linked to natural processes is a productive force, but violence for its own sake, or in order to perpetuate a destructive status quo, is the target of *Earthsong*'s fierce critique.

In opposition to the destruction that the Linguist and Terran men wield, the Linguist women enact a highly sophisticated schema for rebuilding human society from the ground up, reshaping its socioeconomic, ecological, cultural, and linguistic institutions. This reconstruction has broader implications as it both saves humans from extinction and makes Terrans fit for intergalactic society. This plan within a plan couples the spread of audiosynthesis with an alliance with the PICOTA, the alliance of numerous Native American peoples whose spiritual gifts first enabled Delina to contact the deceased Nazareth and begin the quest for an alternative to violence. Nazareth's suggestion, as reported by Delina, that the women of the Lines begin marrying the men of PICOTA is described by Chief Bluecrane as "the marriage of the highest of technologies" (35). In contrast to the Alien and machine technologies, which cause the Icehouse Effect (151) and generally fail in unfixable ways (105, 40), these technologies—linguistics, spirituality, and alternative forms of healing—are part of the fabric of human interaction, possessing the power to transform society instead of destroying it.

The alternative technologies the women wield embody the nature of lasting change, which is not merely additive but transformative. Linguistics provides one metaphor for that kind of global transformation: "Translation, you know, is not a matter of substituting words in one language for words in another language. Translation is a matter of saying in one language, for a particular situation, what a native speaker of the other language would say in the *same* situation. The more unlikely that situation is in one of the languages, the harder it is to find a corresponding utterance in the other" (6). The women's invention of Láadan provides the most powerful example of this process. As Delina recalls:

So . . . remember how, after we began speaking Láadan, and after our little girls began growing up speaking it, how we changed? It wasn't that we were *the same women with a different language added on*, Sarajane: we were *different*. So different that the men could no longer bear to have us with them for more than half an hour at a time . . . so different that they built the Womanhouses for us, to keep us separate. Remember? (74)

The implication is that people are something like native tongues: given a change of sufficient magnitude, they will be *translated*, so that certain perceptions or expressions would be more (or less) thinkable. This, then, is the hope of audiosynthesis, which Delina explains in a conversation with Sarajane:

> "The point," said Delina, "is that the creatures we are . . . and perhaps most especially the *male* creatures . . . seem unable to set violence aside. But human beings who have never eaten mouthfood . . . who have *never* had to say to themselves, 'This substance in my mouth was once a living creature like me, until it was caught and killed and cooked for me to eat' . . . Sarajane, they won't just be the *same* creatures eating a different diet." . . .
> "You are saying . . . evolution."
> "Yes! Evolution. Exactly. It wouldn't have had to be audiosynthesis, Sarajane—any change of sufficient *scope* would have done it." (74–75)

Like audiosynthesis, like language, a well organized local faith can also produce translating change. When Delina learns about audiosynthesis, she realizes that she hasn't found something entirely new, but rather rediscovered something that had been hidden in plain sight in holy books for thousands of years (53). As the women of the Lines spread audiosynthesis secretly, they do so by way of a new religious branch of women: Our Blessed Lady of the StarTangle. Presumably aligned with the Catholic Church and comprised entirely of women of the Lines, the Order takes as its mission the creation of Music Grammar Schools, which in turn allows them to nourish children aurally and thus institute audiosynthesis secretly. As its name implies, the Order takes seriously the women's addition to the traditional rules of research and analysis: "find the one critical end of the tangled string. The one you pull to make the entire knotted mess fall into orderly disorder at your feet" (39). Hunger is the string the women pull—by means of audiosynthesis—to untangle the mess that is human violence. And faith is another form of translation, another technology of transformation. As Chief Bluecrane observes when Delina emerges from her vision quest, "She was no prettier than she'd been when she first showed up to torment him, but right now she had the uncanny translucent elegance that goes with a sacred procedure done properly and all the trimmings laid on. She had not only survived . . . she had *improved*. And that was how it was *supposed* to work" (33).

A third technology of transformation is entrainment-based medicine, or resonance healing, with which the women have replaced the medical knowledge that the men have taken from them through the restrictive move of masculinist professionalization. The men's strategy of restrictive professionalization, first seen in the realm of medicine, is something that the women expect them to repeat in their response to audiosynthesis. As Willow explains to Delina:

> Think . . . what happened with medical care. It wasn't because people couldn't learn to do it themselves that men made it a crime to practice medicine "without a license," and set the cost of the license so high that most people couldn't even dream about getting one. And made it impossible to order medicines without a medsammy's permission. And sent women to prison for tending other women in childbed. (60–61)

To the male medical professionals, resonance healing lacks proper professional authorization. It is transmitted not through approved textbooks but through "*poems* and cute little stories," taught not through proper professional education, but through the Linguist women's network of the music schools (97). But to the women of the Church of Our Lady of the StarTangle, who live as missionaries on distant asteroids or struggle to build a way of life not reliant on Alien and machine technologies, resonance healing offers a crucial—if for a long time unvoiced—alternative to the dwindling pool of bedside healthies or working medpods:

"Nobody suggested that the women of the Lines would have to take over with resonance medicine; nobody suggested that they would have to open medschools and train people in that skill. Just thinking about it was overwhelming; they were determined *not* to think about it" (105).

These technologies of transformation rely on another theme of the novel, indeed of the entire trilogy: connectivity. The things that *work*, here, all presume and rely on connections between humans. Delina's vision quest assumed a connection between life and death, the living and the dead. The intermarriage of the women of the Lines and the men of the PICOTA formalized a connection between similar worldviews. And finally, the technique of resonance medicine and *entrainment*, the production of resonant vibrations in another object or being, demonstrates the inherent connection that can be produced between two people. Strategies that do *not* depend on connectivity, figured in the novel as various kinds of violence, ultimately fail by making the problem worse. The clear implication is that successful change and response require networks of people used effectively.

Earthsong, then, is a map for change, a demonstration of the principle, if not the actualities, of transformation from violence to sustainability. The tools of this change are connectivity, language, and faith, tools every woman, and every revolutionary, has at her or his disposal. Made possible by the feminist commitment to linguistic and social transformation, these movements for effective change and revolution are not, Elgin suggests, large-scale events, but a series of small alterations, seemingly unrelated, that combine to shift human relationships into a new space and a new understanding.

Teaching Revolution

The Native Tongue trilogy offers many areas of exploration to the contemporary classroom. As Elgin herself notes, the novels could be used in a linguistics class to introduce basic principles of the field. The trilogy might also be used in a political science class with emphasis on political change, utopias, dystopias, or revolutions. Any class in literature and medicine would find the entire trilogy valuable for its examination of the social treatment of aging, the role of physicians, the effects of medical technology on the doctor-patient relationship, and the relationship between medicine and spirituality. Classes in feminist science fiction would find Elgin's trilogy a good choice to pair with Octavia Butler's Xenogenesis trilogy, Joanna Russ's *The Female Man*, and Margaret Atwood's *A Handmaid's Tale*, as well as Donna Haraway's *Simians, Cyborgs, and Women* and *Modest_Witness@ Second_MillenniumFemaleMan©_Meets_OncoMouse™*. Such a course could explore the variety of boundary relations mapped in these different science fictions: human/alien, human/animal; fiction/theory; female/male; black/white; third world/first world. Elgin's fiction, like Atwood's and Russ's, articulates second wave feminist thinking, while Butler's work, like Haraway's, articulates the perspectives of postmodern feminisms. There are crucial theoretical and practical reasons to teach second and third wave feminist histories *together*: the resulting juxtaposition of feminist visions both enriches and challenges us.

Overall, the Native Tongue trilogy will be most useful and engaging in a class exploring feminism, whether a literature course, a women's studies course, or a theory course (or some combination thereof). The trilogy demonstrates and explores many of the questions that are basic to a feminist perspective of the world through both its thematics and its unusual and increasingly nonlinear structure: What is patriarchy? How does language participate in women's oppression? How can we simultaneously engage women's equality and difference? Is there an essential female connection we can draw on to intervene in patriarchy, or should we seek a feminist connection not necessarily entrenched in biological difference? How can we intervene in patriarchy when patriarchy is all we have? While these questions can be difficult for undergraduate students to grapple with, the novels can provide both an unfamiliar and fascinating example to work through and enough parallels with our society for students to draw connections.

More advanced students can use the novels to explore the ways both feminism(s) and US society have changed over the last few decades. The dichotomized gender roles of the novels are not as convincing today as they might have been at publication, and the assumptions about women's inherent connection made explicit in the earlier novels and questioned somewhat in *Earthsong* are now much more problematic. By demonstrating these changes in feminist perspective and feminist theorizing, we can encourage our students to articulate and continue the struggle to address the problems within feminism today. Moreover, we can use the novels in the classroom to encourage our students to produce change locally and consciously, in the service of making the world safe for people of all kinds.

Susan M. Squier and Julie Vedder
May 2002

Notes

1. Suzette Haden Elgin, personal communication, 20 January 2002.
2. Suzette Haden Elgin, personal communication, 20 January 2002.
3. Darko Suvin offers a critique of the novum, a distinguishing feature of science fiction, arguing that it is "obviously predicated on the importance and potentially the beneficence of novelty and change, linked to science and progress," in his essay "Novum Is as Novum Does," *Foundation: The Review of Science Fiction* 69 (Spring 1997): 26–43, 36–37. While we grant the point of Suvin's remarkable self-critique, we would argue that his point still stands if we take the term in the broader sense—as the "machine for thinking" through innovations of all kinds, including the feminist innovations central to Suvin's own critique—that science fiction offers to society (Suvin, 34–35).
4. William Shakespeare, *Twelfth Night*, act 1, sc. 1.

Work Cited

Elgin, Suzette Haden. 1999. "Waterships All the Way Down: Using Science Fiction to Teach Linguistics." In *Language Alive in the Classroom*, edited by Rebecca S. Wheeler, 157–66. Westport, CT: Praeger.

More Classic Works
from the Feminist Press

But Some of Us Are Brave: Black Women's Studies
edited by Akasha (Gloria T.) Hull,
Patricia Bell Scott, and Barbara Smith

Changes: A Love Story by Ama Ata Aidoo

Daughter of Earth: A Novel by Agnes Smedley

His Own Where by June Jordan

**I Love Myself When I Am Laughing . . .
And Then Again When I Am Looking Mean and Impressive:
A Zora Neale Hurston Reader**
edited by Alice Walker

The Naked Woman by Armonía Somers,
translated by Kit Maude

Still Alive: A Holocaust Girlhood Remembered by Ruth Kluger

Thérèse and Isabelle by Violette Leduc,
translated by Sophie Lewis

Touba and the Meaning of Night by Shahrnush Parsipur,
translated by Havva Houshmand and Kamran Talattof

Witches, Midwives & Nurses: A History of Women Healers
by Barbara Ehrenreich and Deirdre English

The Yellow Wall-Paper by Charlotte Perkins Gilman

You Can't Get Lost in Cape Town by Zoë Wicomb

The Feminist Press is a nonprofit educational organization founded to amplify feminist voices. FP publishes classic and new writing from around the world, creates cutting-edge programs, and elevates silenced and marginalized voices in order to support personal transformation and social justice for all people.

See our complete list of books at
feministpress.org